When Spirits Break Free
AndyEvans&VesnaKovac

This book is a work of fiction. People, places, events and situations are the product of the authors' imaginations. Any resemblance to actual persons, living, or dead, or historical events is purely coincidental

© 2010 Andy Evans & Vesna Kovac. All rights reserved
No part of this book may be reproduced, stored in a retrieval system or transmitted by any means without the permission of the authors

ISBN 978-1-4467-2442-2

Special Thanks to the following people;

Alison Hirst for patiently doing the initial grammar checks when the manuscript was in its initial stages.

Ben Morgan, an ardent reader of fiction who gave the idea for the opening chapter and encouraged us throughout the time of writing.

Diane Hall, author of Son of the Ringmaster and professional proof-reader.

Finally to all friends and colleagues who supported us along the way.

When Spirits Break Free Contents

Chapter One – Life for a Life

Chapter Two – Molly

Chapter Three – The Dragon Slayer and the Beast

Chapter Four – When the Dead Came Calling

Chapter Five – The Path of Adventure

Chapter Six – Just the Two of Us

Chapter Seven – Radio Waves

Chapter Eight – Over the Rooftops

Chapter Nine – The Wind of Change

Chapter Ten - Do You Remember Me How We Used To be?

Chapter Eleven – The Partisan

Chapter Twelve - Pit Heads and Cobble Stones

Chapter Thirteen – The Genie and the Smoke

Chapter Fourteen – Spirit of the Age

Chapter Fifteen – When Spirits Break Free

Chapter Sixteen – The Changing Times

Chapter Seventeen – No Turning Away

Chapter Eighteen – The Blackbird and the Clock

Chapter Nineteen- The Human Apple

Chapter Twenty- Lonely This Christmas

Chapter Twenty One – Life For Life

When Spirits Break Free

By

Andy Evans and Vesna Kovac

Chapter One – Life for a Life

The sheer strength of the man was obvious to all who looked on, as he fought 'Mohammed Ali' in the ring - a fight that would determine world-class heavyweight status. The two fighters were locked in combat, neither one taking the respite that their corner offered.

Distracted by a screaming woman in the audience, the doctor felt a crushing blow that hit him squarely across the temple.

"One, two, three, four," the count advanced to victory and darkness reigned.

The bell sounded, sealing the fate of both the victorious and the defeated.

Pain bore into him as Doctor Forster slowly opened his eyes. The boxing ring faded from view and the animated chants from the crowd became subdued, transforming into the ring-tone of the telephone that lay on the cabinet next to the bed.

Still under the induced effect of morphine, the doctor lifted the handset from its cradle.

"Hello, Doctor Forster's residence," his voice slurred as he stifled the yawn that rose from within him.

"Doctor, we need you to come quickly!" Milan's voice was clearly recognisable despite his laboured breathing, having run through the dimly illuminated streets to the nearest public call box.

"It's young Molly, Doctor," the eastern European accent was exaggerated within the voice.

"Take your time Milan, what's the problem?"

"It's the baby, and little Molly's in so much pain with the birth." Milan's desperation was evident.

Doctor Forster realised immediately that the child was in danger and he knew from experience that only time could prevent death.

"Go back to Molly and reassure her that help is on its way," he ordered, his professional undertone rising.

The pregnancy should have continued for another four weeks; his ingrained knowledge told him that the baby may have become breeched, before concluding that both mother and child were in immediate danger.

Another possibility was that the umbilical cord had become compressed. Any delay would further heighten the risk of foetal distress and the brain would be starved of much-needed oxygen.

The doctor knew, regardless of his own pain, that this was one house call he could not afford to miss.

At the age of sixty-four, he treasured the existence of life like he had never done before.

His cancer had slowly entered his lungs and marked its presence twelve months before. He knew that his own end was imminent.

"You should see a doctor," Mrs. Forster would say, concerned that her beloved husband lay in pain and discomfort.

"I am the doctor, my dear," he always replied, carefully concealing the blood-stained handkerchief after wiping his mouth.

The doctor's wife had learned to live with the fact that their nights together would be disturbed and turned over, pulling the duck-down duvet over her shoulders to ward off the cold.

Never mind, she'd remind herself, her honourable husband would retire shortly and then they'd have the rest of their lives without interruptions.

Careful not to disturb his wife further, Doctor Forster quietly eased himself out of bed and hurriedly dressed.

"Sleep, my sweetheart," he whispered, leaning over to kiss her before closing the bedroom door.

Doctor Forster was the last of the old village doctors, a dying breed that would take the time and patience to get to know their patients on a personal level.

He had confirmed Molly's pregnancy eight months earlier and toasted the news over brandy with Roger, the proud father to be.

He had been aptly named 'Old Reliable' by the townsfolk, for his ability to always reach the patient in their time of need.

Despite his own suffering, tonight would be no different and he would reach the patient regardless.

Pain raced through his dying body as he hastily donned his overcoat. Hesitating, he reached for the briefcase that he kept on the breakfast bar dominating the spacious kitchen.

Unzipping the side pocket slowly, conscious the noise could alert his sleeping wife to his terminal plight, he pulled out the vial of morphine.

The glass felt cold to the touch as he carefully broke the seal, exposing the delicate needle that would convey comfort and warmth, despite the fear and dread it would generate into many.

Like a schoolboy inhaling a cigarette away from his teacher's gaze, Doctor Forster quickly looked round to make sure that he was truly alone.

Satisfied that his secret would remain his own he plunged the steel strand into the muscle of his thigh. The heavy weave of his trouser fabric offered no resistance as the sharpened point found its target.

From a medical perspective, he knew the immediate hit would always manifest itself from injecting into the blood stream and go directly into a vein. This time, however, the doctor knew that it may be some time before he was to return home, so an intramuscular administration would release the pain relief at a slower rate into his ravaged body.

"Besides," he thought to himself, it was now difficult to find a suitable blood-carrying vessel that had not collapsed through his regular injecting.

"And one for the journey," he whispered into the darkness.

This time he carefully injected directly into his neck, just below the collar line so that no marks would be visible.

Immediately, a deep sense of euphoria washed over him and he held onto the work surface for support.

Without further hesitation, he discarded the needles into the sharps-pouch that he always carried within the medical bag.

He felt as if he was floating across the carpet as he made his way to the door. Anxious not to make any noise with his bunch of keys, he quietly turned the lock before peering outside.

The weather forecast had been correct and a thick blanket of snow had fallen, smothering everything beneath its protective covering. Only the blackbirds that sat on the wooden fence remained uncovered as they watched him, unafraid.

Careful not to slip on the freshly fallen snow, Old Reliable stepped out onto the covered stone path and proceeded down the garden to where he was needed the most.

Molly slowly opened her eyes to the movement immediately at her side.

Straining to focus her vision she slowly picked out the unmistaken features of Doctor Forster.

"Hush child, I am here to help you," he whispered as he spread the contents of his medical bag on the bed beside her.

"I was so frightened you would not come," her deep relief evident in her hushed voice.

"Relax Molly, and let me take care of you one final time," Doctor Forster soothed, his words having an almost hypnotic quality.

The first baby cry rang out into the silence at 3.05a.m. - announcing that a new life had entered the world.

Taking a much-needed rest from the vigil that had begun the day before, they had taken advantage whenever Molly drifted into light sleep.

Alison was the first to hear the infant's crying wail as she poured boiling water into cups. Scalding her hand in haste she ran up the stairs. Although the bedroom was still in darkness she could clearly make out the sight before her.

Molly was awake, nursing her newborn son.

Roger and Milan, who had been smoking in the garden, followed closely behind and excitement rose in the crowded room. The child was crying in his mother's arms, the umbilical cord still making the connection that had transmitted life throughout the pregnancy.

"We need to get you both to hospital!" Alison screamed in panic.

"But everything is fine, mam," Molly replied, exhaustedly, "let the doctor take care of everything."

"The Doctor?" Alison looked at her, confused. "Mr. Forster never managed to get here; it must have been the snow that prevented his journey."

The ice-cold draught woke Mrs. Forster and she climbed from the bed, wrapping the thick blanket across her shoulders.

Wearily, she descended the staircase and was met with an icy blast as she slowly opened the kitchen door. Her husband was slumped across the carpet, eyes wide, as if staring in disbelief. Beside his body the medical briefcase revealed the sharps pouch that remained open, exposing a hypodermic syringe. Tears of utter grief streamed from her eyes as she knelt and embraced her lifelong companion for the final time.

Looking out through the open doorway, she saw that snow had settled, looking almost picturesque without the contamination of footprints.

"At least my dear," she said fighting back the sobs of anguish, "you made it home before the snow fell."

* * * *

Chapter Two - Molly

Molly looked down from her bedroom window and watched the two boys until they rounded the road's bend and disappeared from sight.

She loved her son dearly, and it weighed heavy in her heart that he was transforming from the playful child he had been into a young man.

He would always stop and turn as he quietly closed the wooden gate, knowing that his mother would be watching his departure.

"Mam, stop worrying, I have to go," he shouted up to her silhouetted figure, outlined behind the lace curtains.

"I know, my sweetheart, but you are still my baby, and I worry so much," she whispered just loud enough for him to hear.

"Mam," he said, turning one last time.

"What baby, what have you forgotten now?"

"Just to say, I love you too." With embarrassment clearly etched across his face, he looked both left and right, making sure no one else had heard his words of honest affection.

Her gaze wandered further across the road and out onto the open fields towards the colliery. The spinning wheels of the pit-head caught Molly's attention as if reaching out to remind her that they would soon be sending her beloved Billy to the place he was destined to go.

His destiny, she knew, would be to join the countless generations before him deep below the earth, to win over the nation's fuel.

She missed the days of yesterday when Billy was a mischievous child, and remembered that from the age of four years, he had somehow been different from those who played in the streets below.

There had been something about her son, something that had separated him from the crowd of children his own age.

The others had blended into each other as one, like mirror images of the stereotypical expectancy, but not Billy.

Something seemed to surround him, enhancing his presence with mystique and magic that she never could explain.

Roger, Billy's father, had refused to believe that anything at all was wrong.

"You watch too many horror films, Molly," he would mock. "Maybe you should apply for a job as one of those fairground mediums," sarcasm and ridicule evident in his voice.

She had accepted his scorn and quickly realised that it would need something catastrophic to happen before her husband would change his rigid thinking. Until then she would simply have to suppress her own fears and anxieties.

The voices that seemed to creep like an invisible mist from the shadows of the night, had only been the beginning.

At first these had only been audible to her son and he would idle away the darkest hours, immersed in what appeared to be one-sided conversations.

Slowly, however, as if gaining strength and confidence, the voices gradually spilled into her own range of hearing. It was as if the speaker knew that the story was never to be accepted by others. That the narrator now had power, and control, over its vulnerable audience.

The visions had always been the worst for Molly to accept - how her son seemed to have the ability to seek out someone's fate, simply by looking into their eyes.

He had foretold of impending death on several occasions, and she had ignored his words. Those words she would regret for the rest of her life.

Only when years later her husband finally accepted that all was not as it should be, the link would be finally broken.

The move from the Victorian cottage seemed to put an end to Billy's isolation, and the voices simply died away into the night.

His laughter and frolics would now reverberate throughout the streets and recreation areas; dreams of death and decay would be replaced by those of childlike innocence and fun.

He was always so full of energy, she fondly recalled, as if constant charges of electricity were being pumped around his body instead of his blood.

"Keep still," she would say, trying in desperation to dress him or tie up his shoelace.

"Anybody would think that you had ants in your pants!"

Each and every day was a fun day for young Billy, and she would sit and watch him fondly as he played with his favourite friend who lived further down the street of ageing terraced houses.

Blake was two years older than Billy, but the age gap meant nothing to the two boys. Their never-ending play echoed along the street into the open windows of the houses.

This was, at times, irritating to the occupants when drearily viewing their soap operas and quiz shows on newly installed - and prized - colour television sets. Unlike the other young mothers, Molly did not welcome the times when young Billy wanted to leave the safety of the family home.

Some would relish the tranquillity that was offered when their young charges chose to stray, seeking out pastures new.

Out of sight and out of mind was the preference of many, and allowing the children to wander from view was commonplace.

Not with Molly, however, she would keep Billy within her sight at any cost, even if it meant that she was to be overrun in her own home by the local children.

War games were his favourite. She smiled as she remembered how young Blake would knock on the door ready for the day's action.

His father was an accomplished blacksmith at the colliery and would construct rifles and hand grenades that were impressively realistic.

She would ponder that Blake's father spent more of his work time fashioning weapons for play than he did doing the work he was being paid to do.

"It's no wonder coal production was low this week, young Blake," she'd say with a smile, as the youngster waited for Billy to tie the laces on his fabric plimsolls.

"Your dad must have kept even the Colliery Manager waiting whilst he idled his time away making these," she added, admiring the beautifully crafted weapons that he held at his side.

Even in the open combat of child's play, Billy had never blended into the fold.

The choice of either being the ever victorious British commando, or the inevitably defeated storm trooper, would always be declined.

He wanted to be the freedom fighter that would rise and defeat all, regardless of standing alone amongst the overwhelming odds which the other children presented.

The constant rat-a-tat from make-believe machine guns would drive Molly to the brink of despair until, regardless of victory or defeat, young Billy would seek her out and run to her open arms.

"I love you, mam," he would announce as she held him tightly.

His grip was always the same and would never weaken until she responded with her own enthusiastic reply.

"Love you too, baby, now go and play," she'd say, with motherly affection.

Molly looked back at her own life with a regrettable sigh. She had been the free spirit of laughter and frolic wherever she went.

The granddaughter of a coal miner, she had never quite fitted into the expectations of those around her.

Her own life had fallen apart the day that she had returned from school, only to find her grandfather laid out dead on the kitchen table. The local women had busied themselves, cleaning the broken corpse in preparation for the drab coffin of a working man.

"Take the child away." Molly remembered those words from the old woman as she paused from her macabre work to look at the little girl with contempt.

"Only when the body is ready shall it be seen with prying eyes," she added, hurriedly buttoning up the suit jacket that was reserved for exceptional occasions only.

John Thomas had suffered the same fate of countless men before him. A sudden shift in the roof of rock above him had sent tons of crushing limestone in a downward fall of death.

His gallant comrades had desperately clawed their way through the debris only to convey the shattered body to the surface.

Tradition was that the body would be returned to the family home, as if to complete the working day with a macabre: "I left for work and now I return."

She also regretted how she had succumbed to tradition and married young.

Billy's father, Roger, had charmed his way into her affections from an early age. Two years older than Molly, he had paid for her attentions with the wages he earned working at the town's colliery.

She had been sixteen and in her final year at school, and loved the extravagance of a waged man who could take her to the cinema and spend money taking her to the many ale houses in the local, music-filled town.

Luxury, however, came at a price to Molly and on her seventeenth birthday the over the counter pregnancy testing kit confirmed her fears. Young Billy was conceived on some grassland either at the village cricket pitch or on the colliery railway sidings, places of fertility amongst the local women.

"A father!" he announced with glee, "me - a father!" Roger had shouted with delight as he held her close to his chest.

"I'm going to be a father," he called out to everyone that passed by.

That evening, on his journey home, he had taken celebration within the many bars and clubs that lined his route.

Initially, Roger had been the gentleman of customs old. He had been the husband, father and provider for Molly and the demanding addition to the family home.

The father figure that was central to a community that worked hard, and played even harder.

He would bounce his young charge upon his knees. The same knees that fuelled the grateful nation as he went about his daily work, winning the coal that kept the home fires burning, day and night.

Unfortunately, the novelty of fatherhood soon began to falter for Roger, and he slowly withdrew himself into the age-old tradition that parenthood was a female practice. The man's world that he saw himself surrounded in, needed a man's logic and thinking.

"Just give a working man the peace he deserves," he would often say whenever Molly attempted to engage him in conversation.

Soon the days of family togetherness, walking the ever-learning Billy around the local countryside, were replaced by Roger spending his time becoming detached from the family unit. He now preferred to spend leisure time watching sport on his precious television set, or drinking with his beloved work mates in the local Working Men's Club.

"More coal gets cut over a good pint in the stories told in that club," he would joke on his return, more often than not a little under the influence.

Molly would be expected to stay at home and busy herself with the endless housework that a home and motherhood presented.

Despite his lacklustre attempts at being the pinnacle figure within the family, Roger expected everything to be perfectly organised in his own home.

The family house needed to be pristine whenever he returned and a warm meal to be waiting on the table, without delay, as if it were ordered at a fast service restaurant.

"Why must I always wait to be fed, Molly?" became his catchphrase, as he sat impatiently in front of the television set.

Conversation became limited, and by the time young Billy had reached four years of age, interaction between husband and wife could be counted with each word on one hand.

Roger would rise into a rage at every opportunity and Molly would gradually believe that she was to blame for the maddening outbursts.

Over the hurried breakfast of cereal and toast, the merest spillage from Billy would send him into the darkest of moods that would continue for the rest of the day.

In limited response she would cradle her son in her loving arms, safe within the sanctuary that she had created in the bedroom that was now Billy's little piece of space, in a town of drudgery and biased traditions.

With the mood set, Roger would not be appeased, and mother and child would be wise to wander afar from his gaze, until the sun gave way to darkness, and sleep offered the solitude of forgetfulness.

Deep down, Molly knew she was not without her own faults.

She too had the fire of contempt within her own gut. If Roger wanted the fight, she was all too willing to enter the ring. Constant bouts of anger filled the house. She would spend endless moments comforting, and apologising, to the sleepy Billy as he wrestled for slumber away from the raised voices of anger. She would whisper, as if the magic of some other place had washed over her.

"Say goodbye to the colliery heaps, say goodbye to the rain, me and Billy are to live in the USA."

The magic never failed to work. He would send out the gentle snores of a child, chasing the coloured dreams that only childhood permits. Molly would lay with her son and listen to the ticking clock counting the rhythm of life itself. She would close her eyes and bring upon dreams of summer days spent when she was again the child of sunshine and warmth.

* * * *

Chapter Three – The Dragon Slayer and the Beast

Molly's stepfather was considered an alien by those around him. A bear-like figure whose love would envelop all that he met, regardless of their own initial thoughts and response to a man that they could never truly understand. Milan had simply appeared in England with no past or stories to tell.

He was the father that would sit with the child he loved as if she was his own flesh and blood but could utter no words. There were no stories to amuse of antics long lost, when he also was the child of former times. He was the unspoken magician with no song to recite.

His words were those of knowledge of now and next. Words of the past were non-existent as if history itself had died before him in footsteps that he never was to tread again.

Molly would tease him constantly attempting to pry any indication of his former life before World War Two in the former Yugoslavia.

"U laži su kratke noge," he would sigh, the smile cascading warmth and love.

"You lazy stew…" She tried in vain to hopelessly recite the words through restrained laughter."

"What does it mean, granddad?"

"The lie has little legs," his eyes, as always, were full of hope and promise.

Milan would allow her game to continue and would talk of mythical monsters he had fought on the wooded mountains of his homeland. The fire-breathing dragons he had slain in defence of the village children. Of rivers, so clear there was never the need for a looking glass to see one's true likeness.

"You will see one day, my child," the look of hope and longing reaching out from within the eyes that absorbed her own enlightened stare.

"You will one day travel to the place where now only my heart remains."

Young Molly would look, as if transfixed with delight each and every time the stories were told. Sadly, as the years slipped slowly by, the belief of monsters and dragons faded, and the stories slowly drew to a close.

Whenever she visited the ageing Milan now, she always felt saddened.

The fire and dreams remained in his eyes, but his body was failing in time. The bear was becoming tamed as if it had spent its mundane life caged in some rundown zoo. Molly would wish that she could once again sit on his lap, and stare in wide-eyed belief how the man had actually been a dragon slayer.

She looked at the sleeping Billy, so peaceful and at solace in sleep, and she wondered with a heavy heart what tomorrow would bring.

Roger's mood swings had become a regular thing, and she had begun to dread Old Red the rooster's announcement that morning had once again arrived.

Whenever he was not on the early shift at the mine, Roger would expect nothing less than a cooked breakfast waiting for him on the table as he descended wearily down into the kitchen.

"Mmm, smells almost good enough to eat," he would announce as he sat, waiting to be served.

"A man could die of starvation," his impatience evident, whenever there was even the shortest of delays with the plated offering.

The slightest miscalculation on Molly's part would result in a rage that would last until sleep offered its sanctuary.

Each day she would pray that the darkness had lessened the previous day's mood, and that Roger, the man that she had known and loved, would arise once again.

Each and every day was the same and Molly began to realise that the times of joy and romance were possibly behind her, as were the stories of dragons and misty, wooded mountain slopes.

Maybe, with the diminishing glow of the dragon slayer's keen eye, so too was her own passion for the life she had known and had always been accustomed.

Perhaps, she thought, luck would have an unexpected turn for her and her loving charge.

She would often fall into her own thoughts of a childhood lost - hazy days of summers long gone from memory, where the sun never failed to smile its warm caress on those beneath. Distorted images of the butterfly and bumble bees, buzzing their own paths amongst the carefully laid out rows in Milan's garden of apparent happiness, were always foremost in her childhood recollections.

The dirt and the filth of her natural surroundings always became lost in this place of never-ending happiness.

She would wander, as children do, along the cut paths of wild grass, so neatly neutered, as if it was someone's prize lawn. A place they would entertain their guests, during balmy summer evenings.

"Come, my child, and enjoy with me what nature's mother has offered to us," his voice, forever hushed, with a gentleness that only added to the serenity of the surroundings.

She would walk, carefully treading the recorded soil imprints before her, amongst the tender cabbage leaves that yearned upright for the sun.

Through the delicate lettuce that needed constant attention, and, most curious to young Molly, the imposing alien to her own understanding of the plant world, the tall plants that yielded tobacco.

"Are these the magic beans from the story of the giant?" she'd ask with childish innocence.

"No my precious," he'd answer. "These are the magic beans from a faraway place called Herzegovina."

As the sun reached its zenith, Milan would invite her to sit by his side in the shade that the old apple tree offered. He would carefully wipe the freshly picked apple with a cloth, dampened from the well nearby before giving Molly the shiny offering. His wide grin would win her over and fill her heart with love and affection.

"My child," he would say, his accent strong despite the years he had lived in England, "eat what the earth has given you."

It was always the same; the shade from the old tree, the offered fruit, and then the story.

Milan would tell his young charge of a time, long ago when the world was new, where everything was bright and colourful. He would speak of two foolish men who would spend their tireless days getting into mischief of all kinds.

One day they had ventured into Milan's homeland and, whilst walking along a trail of flower petals, they stumbled upon God's very own fruit bowl, perched high upon a mountainside and illuminated so brightly from the golden rays of a beautiful summer's sun.

Full of mischief, the men climbed the heights and took from the bowl the most delicious orange. Laughing and throwing their prize to each other in turn, they descended back down into the lush valley below, where their game of pitch and catch continued until the sun dipped down and the earth became enveloped by the darkness of the night.

Next morning, God was resting from his arduous task of creation, and decided to sit under the old apple tree to shelter from the hot rays of his mighty sun that lit his new world with warmth and prosperity. Feeling a little hungry, he reached and tilted his precious fruit bowl towards him. With utter disbelief, he found that the orange had been stolen. With rage and anger, he raised his arms and sent out bolts of lightning which reached out across the lands in a wrath of fire. The playing men were consumed in flames, and the orange was catapulted high into the air, breaching the earth's gravitational pull, and came to rest high up in space. As it cooled from the impact its colour faded, and it began to turn slowly to further protect itself from the rays of the sun.

Knowing that his beloved orange was spoilt forever, God wanted to preserve it as a reminder of the fateful day, so he gently blew a warm breath to carry it further from the harmful rays, casting a magical spell that it only appeared when the sun had sank into the ground to slumber.

Lazy, hazy days of summers lost were behind her now, and the realisation was gradually casting its gloomy shadow across what she had always wanted, and believed.

Milan had not been Molly's natural father, but had taken on the role with determination, enthusiasm, and passion.

Her own father, Dennis, had been a local entrepreneur who had made his fortune fleecing anyone who was unfortunate enough to be taken in by his banter and charm.

Born within a mining family, he had quickly learnt that sweat and toil was not the only way to earn a living. There were far easier ways to earn an income than crawling in the bowels of the earth, for a meagre pittance.

"Why work and break the spirit?" he would announce to all that cared to listen. "When you can live, and thrive from the backs of others."

Dennis' first breakthrough came following the ceasefire of hostilities in war ravaged Europe in 1945.

Maybe by sheer cunning, or by chance, he realised many thousands of soldiers had been killed and would have no further use for their boots.

"The local miners could make full use of the reinforced footwear," he would convince himself.

Dennis saw his chance and took it without conscience.

Boots would be taken from the fallen heroes and sold onto the eager colliers at what they saw as being a bargain price. Aching feet were saved, and the purse grew fatter.

With a pocket full of cold brass pennies he had purchased dead men's feet, then a rundown grocers shop.

The once proud owner had succumbed to a fatal heart attack, leaving his wife not only distraught with loneliness, but also with little experience of running and maintaining a thriving family business.

Soon the shelves had become starved of the fresh produce that had filled the aching bellies of countless generations before, and with this, the ringing of the bell above the door to announce an eager customer had slowly uttered its dying breath of silence.

Dennis eagerly watched the grocery shop's slow demise with baited breath. Like one of nature's predators, he had quickly realised in his quest for riches that in order for an easy survival, it was the weakest that should be observed, and he therefore monitored closely from a distance.

He knew that with the dying animal came the vultures that would recognise from afar that easy and rich pickings were soon to be had for the feast.

Speculation amongst the locals had been growing that the poor grieving widow would soon have to give up the ghost of her departed husband's vision of success and community standing.

She would have to succumb to the inevitable that she simply could not survive alone and that the family business was crumbling before her very eyes.

Dennis knew, that in order to make the kill that he desired he would have to lunge at exactly the right time.

Too soon, and the end could be at a greater cost than he had anticipated; too late, and he would see the feast being taken out of his hands, consumed with relish by an equally conscience-clear rival.

With a full understanding of the woman's plight, he had pounced with neither guilt, nor shame but cunning, knowing all too well that she could not maintain both her young family and the arduous tasks of business. He clawed feverishly at what he saw as his own opportunity to make the kill his very own.

Dennis offered the unsuspecting woman a lifeline.

With reckless cunning, he offered the unfortunate widow a way out of the misery that was slowly engulfing her.

"It's a gift from my own heart," he'd said, as he held the grieving woman close to his chest. "Only I can lose."

The rehearsed serenity, evident within the words of a man that was prepared to rob the soul.

Shrewdly, he had offered to provide the once thriving grocery shop with the much needed fresh supplies. He promised that this would turn the shop once again into the centre of business that it had once been renowned for.

She would have no payment to return for the duration of six months. This way, Dennis had smiled reassuringly, she could concentrate her efforts into her family and after the six months the business would again be profitable enough to pay off its debt to him. After all, he had said, it was from the truth of his heart that he had offered this, as no profit would be reaped from the friendly gesture and that he was simply a concerned onlooker that had taken pity on her new-found plight.

With his first victim in the bag, the widow had unwittingly shaken the gentleman's agreement, had signed the contract of deception that inevitably would take her lifelong assets and future dreams from beneath her very eyes, with nothing in the sense of remorse for his cruellest of actions, nor any way out of the inevitable collapse of her mere existence.

The coming weeks went well. The shop became stocked as it had been in the glory days of a man proud to serve the community that he had loved and cherished. Dennis, it seemed, had been the champion, the rescuer of those in need. No longer was he deemed the exploiter of dead men's feet by the local onlookers, but was now seen as the saviour of widows lost to despair.

Unfortunately, the saviour had his own devious ideas about the bustling shop and these ideas were not the ones that would establish himself a seat amongst the righteous following his own eventual demise.

As the weeks passed by, Dennis began to play his hand in what would be a game of betrayal and cunning.

He began to acquire inferior goods for the shop. Fresh produce would be replaced with fruit and vegetables that had passed their better days.

He would blame the suppliers and spend countless hours in artificial negotiation with local market gardeners and warehouses. Eager customers would soon turn their backs on the inferior supplies, opting to travel the several miles to the new supermarket on the fringes of town where quality would be guaranteed. Outgoings soon outweighed incomings and by the time that the agreed six months drew to an end the unwitting shopkeeper was heavily indebted to its scrupulous saviour.

The vulture seized his golden opportunity. He offered what he claimed was the only lifeline available.

The shop would have to be sold. He now took on the role as master actor, giving an Oscar-winning performance to his unsuspecting prey.

"After all," he said in earnest, "it is your best interests that I hold close to my heart."

Due to its rising unpopularity amongst the local community, the store had become a burden too heavy for the unfortunate widow.

She was heavily indebted to kindly Dennis and readily accepted his proposal. He would purchase the shop from her at a price that he explained was fair and generous, given its lost favour and lack of custom.

Without realising it, she would almost be giving away her assets without ever realising that she had been taken for a fool. The shining knight in armour had again offered the lifeline that would save her and her family from ultimate ruin, and kindly Dennis, in her eyes, would sacrifice himself in order to save her.

In reality she had been the unwitting victim of a class deceiver.

She had played into Dennis' cruel hands without the realisation that her rescuer had set out to take her life's blood, devoid of even a sliver of remorse.

He had purposely run the shop into the ground. So rundown that it no longer offered any temptation to the less scrupulous local businessmen that enjoyed the easy kill.

With his offered lifeline, he again appeared as the valiant saviour, and toasts were made in his name inside the local public houses.

The widow had been saved from her own misfortune and the caring Dennis had taken over her burden. It certainly seemed as though she had been saved from her downfall.

Once again the thriving business flourished. Each ring of the bell from the hand-operated till announced that business was booming.

As the business grew, so did the need for Dennis to take on waged help, and he promptly offered employment to a young village girl, Anne.

Her father had been a close friend to Dennis until his untimely death from a heart attack.

Again he was deemed the saviour of those in need. He offered the girl a way out of the poverty which often followed death for those within the mining communities.

At the age of nineteen, Anne had found herself admired by many of the young colliers. They would flash their hard-earned money in the hope that she would flutter her smouldering eyes in their direction.

She had been a lively, carefree soul, the centrepiece at any party. This gradually changed and she seemed to submerse herself in her new-found opportunity, working alongside the middle-aged Dennis.

Extended hours were spent doing regular stock takes, and it did not take long for local speculation to emerge that perhaps Dennis had other desires than those of a local saviour.

The truth was that he had his own thoughts and plans for the young Anne.

The same cunning that had stole the once prosperous family business from under the grieving widow's feet was to emerge again.

As always, the trap had been set, and the prey had unwittingly placed her innocent foot in the jaws of her new-found saviour.

Molly's mother knew all too well what was happening.

"Who am I to complain?" she would convince herself.

Although her husband had not been the loving father, he had, sometimes, begrudgingly honoured his paternal instinct and provided for his forgiving wife and offspring.

He did, after all, provide the roof of security over their heads, the necessities for sustenance upon the table and the safe environment of a family home.

Dennis would return each day from his work and provide the coffers of a working man to his eager family in return for the respect that a working man deserved.

All too soon the time that Dennis graced the family home with his presence grew less and less. The never-ending jobs that running his new found empire required, he told his wife, would have to take precedence over daily chores within the home. Looking after young Molly, after all, was woman's work and it was the wife that should stay home to keep the fires burning.

Molly would never forget the day when Dennis, her father, returned to the family home for the very last time.

She would look back with grief and tears when the smartly dressed Dennis left his final farewell, casting misfortune on the family that needed him the most.

She had returned from her day of schooling as usual, although today she had not been greeted with her customary slices of freshly baked bread and strawberry jam. Today, however, the young Molly was faced with the realisation that all was not right.

She passed her father, Dennis, on the Yorkshire stone flags leading to the front door of the house. As she walked towards the house, he walked past her.

"Goodbye," was the only word spoken as father and daughter parted for the very last time.

With not even eye contact, he continued, opening the rickety gate, and climbing into his waiting car before driving down the cobbled street.

Without the slightest of remorse, Dennis, Molly's father, had gone from her life in a selfish act of self-indulgence and heartlessness that would split the family apart for eternity.

* * * *

Chapter Four – When the Dead Came Calling

Molly had always known that Billy was different to the other children around her in the tightly-knit mining community.

Okay, she thought at first, children do have times of need and discomfort, and friends from their imagination can take away their sorrows and despair.

Billy's friends of make believe manifested themselves at an early age. She recalled the day when the excited youngster had charged into the living room with an empty tumbler asking her for water.

"Are you thirsty again Billy?" she had asked.

"No mammy, it's not for me," he had replied with excitement.

"It's for the poor man, so that he can wash the muck from around his eyes."

With childish enthusiasm he went on to explain that there had been a man, sad and dirty, laid down to rest upon the kitchen table. The poor man, Billy said, had asked in despair for his face to be washed from the coals that had blighted his life and that of his family through their times of strife.

These innocent words shook Molly to her inner core; the hairs at the back of her neck stood as if jostled by a sudden charge of electricity.

She was taken back to her own childhood when her own mother had told her of the fateful day when she had returned from school to find, with sheer horror, her father, Molly's grandfather, laid dead upon the old oak table in the family kitchen. The elderly local women were working to clean the dirt and coal grime from the shattered corpse.

"Billy's account confirmed Molly's suspicions of his ability to communicate with the spirit world but this suddenly brought home his clear ability to communicate with the spiritual world.

"Who are you talking to Billy?" she'd ask, as he sat alone on the bed, idling away the hours.

"The shadow people, mammy," he'd reply without further explanation, regardless of how deeply she delved for a better answer.

She sat with amusement as he apparently talked to, and played with, those of an invisible world, a world that only Billy could see. But now… things were quite different.

Her child's invisible world made him happy, and to Molly, Billy's happiness was all that mattered. She often wished, as she watched him, that she could be offered the slightest of glimpses into the world that he became drawn into as he tirelessly played.

He often said to her, as he noticed her scrutinising gaze, that she should just close her eyes and free her mind of all the thoughts and trappings of her earthbound existence. Only then would she be offered the glimpse of what he could experience and see.

"Close your thoughts, mammy, and allow them to enter your mind," he'd said.

"Only then will the shadow people rise and come forward to retrace and capture what they once had lived and loved."

At times Molly would hear the slightest of noises as she sat in complete silence watching over the playing Billy. A whisper that came from nowhere in particular, the laugh of a child in some faraway corner, or the cushioned sound of a footstep.

The strangeness that seemed to envelop Billy had made its presence known almost as soon as he had entered this world.

Molly and Roger had the fortune and luck to purchase an old two-bedroom cottage at a knock-down price when they discovered that she was carrying their unexpected child.

Whilst the pregnancy developed they would tirelessly spend hours renovating the property to the standard that Roger's income from the colliery would provide.

"Our very own castle," they'd say in spontaneous unison, whenever they entered through the door to begin yet another day of wallpapering and painting.

Upon leaving the maternity unit of the local infirmary the happy couple moved into the freshly painted and newly-carpeted property to cradle their newborn with love and pride.

All was perfect now. The young couple, so much in love, a newly-renovated home of their own, and their newborn charge to focus all of their loving attentions on.

To bring in the much-needed income to maintain his new-found kingdom of bricks and mortar that was to support his new family, Roger had asked to work the nightshifts at the colliery.

Working through the night led to higher wages as the hourly financial rate was equalled at one third its value by an unsocial hour's payment.

Not only were there financial rewards for Roger, but he soon found that the burden of a hungry baby crying through the small hours of night could also be avoided if he were away from home, labouring for the much-needed money that was needed to sustain the family into survival and prosperity.

Molly soon found that, at best, she was left alone with the attention-demanding Billy. At night she was the single-handed carer, feeder and guardian for the persistently needy baby. During the daylight hours she found herself overburdened with carrying out the day-to-day chores of family life, added to the extra weight that everything had to be done with the minimum of noise, so as not to disturb her sleeping husband; after all, he often reminded her, he was the one having to work, whilst she stayed home sleeping the night away.

The days for Molly were filled with the never-ending chores of housework, tending to the ever-demanding Billy and making preparation so that everything was in order for when Roger returned from his day of work. That he could survey his new-found kingdom with a careful eye to make sure that idle hands had not entered the family home whilst he was away, and all was as it should be. He would often quote his favourite saying: "A tidy home is a happy home."

As the winter evenings slowly settled their gloomy presence over the rooftops and streets of Castlefields, Molly felt the burden of motherhood lift. Although the growing Billy had no knowledge of mechanical time, his natural, in-built time piece recognised the difference between the daylight hours and darkness. Daylight meant constant nourishment and attention and the dark hours were for interrupted rest and dreams of never-ending play that were to come.

With the rigours of every day dipping to a close with the dying winter's sun Molly would look forward to the punctual announcement that Roger would offer - the usual kiss on the cheek and the take up of his newspaper-wrapped sandwiches that she had prepared as he left again for another night, deep underground winning the coals of a grateful nation.

"You're a lucky woman, Molly," he would turn and say, before disappearing from view around the corner.

"No work and all play," he'd add with a hint of resentment.

As the door closed so too did Molly's inner feeling of warmth and happiness. She would settle the tired Billy after his last feed of warmed milk and comfort him in his crib until the last of the fight had gone from him and his blue eyes slowly blinked to the close that sleep offered.

She'd sit with him, gently caressing his tiny hands until she knew that sleep had taken its grip and the twitching of his tiny feet meant that he entered the make believe place of fun and play that babies succumbed to when only in the deepest of slumber.

Slowly, taking tiny steps, she'd leave the dreaming Billy to his own play and merriment and creep down the stairs, avoiding the places that let out an eerie creak whenever stepped on, so as not to interrupt his slumber.

Safely in the comfort of the living room she would settle herself before the glowing embers of the coal fire that warmed the family home and offered a constant supply of boiling hot water whenever it was needed.

It was during one of these brief respites that Molly first heard the voice of what sounded like an elderly lady. The voice was faint and seemed quite distant, so she switched her mind to concentrate on her favourite weekly television programme that was being broadcast.

Sipping on her nightly treat of red wine she was again snatched from her thoughts by the sound of the elderly voice. This time it sounded nearer and seemed to be coming from the house itself. Perturbed, she quickly rose from the comfort of the armchair and reached to turn down the volume on the television. As the silence fell around the room so too did the voice.

All in the house was quiet except the occasional passing of a car on the road immediately outside.

Silly, Molly thought, as she again turned on the television's volume and settled herself in the comfort of the chair. Maybe the wine was a little stronger than she had thought, or just maybe, she had drunk a little too much.

She quickly dismissed the imaginary voice and her thoughts once again focused on the leading character that the weekly serialised drama was portraying, sitting in his local public house, amusing those around him with stories of fun and mayhem.

No sooner had she settled once again when the voice returned. Startled, she rose quickly from the armchair and turned off the television completely.

As if playing some bizarre game of cat and mouse, as the dying voices of the television faded away, so did the elderly voice, only this time it continued long enough for Molly to acknowledge that, not only had the voice seemed to come from upstairs, but that it resembled the speech of an elderly woman speaking to a child.

Motherly instinct rose within Molly. She raced out of the room and bounded, with giant leaps, up the creaking staircase. With effortless ease she leapt forwards, crashing through the door that she had left ajar and raced towards the crib.

Billy's wide, blue eyes looked up at her and a wide, toothless smile beckoned a warm and heart-stopping greeting.

With the love that only a mother can offer, Molly reached down and scooped Billy into her arms, holding him tightly and protectively to her chest.

Once he was safe in the warmth and shield of her embracing hold she scanned the room for the intruder. Everything was how she had left it, nothing had been disturbed.

Walking to the window she checked the latch - locked as it was when she had first turned the arm, hours before.

Molly felt a cold shiver run down the whole of her body, as if an ice cold glacier had burst its restraints and was streaming through her veins. With panic, she fled from the room and ran as fast as she could safely go, down the staircase that she had, moments before, ascended with curiosity and suspicion.

Once in the apparent safety of the living room she immediately turned on all the light switches, bathing everything in white light which forced back the invading shadows.

Despite her own excitement and fear, Billy lay, as if breastfeeding, tightly against her chest, the toothless smile still beaming across his entire face. Whatever had happened just then, she thought to herself, had not startled or upset him in any way.

On the contrary, whatever it was that had sounded within the bedroom, it had been warmly greeted and appreciated by the inquisitive baby.

Slowly, and fuelled by the warmth of the room, Molly's senses returned to normality, her heartbeat fading into the rhythmic tone that nature had intended for its bearer's future survival.

The occasional monotonous drones of passing traffic were now the only interruptions that drifted into the brightly lit room and Molly eased herself down into the armchair, careful not to disturb the now sleeping Billy.

With everything again as it should be, she regained her composure and gathered her scattered thoughts together.

Surely she had been mistaken? She and Billy were the only people inside the house and no one had entered, nor had anyone left unnoticed. Besides, she remembered, she had carefully locked and bolted both doors, as was her routine as soon as Roger left for work at the colliery.

Thankfully, the rest of the evening passed without further incident. Billy continued his slumber through to the slow rise of the winter's sun and there were no mysterious whisperings of elderly voices drifting through the stillness of the night.

Despite normality returning, Molly found it difficult to slow down her racing thoughts enough for sleep to take its weary grip and she slept very little. Whenever she closed her eyes she was taken back to moments earlier where she'd sat in the comfort of the armchair, enjoying the serenity that had settled around her, the warmth of the glowing coals from the fire keeping out the winters chill.

The voice had been unmistakably real. It had been as real as her own voice had been when scooping up Billy in motherly protection as she had entered the bedroom.

Although Molly knew what she had heard, she wondered what she should say to Roger on his return from his night of toil. Her previous experience of his deep ingrained beliefs told her that her concerns would be met with scorn and ridicule.

He had always been a man of logic and reasoning. She had recalled the times he had chuckled with relish whenever he had relayed conversations from colleagues during his working day.

How he had mocked them whenever they had made reference to ghostly encounters deep underground with miners long lost to some tragic accident that had stolen their lives prematurely, without pity or remorse.

No, she decided. Whatever she had heard would be best kept from Roger's attention. Besides, she thought, it was probably a one-off occurrence and would not be repeated. Some fluke of nature or rogue radio signal, amplified in the stillness of the night that had caused the strange phenomena.

*   *   *   *

Chapter Five – The Path of Adventure

Thankfully, over the coming days, everything remained as it should have been within the family home. Roger would be working, sleeping or spending his valuable leisure time enjoying the fine beers offered at the local Working Men's Club, preferring more and more the company of his colleagues than that of his needy family. After all, he would remind Molly, "A working man need not suffer the burden of parenthood as well as provide the necessities through hard work for the family," the voice of authority coming from within him.

His explanation would continue that putting the food on the table and clothing on their backs was the man's sole duty he had to perform. Motherhood was the woman's role within the household and if he were to help around the house, he would become the butt of the masculine laughter that frequented the mine and its workforce.

As the darkest of the seasons dragged its weary path ever so slowly forward, winter's grip began to beckon its prey into its icy clasp.

Although the days were shorter, time seemed only to slow for Molly. No longer did the welcoming local park offer solace and company, the haven that she too had known and loved as a child.

How she had run excitedly over the neatly mown grass, along the impeccably kept hedgerows down towards the small, man-made boating lake where she would lose all real sense of time and purpose, dredging the green waters for the myriads of tiny sticklebacks that seemed to make the water shimmer in their vast numbers.

The tiny fish were scooped in their dozens in the cane-handled fishing net and quickly released into the water-filled glass jar where they would spend their new-found day of captivity until it was once again time for their release as darkness beckoned.

She remembered fondly how Milan would walk with her along the path of adventure on their weekly forage into the communal haven that was the hub of the community. The path of adventure, she recalled, was a journey she relished with glee and would skip merrily home from school on Fridays knowing that this route would be taken the following morning.

In essence the path was merely that of a walkway that ran along the perimeter of the town; a tar-macadam lined path which ran parallel to the main road that was the central hub of the town.

The route dissected much of the town's allotment gardens. The allotments had been a gift from the coal owner to his loyal workforce one hundred years before. The gardens were a collective form of one's independence away from the grit and grime of Castlefields.

Here the amateur farmer could sow his seed without the pressure to supply. Simply, if the carrot did not grow, then lessons would be learned without hunger, for the following year's harvest.

She again smiled as she recalled taking the path. With the inner feeling of warmth she remembered the heart-stopping fear she had felt as the devilish beast had called to her. Her heart had stopped each time she had rounded the corner to face the demon himself.

The devil in Molly's case was a goat. Milan's allotment neighbour had taken the easy option.

"Why dig and break the back?" he would say with a smile.

"Keeping animals on the land was the easy answer." With pride he would point over the flock of demon-eyed wanderers.

Here, the goat was king. The goat would pick out its unwary prey and, with the blink of the devil's eye would, without warning, lower his head and spring forward with the speed of the wind itself. The unfortunate victim would be catapulted forward as if hit head-on by an oncoming express locomotive and would suffer bruising to the buttocks for days afterwards.

Molly was snatched from the happiness of her memories with the sound of amused, childish laughter from Billy, whom she had left asleep in his crib upstairs whilst she settled into the routine of her morning's household chores. Returning the cleaning cloth to the locked cupboard she made her way up the staircase and opened the door to the dimly lit room where she had left the sleeping child some thirty minutes before. She was aghast at the scene that met her.

Billy was stood upright against the side of the crib. As if taking part in some showtime audience he was excitedly clapping his hands in rapid applause whilst letting out the squeals of delight and relish.

His eyes were transfixed to the wall opposite the bedroom window, as if enjoying the antics of some circus performer taking in the appreciation of the final curtain call. Molly stepped back against the door she had just entered and watched in fascination the scene playing out before her eyes. Although nothing to her was visible against the backdrop of the wall, whatever Billy could see had obviously drawn in his entire attention, as he seemed oblivious to the fact that anyone else had entered the room. His eyes were transfixed, as if locked on to some invisible point of light that danced its merry, mysterious dance in circular motions across the surface of the wall.

Intrigued, she took a step closer, to see what it was that had captured her son's attention so much that he seemed transfixed to the invisible scene before his childish vision.

Before she had time to gain her composure, Molly froze, as if a glacier had forced its way into her blood supply. The sensation that the hairs at the nape of her neck were being lifted by some unseen force startled her senses and with a dreadful screech of, "NOOO," she felt herself being pushed back with a ferocity of aggression and hostility. She felt her back make connection with the door in a sickening thud, jolting her entire body and sending her crashing to the ground. In panic and desperation she fought against the fear and pain and heaved herself to her feet.

Motherly instinct to protect her brood rose above all feeling of self preservation and she leapt the short distance to the crib, scooping up the now-crying Billy into her arms, clawing the frightened child tightly towards her in a mother's protective embrace of safety and comfort before making a hasty retreat out of the bedroom and down the staircase.

Once in the living room she quickly closed the door and leant against it as if to barricade them both from unseen danger.

Although the room was lit by a small lamp she leaned across and turned on the central ceiling light, bathing the area with a brightness that momentarily dazzled her and forced her to blink her eyes in rapid succession until her sight accustomed itself to the artificial brightness.

As she focused, Molly took in deep breaths to calm herself and began to take stock of her racing mind. The house was quiet, exaggerating the heavy sound of her heartbeat which seemed to fill her ears, as if part of a procession of drummers in some colourful street parade.

Surely, she thought, whatever had happened just minutes before had a completely rational explanation. Unexplained phenomena, after all, was a thing of vivid imagination or televisual wizardry, not the usual evening's experience of a working-class mother left alone to ponder the day when relaxing in the comfort of the family home.

Despite the reasoning in her thoughts Molly simply had no answer to what she had both seen and heard. Billy had been fixated and unable to distract himself from whatever scene had been playing out its act before his eyes.

It was as if an unseen dancer had been weaving its trance-inducing steps before him, only to be interrupted when the final curtain was lowered.

The terrifying protest of, "NOOO," had filled Molly's ears with both clarity and reality, as if she had called out this herself. The back-wrenching push that followed and the resulting impact as she crashed into the door simply held no explanation other than brute force had played its part.

The night drew out its weary path without further incident. Afraid to return upstairs to the bedroom Molly slept huddled on the couch nursing Billy against her chest.

Sleep did not, however, offer her the respite from what she had experienced. As she drifted into deep slumber she found herself again dreaming of walking the path of adventure, hand in hand with Milan as they merrily made their way to the flower-bedded park and the lake.

Once again she was snatched from her thoughts by the sound of laughter resounding from the bedroom above. As before, she made her way up the creaking staircase and entered the room. This time, however, the scene had taken a sickening turn and as her eyes accustomed themselves to the gloom she made out the figure of a woman facing away from her, gently rocking from side to side.

Shocked, Molly took a step forwards. As her foot rested on the carpeted floor the figure turned. The fear inside Molly exploded into a sickening scream as she focused on the figure's grim face. Her eyes locked with the eyes of death itself.

The face that met her gaze was wizzened and unreal. Deeply wrinkled and pale grey, as if its very life had been drawn from it in some macabre ritual of torture and disfigurement.

Fear rose within Molly as she was drawn into the colourless eyes that bore their gaze into her own. As she felt herself being slowly pulled towards the impenetrable gaze she felt the sickening feeling of cold, unseen hands reach up over her arms and trace their way slowly across her shoulders towards her throat.

"NOOO!" She screamed out in blind panic, looking into the colourless eyes with a plea for mercy.

As if her plea had been answered and acknowledged, colour slowly fused into the lifeless eyes of her attacker and the wizzened, deathly pale features took on a life and warmth that she slowly recognised through her own panic and despair. Roger was standing above her, slightly bent, with his hands resting on her shoulders.

Relief raced through her body, quenching the panic that had exploded from deep within. Sobbing, with deep breaths, she reached up to take on the embrace of safety and reassurance, taking in the warmth and life of her husband's touch. Whatever demons had been lurking in her dream-like state, they slivered back into the depths of her imagination to be replaced with thoughts of normality and safety.

"Maybe you've been watching too much television," Roger said, a grin upon his face.

"Your head is full of dreams," he mimicked, as he sat down on the armchair beside her.

"Anyway, now that you're awake," he said, the smile widening across his face, "Be a good girl and make breakfast. I'm starving."

* * * *

Chapter Six – Just the Two of Us

Silent, radiant flakes of sunshine settled gently across Molly's face. "All around the golden sun, flakes settled on the ground, misty mornings and mysteries……." Molly opened her eyes. "Hark to the sound of the dog fox, gone to ground…." As she felt herself drawn away from the picturesque meadow that she had lay; as her vision returned so too did reality. With a yawn she rolled over and took stock of her thoughts.

How she wanted so much at that moment to roll over into the comfort and peace that the water meadow had offered in her dream. To lay, undisturbed with the summer sun dappling its warm dance across her face was a dream she would gladly embrace for all eternity.

Now, not in slumber, the reality settled its weary path, replacing the golden flakes of what was never to be, to what was here and now.

With a weary yawn Molly leant over and turned off the music system that Roger had bought some weeks before. Castlefields at last was waking to the dawn of modern music which had slowly crept to the fold. Stuck in the time warp of rock and roll the town had slowly let in the newcomers. Elvis Presley had reigned; his supremacy was God-like throughout the small-minded miners of Castlefields. But now the new age musicians were slowly creeping their way into the kitchens of weekend leisure.

Molly had discovered the music of Pink Floyd whilst listening to the morning radio station that helped her through her chores of repetitive housework.

Despite her enthusiasm for the music that ebbed away at the grime and uniformity of her drab environment, Roger always showed his distaste by turning over the radio channel or switching off the music system whenever he entered the room. Like most coal miners of his time he was deeply stuck in his ways. The same ways in which his father, and his father's father had been set. He had become deeply socialised to his surroundings and change was met with contempt. Roger would ridicule Molly whenever she listened to the new music that was sweeping the nation. He would jibe that maybe she would be more suited to living in a commune where she could frolic naked and smoke marijuana whilst chanting some ritualistic pagan verse.

Molly took this in her stride and his remarks deflected from her like water from a duck's back. Besides, whenever she felt hurt by the cutting remarks she would confide her woes to the understanding Milan. Although he could no longer sit the child upon his knee and cradle her reassurance, he would offer her his wholehearted support and opinion whenever this was required.

Milan had become the rock for which she had desperately searched when her own father, Dennis, had fled the family nest to seek out his own pleasures of self satisfaction and mirth. Milan, with no past of his own, had stepped up to the mark and had offered his new-found family his very heart and soul.

Molly was brought from her thoughts by the sound of Billy's laughter. She slowly rose from her position of comfort on the plump suede couch and took stock of her surroundings. Pink Floyd continued their hallucinogenic offerings amplified by the dual speakers that modern technology offered.

As gentle haze was replaced by clarity she took in the sight of her awakening. Billy was stood, rigid in stance, looking high above the empty fireplace. As Molly focused her own sight on what was not there to see, Billy turned and whispered, "It's okay mam, she's gone to heaven again, she only came to say 'hi'."

Molly had grown used to Billy's friends of his imagination. She had even grown used to the imaginary elderly lady that he would idle away the hours chatting to as she set about the chores of never-ending housework. From time to time, however, her thoughts would drift back to the evening when she had felt the cold grip that had touched her, sending her with violent force crashing into the door when she had tried to interrupt Billy from his play.

How she had felt true fear that night, fear that had followed her and entered her dreams - only to be repelled when Roger had returned in the morning from work.

Roger, the joker as always, laughed and mimicked the frightened Molly. He spent the following weeks waiting round corners. With mirth he would surprise her with the obligatory "Boo!" of lifelong fear and childish merriment.

Eventually, even he grew tired of his latest form of amusement and the waiting round corners gradually stopped as some other form of antic sought out his attention.

A warm breeze gently blew as mother and son walked slowly through the bustling streets in the early morning's warm rays of sunshine that spring bestowed on the town's inhabitants. Despite its grit and grime even Castlefields looked a more pleasant place as nature began to shed its winters coat and opened itself up to the radiance that the approaching summer offered. Soon the farmers would be busying themselves in the fields that surrounded the small town, breaking up the fertile earth that would produce rich crops when summer and the stirrings of autumn embraced together.

Soon the pair were walking the path of adventure. With the safety that the path offered away from the busy main street, Molly allowed Billy to run along in front of her.

There was a distinct spring to his step as he always looked forward to these visits to see his grandfather. The same bond that had connected Molly and Milan together had passed down to Billy and had strengthened to form an unbreakable cord. The pair would sit away countless hours amongst the vegetables on Milan's allotment. They would emerge as the sun settled to rest at the end of the day, reddened by its day-long warmth. Molly's mother, Alison, would shake her head in mock disapproval as Milan would pour himself a well earned tumbler of his beloved whisky and, before drinking, would offer the glass to the eager Billy who would reach over and inhale its powerful vapours before passing the glass back. Both rejuvenated from their day's toil they would then always settle to play the obligatory game of chess that always followed. Milan would give out the ritual sigh of surrender in checkmate as each game drew to its close. To the observer it was always obvious that Milan had given the game away with reckless moves of defeat, but to Billy he was the champion of champions, the David that had again defeated the Goliath.

Molly smiled with pride as she looked in front of her. As always Billy had saddled himself into the reins of his favourite charger. The white stallion that would beckon his call had again obeyed the summons and had taken the master aloft. She smiled as his knees slowly rose in mock horse-riding as he play-galloped along the path.

Billy had now become the fearless dragon slayer of Milan's stories. The thin, stripped whip-like branch of English willow had become a glistening sword and the brave warrior knight lashed out at the never-ending enemy that lay before him. With feverish slashing and cutting, the dragon slayer cut through the barrier of stinging nettles that lined the path as nature fought back to reclaim what she had lost when the path had been constructed some hundred years before. As always, the battle concluded in carnage. The path would be littered with newly-cut foliage and the deadly sword would finally succumb to its inevitable end, breaking under the overwhelming odds that it had faced. With the moment's magic gone the fearless knight would quickly dismount and run to hold his mother's hand and accept the offered chocolate with childish glee.

As usual Molly's mother was busy making bread in the main room of the house which doubled as a kitchen and living room. Molly had always been fascinated watching Alison baking the family bread. She would pass Molly a piece of the warm dough and mother and child would knead the gently rising mixture in unison.

Each and every time, Molly would sit impatiently next to the large earthenware pot that was covered over with a damp towel and left to warm, as the dough was left to rise.

Molly would let out a childish gasp as Alison drew back the towel like a magician exposing a rabbit from a hat. It never ceased to amaze Molly how the contents had grown before her very eyes. Magically, when the damp cloth had been removed, its contents had always trebled in size. Alison would tell her that the invisible fireside people had added to the mixture as it rested underneath its cover. Molly smiled to herself, now remembering that she had been almost twelve when she had first found out that the fireside people were imaginary inventions of her mother's playful mind, and that it had been a cookery lesson at school that had finally educated her with the knowledge and understanding of a simple chemical reaction. It was the work of yeast, not invisible hands that forced the dough to rise and swell.

As the magnetic bond that had formed an unbreakable chain between Milan and Molly had been passed down to Billy, so too had the love that was reflected between Alison and her grandson. Now it was Billy's turn as he sat eagerly awaiting the slightest of glimpses of the magical people that would now be feverishly working away, adding their own offerings to the warming earthenware pot nestling by the coal fuelled stove.

Each day would finish with the master storyteller taking stage before his eagerly awaiting audience.

Even in adulthood Molly would feel herself drawn to the magical mysteries that Milan had to offer and would sit beside Billy for the show to begin.

Whisky glass charged with his beloved amber liquid, Milan would begin his story of the day.

He would speak of his own childhood in a faraway place that had been his own paradise lost. He recalled the child that he had once been, surrounded by beautiful meadows and mountain streams. Flowers had danced their song of colour as they strained to rise up above the long grasses to take on the warmth of a sun that had filled the valleys with its love and life. The rolling hills of beauty settled gently as they rested onto the banks of a beautiful lake.

Milan's voice would turn into that of a whisper, forcing the listener to lean towards him; transfixing them, wanting never to miss a word that he spoke.

He would continue, in hushed tones, to say that local legend depicted when God had been creating the universe above he ran out of the rocks needed to create the crescent moon. Being the master of all creators he had decided to dig out its shape from the earth's surface and allow water to fill in the void, creating a natural lake so that his own miscalculation would never be revealed. He would call this place Olic, the lake of miracles and never-ending stories.

The glint of sadness would shine in Milan's eyes, as it had done so when Molly had been a child, as he recounted the place of his youth in story. Billy would nestle up close in comfort as the story continued.

He'd tell of the lake taking the shape of the crescent moon - which would shine its presence to any onlookers that roamed the mountains rising up from its banks. Flowers of many colours had thrived on the water's surface and their reflections gave the appearance that hidden treasures of golden finery had been abandoned deep within its bottomless depths.

At this point Milan would always blame the fiery hot liquid that he drank for the tears that would rise up from deep within him. As Molly had grown she had realised that the tears were simply that of a man who had loved and lost a place that he cherished deeply within his aching heart.

He would recall hot days of summer, the smell of freshly cut grasses used to feed the cattle during the extreme harshness of the winters to come. The same cattle that he had been given the task of tending, as the heat of the summer's sun bore down on drying soil below.

Taking in the pungent liquid that the refilled glass offered, Milan would recall that as a child he had been forbidden to stray anywhere near to the crescent lake, as it was said that it held no bottom and that mysterious whirlpools would catch any swimmer unaware, sucking them down into its darkest depths.

He had heard countless stories that the lake had snatched three local swimmers to their watery graves and that its pull had been so strong that drinking cattle had fallen beneath its surface, never to be seen again.

As the sun had bore down with its never-ending heat, the cattle in his charge would always remember the cool waters and the sanctuary from the never-ending rays that beat down from the skies above. No amount of attempted dissuasion from the stick would deter them from their route and Milan recalled that most days would result with a visit to the forbidden lake.

He would become lost in his own story, oblivious now that he was playing to a waiting audience that had become captivated by this magical place of his words and memories.

A smile would slowly spread across his face as he recounted that more children and their cattle would congregate around the lake, each unable to restrain the animals that sought the cool waters in which they drank with a feverish thirst.

As the cattle drank and basked in the muddy shoreline the younger children would frolic in the cooling shallow waters along the lake's banks whilst the older children would venture deeper to seek out the small terrapins that thrived in the nutrient enriched waters.

Milan's smile would broaden as he recounted that only the bravest of the children would venture far out into the water's depths on the home-made rafts that they fashioned from old timbers tied loosely together with reeds collected from the surrounding marshes.

The brave would venture out into the deepest of the waters in the faintest hope of catching sight of the legendary Babushka that was rumoured to inhabit the dark water at the lake's centre.

It was also said, through stories of those that had seen this mysterious and illusive fish, that its head was like that of an old woman, and many unwary swimmers had been forced into a deep state of shock at its sudden appearance beside them as they swam the cooling waters.

The smile would give way to a wishful sigh that only the happiest memories could arouse as Milan recalled that, at the end, the children, weary from their fun and games would slowly walk the cattle back across the meadows of beauty. Fearful as always that their parents would discover they had spent the hot summer's day at the forbidden lake they would place their wet underwear on broken branches and swing these high above their heads to dry in the gentle breeze as they walked across the blanket of flowers to their respective homes, nestled higher up the sloping forest-covered valley.

Molly would reach out as she had done so countless times before and clasp the hand of the story teller.

"Please, will you ever take me there one day?" would be the question, hoping that the answer would be what she had always wanted to hear.

Milan would gaze deeply into her eyes and his pause would always be the same as he reached with his other hand to gently touch her cheek.

"You will see my place of wonder and mystery one day."

The smile would slowly diminish but the gleam in his eye would remain.

"I will guide you there from the stars high above that shine throughout the night......"

Then Milan would rise slowly and make his excuse that he needed to visit the lavatory.

Alison broke the silence as Molly and Billy sat - like an audience would often sit in silence immediately after an act had left the stage, hoping and waiting for the encore that would never appear.

"Billy, the fireside people, remember?" she said, as she pointed to the earthenware pot of dough. The spell was broken and the dream of a paradise lost left the room once more.

Alison had been brought into the life that she had been accustomed to in the hardest of ways. The daughter of a coal miner in the dying years that Victorian rule had left behind, she had learned from an early age that survival reigned above all else. Happiness was a simple word which merely meant the pleasure of feeling the morning's sun settle upon her face as she hurried about the constant and relentless chores of the damned.

In an age of poverty and mortality children were seen as extra hands to lessen the burdens that the adults were to carry in their daily strife. Playtimes and frolicking were way down in the line of priority and Alison, as was customary in those harsh times, was put to work at an early age. Young girls were looked down upon as the unfortunates of the family unit. The campaigners had been victorious and thankfully for Alison, females had been excluded from descending into the dark mines years before. Boys now were the family pride. An investment for the future when they could join their fathers and grandfathers to take on the power of nature deep underneath the green and sprawling countryside that was mankind's natural environment.

Girls were now seen as the hands that would take on the menial tasks that would at least help towards their keep until they could marry and bear the sons that would fuel the nation, adding to the financial pot that could keep the cycle of simple survival alive and sow the seeds for the coming generations to flourish.

Alison's own life had been torn apart and dismembered the day that she had returned from her day of work at one of the nearby farms. At ten years old her natural expertise, like that of the other girls in the village, were highly sought after. Dairy farmers recognised the gentle touch that would persuade the milk-laden cows to part, without fuss, their daily offerings. Milk was ingrained deeply into the staple diet of the simple townsfolk. Small, nimble fingers produced the highest yields and the farmers readily made use of the inexpensive and abundant workforce to line their pockets with silver.

With the passing of time the valuable, gentle touch grew with the child and the working life of the holder was cut short, to be replaced with gentler hands of the young.

Alison's touch had simply grown too old and firm and the profiteering farmer had sent one of his girls to relay a message to the family that their poor daughter was now unsuitable to continue in his employment, wishing the family well for the unsteady future that lay ahead.

As Alison returned for her well-earned teatime meal of bread and home-produced jam she was given the news.

She had simply outgrown the gentle hands of drawing the warm milk from the teats; now, as she grew older, her hands could be put to better use.

Alison's mother had broken the news with only a mother's tear for her daughter. Now, dear mother explained, Alison was a woman of the world. The teats of the gentle cows were behind her and she would now rise above her selected position in life and serve the rich and knowing. Alison was being sent into service, following the route of generations before her. Alison's service was at the stately residence of Major Motram, the last male heir to Lord Boxwood. Major Motram lived in a very different world to the one Alison had known in her ten years of harsh life. The last of the local coal owners, he prospered in the wealth that his thriving colliery gave to him. The huge castle-like home that he shared with his wife and two children lay nestled in woodland. Only two miles from the dreary, one bedroom miner's cottage Alison had known as her little world, but a universe apart in its grandeur and prosperity.

She left her family the following morning with a tearful embrace from her mother and the manly advice from her father to remain strong. Although within walking distance, Alison, as with all girls in service, would be required to live-in as they would be at their master's beck and call whenever they were needed.

The servants' quarters were always situated high in the lofts of the stately homes and would offer the barest of essentials to sustain everyday living.

Alison's early life had been harsh and cruel. She had learned quickly that not to question but obey was the answer, and as the years gradually rolled by, her experience of service life taught her the skills that would carry her forward for the rest of her arduous life.

She had remained in service at Boxwood Hall for five laborious years. She had worked her way up the ranks from scullery maid, doing the most menial, and often back-breaking tasks, to the position of chambermaid. Although the rise in status was well-earned and respected, the quality of life remained the same. The poor servant girl was there to serve and the hierarchy were there to be served.

Alison seized the opportunity that was offered when she accepted employment as an apprentice packer at the copper manufacturers in the nearby city of Glebes. At fifteen she was already seen as a mature working woman and the wealthy employers offered her the going rate that almost doubled what she had been paid at Boxwood Hall. Glebes lay seven miles north-west from Castlefields but was an easy bicycle ride along the flat and picturesque lanes flanked by the waterways that man had engineered years before, to transport the much needed coals to where they were needed.

Alison's parents were relieved, if not worried, to have their daughter back in the family home. Although another pay packet would ease the family burden, space was a problem in the cramped dwelling and Alison found herself having to share a tiny bed with her eldest brother. Cyril, at seventeen, was a typical young miner. Often he would return home from his day of toil deep underground and simply fall into the comfort that bed offered deeply ingrained with the dirt of his profession. Alison would awake with horror. Her skin would be blackened by the dust of coals won whilst she slept. She would hurry to scrub her tainted skin with the harsh coal tar soap until she was satisfied that all was gone. After all, she thought, regardless of breeding and standing, she too was a lady.

At sixteen Alison thought, unwittingly, that she had found her saviour. Dennis was as handsome and charming as they came. Three years older, he would stare deeply into her with the feeling that she was being absorbed into him, his blue eyes melting her soul. Dennis would romance her like no other could. He was the charmer that could charm even the charmed.

Despite her father's foreboding, Alison fell for the never-ending promises to honour and protect her that would result in heartache some sixteen years later.

Dennis was indeed the romancer. He could charm the larks from the sky.

Alison's father saw through the facade of wit and smiles. He looked deeply into the newcomer's eyes and saw only laziness and charity, not the need to cherish and provide for what was to become his.

Alison's father also knew that he should let his daughter follow her own heart and destiny.

Unfortunately she had followed her own misguided heart and not the experienced knowing that her father had gently tried to coax into her thoughts.

The marriage was what the lower working class expected to be offered. The bride and groom kissed and were met with a barrage of local-cut rose petals as they walked, arm in arm and so very much in love, the two-street distance to their own rented home.

Happy days they were not. Dennis soon became the magpie that would open his eyes to the merest of profit. Work was a chore for Dennis and he feigned illness whenever he could line his pockets without the need to sweat and tread the footsteps of honest men and descend to cut the nation's coal.

Years of drudgery followed the unfortunate Alison. Like so many mothers before her, she bore the children as was expected within her role with little if no reward.

Before the age of modern and effective contraception five children were born. The charmer had proved his worth and prowess with his fertility. Dennis had succeeded in continuing the family line and felt that he could now steer from the path of righteousness now that he had sown his seed that would propel his existence long after he had ceased to walk the path of mankind.

Molly's thoughts were interrupted by a squeal of delight from Billy as he hurriedly clambered from his place of watching for the slightest glimpse of the magical people that were invisibly raising the covered dough. "Grandad," he exclaimed as only a child could as he galloped, horse fashion, to the window that overlooked the narrow back street at the rear of the house. Molly rose to see Milan stood at the small gate that enclosed the small concrete yard that separated the house from the communal walkway. Her eyes strained to focus the images to her brain as she slowly comprehended the scene set out before her. As usual the weary Milan leant against the perimeter wall of the secluded yard, taking in the breaths of earned rest from his toil tending the land on his allotment. Flying closely around Milan's head were four blackbirds. Although often referred to as the gardener's friend, helping to rid the soil of unwanted pests, these birds were shy creatures, preferring to hide away from man's gaze. These birds, however, seemed to revel in their closeness to Milan as they fluttered animatedly around him.

Molly felt the slightest tug on her floral dress and she was broken from the unreal sight that was being played out before her very eyes. "They're not always white, mammy," Billy whispered as he looked up, his eyes reflecting back the sunlight that the window offered. "Who, darling?" she asked with a motherly frown of love. "The angels," he innocently replied, "They always change so we can never really know they are really here"....

Shaken Molly made an excuse to leave, saying that she had left the washing to dry and that lately there had been a thief who seemed to thrive on unguarded linen.

Billy protested as he had not yet seen the magic that would make the bread rise. He was, however, persuaded as always, with the promise of ice cream, fresh from the street seller on their return home.

With kisses and hugs mother and son bade their farewells and waved goodbye as they rounded the street corner and headed for home.

The path of adventure offered its usual amusement for the dragon slayer as he added to the drying carnage that he had produced only hours before. Fresh nettle heads, decapitated with the cleanest of blows, rested on the dried out remnants of the battle that had been conquered a few hours before.

With the familiarity of the path Molly retreated into her thoughts. The blackbird and angel comment had stirred her memories and rationale. She drifted back to the night that she had been alone with Billy, with Roger at work. How she had been so afraid to close her eyes after snatching her baby from some unseen force that had captured the innocent baby's attention.

That night had been only the start. Whenever left alone to sleep at night, Billy would wake Molly with his childish laughs of mirth and merriment. The scene was always the same. She would creep into the bedroom to find him stood, holding onto the sides of the crib and pointing in childish relish to some invisible point etched, in his vision only, on the wall. Always the same too, he would wave his goodbye as she hurriedly carried him through the door into the safety that her own room offered.

Although not an ardent believer in the spiritual world of never knowing, Molly did accept, at an early age, that her son was different to the other babies that adorned the prams aligning the banks of Castlefield's duck pond on summer days.

Shivers tingled along her spine as she recalled the day that she had walked past the gates of the colliery. Billy had been almost three years old and had already made her weary from his childish antics as they walked along the busy shop-lined road that was the town's centre. Exhausted, Molly had taken a rest at the bench that offered its welcome to all who entered the colliery's entrance.

Taking in the pleasant mid-morning sunshine Molly heard the sound of footsteps approaching her from the direction of the road that she had walked moments earlier. She recognised the man instantly as he came into view. Peter had been a close friend of Roger's since their school days and they had gone on to secure employment at the town's coal mine together.

Molly waved a friendly greeting to Peter as he neared the other side of the walkway. "Cheer up," she laughed, "a day like today you should feel on top of the world."

Peter looked across and smiled. "Yes, and in ten minutes I'll be at the bottom of the world too." With a grin he turned and entered the first of the buildings in which he would begin his working day, deep within the bowels of the earth, hidden away from the warm sunshine that was bathing the town in its warm embrace.

Billy stopped playing with the wooden toy that he had dragged behind him on its cord since she had bought him it as a special gift for being brave when he had fallen and grazed his knee earlier in the morning. He looked up at Molly and said, "They'll be lonely this Christmas, mammy." Molly looked down and asked who would be lonely. Taking the cord and turning to propel the train, Billy replied, "That man's mammy and daddy." With this he gave out the shrieking sound of the locomotive's whistle and ran, as only children do, along the grass verge, the wooden train bouncing behind.

Molly put the strange remark to the back of her thoughts as she stood and held out her hand for Billy to take as they headed back through the streets of Castlefields on their way home. The wooden train clattered on behind them, coming to grief several times with derailment as the excited driver snatched unevenly at its cord.

The rest of the afternoon drifted slowly by, filled with the never-ending chores of motherhood and housework. Whilst peeling potatoes in readiness for preparing Roger's meal on his return from his work at the mine she heard the front door open and footsteps enter the tiny kitchen. She turned and was surprised to see Roger standing at the doorway. His ghostly expression immediately caught her attention and before she had time to ask whatever the matter was, Roger's eyes welled with tears and he cried out that his friend, Peter, had been killed in an accident underground and that he had to go and comfort the family. With this he pushed past Molly, opened the door and walked slowly down the cobbled backstreet before rounding the corner from sight.

A feeling of nausea rose within Molly as she leant against the fridge for support, dizziness washing over her in sickly and ghastly disbelief. Peter, dead? Her mind raced back to earlier in the day when he had waved his farewell at the mine entrance. "They will be lonely at Christmas, mammy"; the voice reverberated inside her head as she leant forward over the sink, wretched acidic bile stinging and burning her throat as it rose from within her.

The remainder of the day dragged on as if father time himself had momentarily forgotten how to count the cogs of his earthly purpose in remorse for the recently departed.

Billy remained sleeping as he had done so on their return from their walk earlier. Not the best of sleepers during the night, he often made up for this as the afternoons slowly drew to a close with the setting rays of the sun.

Roger had returned two hours after his tearful and sombre announcement, a little the worse for too many drinks whilst comforting the bereaved of his close friend.

Molly sat with him on the sofa as he recounted the day that had ended in tragedy.

The day had begun as usual, comradeship and laughter resounding as the men of Castlefields had speedily descended into the depths of never-ending darkness to pitch open battle with Mother Nature and win out the coals of yet another day.

Tearfully, Roger described that conditions on the coal face had been slowly deteriorating as each day had passed and that the rock strata from which they cut away the coal had become unsteady and open to collapse. One particular collapse had led to concerns and the colliery's safety inspectors had deemed it unsafe to continue production until the precarious rock skyline could be secured and supported in order to provide safe passage for the men below.

Peter had proved his worth in countless situations like this before. Coal mining was within his blood and he revelled in the challenges that it brought.

With a grin and a final spit of the tobacco that most of the miners chewed he lowered himself to his knees and entered the other dimension of life he never knew had existed.

Before the smile had even left his face, nature gave out her sigh of sorrow and thousands of tons of rock descended to erase the man as he was.

Pulverised in a second; it would take days to rescue enough of his remains to line the coffin that would carry him to his grave, only adding to the town's morbidity and suffering.

Peter's long suffering parents were indeed lonely that Christmas to come.

For Molly that fateful day would remain etched deeply within her thoughts of regret and guilt. The foreboding words of Billy would echo through restless nights of her dreams and would haunt her each time she hurriedly passed the colliery entrance and the wooden bench where she had been sitting as

Peter had approached, cheerily, blithely unaware he was to meet his untimely destiny.

Maybe, Molly began to think, coincidence had played its cruellest hand and the events that followed were simply laid out by sheer chance and reasoning. Guilt, however, always gnawed itself way into her thoughts and she would lay awake at night exploring the never-ending 'ifs' that we always face whenever catastrophe strikes and casts its painful blow.

Maybe, she thought, just maybe, there are people put on this earth to guide us safely through life.

The 'what ifs' and 'buts' had become an endless nightmare that tortured Molly as the days, months and years passed slowly by.

What if she had taken heed of Billy's words and had understood the warning that had foretold of the catastrophe to follow?

What if she had called to Peter as he opened the door to his fate and engaged him in conversation, causing him to be late for his final descent into the earth? Realising this, he could have turned tail and spent the rest of the day pursuing his passion for fishing. Surely then, she would deliberate, his destiny could have been avoided and Mother Nature's wrath of defiance would have been thwarted, and the coals of the day would have been won without the need for the sacrifice of life that had followed.

Whatever the reasons behind that day Molly would continue to blame herself for the pain and loss. With rationale she knew deep down that the words 'what' and 'if' should never be placed together but the irrational part of her logic reminded her, on that sun-dappled day, the two words had indeed come together as one, and the final scene of Peter's existence had been played out and finalised forever.

As the memories from that fateful day slowly blurred and clouded with the passing of time it became apparent to Molly that Billy did indeed possess some deep-rooted gift that, at times, enabled him to see what others simply could not. She encouraged him to speak with her openly and honestly and would constantly reassure him whenever he felt that he simply did not fit in with the accepted expectations of the other children around him. His kaleidoscope world would sometimes be ridiculed by the childish taunting of playground amusement whilst within the orderly and disciplined confines at the local school.

Throughout his childhood years Molly had attempted to make the preoccupied Roger aware that perhaps their son was a little different to the expressionless conformity that was accepted as the norm for those children whom were seen only as mere fodder for the mines; the young to replace the old, to be raised like their fathers before them with a tradition to simply descend deep into the earth and fuel the nation's industry and wealth.

Roger would have none of this and would distance himself only further from the family unit. He was, as his father before him had been, staunchly working class and proud to be just that. The realms of the unexplained had no rightful place in his logic and whatever it was he could not justify, he would laugh and make fun of as simply being 'mumbo jumbo' and that it should be kept tightly enclosed within minds of the insane or ludicrous.

The more Roger distanced himself from what was happening, the more Molly felt alone with the added burden that her loving son was indeed different and, she suspected, gifted in some way. That he could see into realms of existence usually only written about or shown to cinema viewers, from the insane and deeply disturbed minds of writers that contained the desire to make their audience shudder in disbelief as they nervously made their way home through the dimly lit streets, truly frightened from the story shown on the silver screen as they slowly devoured the obligatory bags of tasteless popcorn and ice cream.

Each night became the usual practice and routine. Roger would leave for his descent into the man-made hell that capitalism had produced to feed the fat cats of English society in their finery and wealth. Molly would be left alone to complete her daily chores and prepare again for the day that would begin as the dipping moon exchanged an age old golden handshake with its rising cousin of warmth and light.

She would wear herself to the point of near exhaustion, keeping Billy company in his bedroom as he drifted slowly into sleep, bringing her solace and final rest for the day.

She had learned, from his earlier years, that to leave him unaccompanied in his crib would be akin to giving out invitations to the invisible, make-believe souls that would take heed of the calling and amuse the child with their unseen antics of mirth and merriment.

Countless times Molly had been drawn from her evening's favourite television offerings to the sound of Billy's playful voice from the room above. She would creep upstairs and listen to one-sided conversations, eerily coming from within the confines of the room.

So many times she had ascended the staircase to find her son stood, grinning and pointing to some unseen entity that had entered into the boy's realm of both imagination and reality, drawing his entire attention from everything else around him.

Now Molly would sit with Billy as he truly drifted into the deepest of sleep; the sleep where only the dreams of our deepest imagination were truly in control and nothing else mattered.

*   *   *   *

Chapter Seven – Radio Waves

Billy had been seven years old when finally Molly began to think, deep down, that she was perhaps losing her mind. That the post natal depression she had suffered momentarily after the birth of her child had simply withdrawn into her and had lain dormant, growing in strength and resilience to manifest itself in the small hours whenever she and Billy were left alone in the house as Roger laboured deep underground.

The day began as most days did. Sundays were long deemed a day of simple rest for the hard working, hard playing men of Castlefields. Tradition had been for generations that no coals would be cut from the earth on the Sabbath day so the mining towns were, momentarily, given respite from the noise and dust of heavy industry.

The birds could be heard singing and for once the bleakness was replaced by the colours of nature and normality.

Age-old customs of communal gatherings of the townsfolk were relived but now it was the working men's clubs that were to prosper whilst the churches silently fell into recession.

As usual, Molly had woken with the rising sun. Roger, having given himself the treat of the working man, had spent the previous night in the company of friends, drinking away the stories of the week they had spent in the mine. He had stumbled home a little before midnight and now lay snoring, fully clothed, spread-eagled on the marital bed.

Billy was already awake and scampered out of his room, rushing excitedly downstairs as soon as he heard Molly going about her never-ending morning chores.

Roger would rise from his slumber as if by magic, as soon as Molly plated up his Sunday treat of bacon and eggs, and he would sit, eating in silence, as he read the morning newspaper that Billy had collected from the corner shop moments before.

As the morning approached midday again the master of the house would busy himself shaving and washing for the weekly gathering of tradition that would honour the locally brewed beers which would be heartily drank by the thirsty miners whilst playing snooker and darts.

Again, Molly and Billy were left alone within the confines of brick and mortar that had become their world.

With the days chores almost complete, Molly settled down to rest. As usual the television's offerings were scant and offered mainly repeated programmes that she had viewed tirelessly many times before.

Roger's constant snoring throughout the night had allowed her little sleep and soon, in the comfort of her armchair, she began to feel the inner warmth that sleep beckoned to the weary.

Billy, however, was having none of this as usual and, dreading that he would be left alone whilst his mother slept, made it is sole intention to ward off the sleep that was slowly taking her from him. He would tug at her dress in playfulness whenever her eyes closed for more than a blink and soon, for Molly, slight irritation became no match for tiredness. Although she loved her son dearly with all of her heart the need for sleep overcame this and she offered him the reward of ice cream if he were to go to his bedroom and paint her a beautiful picture that she could hang on the wall with pride.

The thought of ice cream instantly appealed to Billy and he promised that he would take his time and paint her the most beautiful painting that she had ever seen. With a kiss between mother and son he gleefully strode the stairs and entered the room where his artistic offerings would emerge.

Molly, tired from her restless night and daily chores, soon succumbed to the inner warmth that sleep offered and quickly found herself basking in a warm summer's day. Bricks and windows were replaced with the freshness of outdoors and her attention was drawn to the rustling sound that was coming from all around as she gazed into a cloudless sky.

"Molly," she heard the unmistakable heavy accent of Milan call out, "Wake up child, you're dreaming." Slowly she raised herself from her place of rest and patiently waited for her sleep-filled eyes to focus. Blurred visions of green became defined and she realised that she had woken under the summer's sun within the idyllic confines of the allotment that offered every variety of fruit and vegetable that nature could offer.

"See the flutter-byes," Milan pointed out, as he offered her water from the crisp, ice cold well that he had dug with his own bare hands years before, after entering England for the first time.

Molly followed the line of his outstretched hand to see. As if by magic she saw hundreds of white butterflies dancing a circular dance in front of her. The beating of their powdery wings was so intense that her naturally wavy hair bellowed behind her in the warm breeze they created.

"Leave the child," came a voice from nowhere. Molly was shocked and frightened with the unfriendly intrusion that had entered without invite. She looked for reassurance towards

Milan but, as she turned, the cloudless sky darkened and her hair was blown by a fierce gust as the startled butterflies broke their circular fluttering and scattered in haste. The allotment was gone and she descended into the darkness of sleep.

"Come here, my gentle child," now the soft voice of the loving Milan was replaced by that of an elderly, gruff female, as Molly desperately tried to fight off the sleep that she had earlier welcomed with relish.

"Here, child, come to the promise of fresh ice-cream that only I can offer you." Again the gruff voice filled Molly's head as she desperately tried to regain the senses of awakening.

Dread filled Molly's subconscious mind as she desperately fought against the effects of sleep. As she slowly withdrew from its grip the tingling of life returned, at first to her fingertips, and then the warmth spread across her whole body and being.

Perspiration beaded upon her brow as she looked around her and gained her composure. Slowly, the realisation dawned on her that she had been dreaming and tears of happiness slowly welled in her eyes as her thoughts drifted back to the happier times that she had spent in childhood. The carefree days of lying in the sun amongst the vegetables in Milan's allotment garden. The ice cold water that would quench even the thirst of thirsts, and the gentle conversation between man and child. How Molly missed those days, she thought with sadness. She had been so happy and would relish the times when Milan sat her down on the earth next to him and relay the stories of the magical land that he had been born into, the mysteries of its people and the fabled dragon slayer that roamed deep into the mountains, sword in hand to ensure peace and safety for the people that he loved.

The story of the fruit basket and the thieves had always been her favourite and as the words were spoken she would stare into the cloudless sky in the faint hope that she would glimpse God as he peered down into the basket of fruit.

"Hush little baby, don't you cry........" Molly was dragged from her happiness as the aged voice of a woman sang out quietly.

"Mama's gonna buy you a mocking bird......" The voice was low but audible and there remained no doubt in Molly's mind that it was coming from above her in the bedroom where Billy played. Motherly instinct kicked in without hesitation and she sprang to her feet and raced up the stairs, her stride taking the steps two at a time. The door to the bedroom was ajar and she tried to stem the gasping breaths that panic and fear induced on the human body in times of fear and excitement. The flight or fight emotion had entirely gripped Molly as she tentatively peered through the slightly open door and into the bedroom.

Billy was laid upon the bed staring up at the ceiling. A wide grin was spread across his face as if his entire concentration was fixed and pinned onto one spot close to the ceiling light.

"And if those mocking birds don't sing......" The voice sounded again. This time, however, it was stronger and seemed to echo around the walls as if coming from no particular direction at all.

Protective instinct raced through Molly's body and she pushed open the door with a force that resulted in it crashing into the wall. Billy startled, rolled from the bed and crashed headlong onto the carpeted floor with a sickening thud. Tears of pain had already began to stream from his frightened eyes as he was scooped into his mother's arms and carried with haste out of the room and down the creaking staircase.

Billy had grazed his head from the fall and with the love that only a mother can give, she kissed away his pain as she sat him on the kitchen's work surface. She reached over and turned on the tap until the tepid water ran cold and held the damp cloth usually reserved for washing the dishes under the flowing water. With one hand steadying the child she withdrew the cloth and squeezed as much of the water from it as was possible and applied it with pressure to the reddened mark that glistened on Billy's forehead.

As the tears ebbed he reached out and placed his arms tightly around Molly's head and pulled her towards him in a loving embrace. The bond between mother and child strengthened and was united in one with the clasp of the closeness that only they could create.

All was quiet now within the house, but every creak of normality that old buildings offer out to the unsettled, raised the hairs on the back of Molly's neck. Her thoughts were a muddled slideshow that had sped out of control. The night that she had been drawn upstairs to the sound of childish laughter and had felt a sickening blow as unseen hands pushed her violently against the door; Peter's cheery wave goodbye as he turned and faced his own cruel destiny that had indeed brought loneliness to his family when Christmas had beckoned - were only a snapshot of circumstances that now played out in the theatre of her mind. The eerie movie of her thoughts recalled the early days when her baby had innocently asked for a dampened cloth to wipe away the dirt and grime from the poor man's face as he lay upon the kitchen table. She had seen the look of foreboding and sadness when she had relayed Billy's words to her mother. The words that brought back the heartache and pain to Alison as her own memories were taken back to the day that she had returned from school to find the shattered and lifeless remains of her father laid out in the kitchen. The local women hurriedly going about their work of cleaning the body in preparation for the final journey to the cemetery, following the fall of rock deep underground that had taken away in an instant what had been cherished and loved and what would be sadly missed forever more.

The recent reference that Billy had made to the spectacle of the blackbirds encircling Milan on his return from the allotment and how he had innocently looked deeply into Molly's eyes and said, "The angels, they always change so we can never know they are really here"....

There were countless chapters in the movie that was being now played out in Molly's mind that she had been unable to explain with rational thinking.

Despite her overwhelming love, the final realisation hit her with the same sickening thud that had sent her crashing into the door. Billy had been different to the other children around him in more ways than one. The differences manifested themselves from an early age. Whilst the other babies at a similar age were still babbling away in the childish sentences of nonsense, Billy had been able to put basic words together enough to be understood. He had taken his first tentative steps that had transformed him from baby to toddler months before the others had finally plucked up the courage to let go of the supports that they held rigidly and refused to let go.

Molly had been so proud of her clever child and would blush with contentment and happiness when others had commented how advanced for his age he really was.

All too soon, however, the unexplained experiences had crept into the essence of the child without explanation. She had relayed her fears and concerns constantly to Roger who had, as usual, dismissed these with a chuckle of mockery. His favourite words had always been that the 'mumbo jumbo' was merely a figment of Molly's imagination and that maybe she should seek out work to contribute to the family's income and focus her mind, eliminating the nonsense that books were made of to amuse and frighten their gullible readers.

It was whilst Molly was holding the calmed Billy tightly against her chest that her attention was drawn to the audio cassette recorder further along the kitchen's work surface. Roger had purchased this weeks before so that he could record his favourite bands that were given airplay on the local radio stations. Glam rock he would constantly announce was now the 'in thing' and the days of Molly's precious Pink Floyd were numbered. After having consumed a little too much alcohol he would now return home singing the latest offerings from bands like Slade and T-Rex, shirt open to his lower chest and strut around the living room as if delighting some unseen audience into a frenzy. Maybe it was the audience that tired of the antics or maybe it was simply the alcohol induced tiredness that finally won the show; before long the great showman of centre stage would slump into the comfort of his armchair and snore out the rest of his performance in sleep.

Gently she lowered Billy to the ground and opened the door that led into the tiny enclosed area that acted as the family garden. The highly prized leather football immediately caught the child's attention and he ran towards it, raising his right foot which resulted in the ball spinning widely sidewards and crashing heavily into the crudely constructed fence that separated the neighbours own space of solitude whenever the summer's sun offered the chance to sit outside away from the confines that the interiors of the small miners' cottages offered.

Molly picked up the recording equipment. The cassette recorder had a built-in microphone which she had found to her detriment last week when she had called Roger to announce that his dinner was ready. He had scorned her without warning for speaking whilst he was recording the latest offerings from BBC Radio One and Molly had tried desperately hard to hide her own amusement when he had played the recording back. As the spellbinding tones of Marc Bolan played out the magical lyrics of Ride a White Swan she could be clearly heard shouting from the kitchen that if Roger did not hurry then his favourite sausages would go cold.

She had an idea. She had always known that the voice of the old woman that she heard was not a mere figment of her imagination and that wherever it came from would capture Billy in some unseen spell that only his eyes could penetrate and see in its entirety. She knew that whatever bond there was between the voice and her child, it was always broken whenever she entered the room. The conversation would cease immediately and Billy would look around in bewilderment seeking out something that was no longer there and had shied away into the darkness that the dimly lit corners of the room offered.

What she had never known was what happened within the confines of the family home when no one else was present, when the emptiness and darkness were finally in control without the interference of the earthly bound realms of reality.

The recording equipment offered the answer. As with its played back warning that the sausages were cooling the small microphone had proved that it could detect and capture audible noises other than the rocking world of radio broadcasts.

Molly pressed the 'play' button and to her surprise and relief the only sound that resounded through the metallic sounding speakers was that of nothingness. The cassette was empty and the white noise sang its eerie tunes of hissing and distraction to entice the unfortunate listener. Luck was on her side as Roger had yet to fill the tape with his favourite sounds of the day.

She rewound the empty tape and placed it with the recording button down to activate the microphone. "Come on, Billy," she called out from the open doorway, "Let's go and see nana and granddad - see what chocolate they have waiting for you."

Without hesitation he spun round, leaving the now discarded soccer ball where it had come to rest against the fence. The thought of a visit to his grandparents never failed to grab Billy's attention, especially when there was mention of a special treat awaiting his arrival.

The path of adventure offered out its hand of amusement as it had done so throughout the years, and today was no exception.

The motorbike had now replaced the horse, and the knight of ancient battles had progressed from a suit of steel to that of black leather, as Billy roared away in front of Molly as she walked briskly along the path's course. Like most boys his age Billy had become fascinated with the fashionable motorbikes that the town's youths would constantly race up and down the main street, much to the annoyance of the more elderly residents. Fresh out of school and with money lining their pockets from employment in the town's mine, they would splash out their wages in fierce competition to see who could make the under-powered, two-wheeled demons the loudest and fastest. Evenings now were a torment of high-pitched mechanical screams as the local road-racing fraternity turned the town's streets into the motor sport circuits of Le Mans and Monte Carlo.

At least, Molly thought to herself, the stinging nettles would be safe and would no longer lose their heads in pitched battles with the armour clad knight as he galloped his make-believe horse, crazily lashing out with the mighty sword of English willow.

Alison and Milan were seated opposite each other, in the plush armchairs they had purchased months before to ease their aching old bones that Milan would announce to all that entered the house, pointing with pride at the newly-acquired furniture of comfort.

Billy ran into the room and threw himself onto Milan's lap with the spring of a young gazelle, kissed him on the cheek and then leapt with equal excitement towards the startled Alison, sitting snugly on her knee as he looked up at her and gently stroked her greying hair.

Coffee and Billy's favourite biscuits were hurriedly served on the table that doubled as a newspaper rack and conversation flowed as if it were some family reunion of people lost to each other only to be returned generations later.

As Molly and her mother exchanged the idle gossip of what had been happening over the past few days in the local town, Milan and Billy got down to the manly pursuit of chess. Like the lost knight of the path of adventure Billy again absorbed himself into the role of conqueror against all odds. It was strange, Molly thought, as she would often watch the pitched battles played out upon the chequered theatre of war that Milan would always allow the child to beat him. Not an ardent chess player herself she had learnt as a child that Milan had indeed mastered the game and was extremely fluent in its many moves of trickery and cunning. It was always, however, the same trickery in reverse that would be used to lure the unwitting apprentice into victory and Billy would charge around the room, the victor of victors, defying the poor defeated to take up the challenge again.

Molly could never mistake either, the twinkle in the ageing eyes of Milan as he simply held his hands in defeat and announced that the greatest player of the two had indeed taken the day in ultimate triumph.

With the ticking of the afternoon's clock drawing the daylight to a close Molly bade their farewell and made the excuse that Roger would have returned from the Working Men's Club, slept and would now be rousing from his slumber, hungry and in need of his light meal of freshly boiled ham and pickle that was his chosen treat of the week. After all, he would announce daily, he was the family provider and should be entitled to at least one treat of his own preference once each week.

The path of adventure now seemed different as the setting sun gave way to the shortening shadows that the chill of late afternoon offered and cast its remembrance of the day that had slowly been laid to rest.

The cockerels now ruled the roost in the many allotment spaces that lined both sides of the path and would startle the unwary traveller with their shrieks of announcement that the day was drawing to a close. Billy was no longer the daredevil motorcyclist as he walked hand in hand, tired now from his childish fun and antics. The yawn now replaced the shrieks of fun and laughter as fatigue began to take its comforting grip.

Molly hurried the pace a little and the two soon came to the railings that announced that they were approaching the town's main road and would within minutes be home.

The house was silent as Molly slowly opened the door. She knew from routine that Roger would have returned two hours earlier and would now be sleeping upstairs. Routine also told her that he would be expecting to be awoken shortly for his late afternoon snack.

Knowing that his father was sleeping and failing from increasing fatigue himself Billy took off his shoes at the door and wearily made his way to the sofa where he stretched, yawned and took up the foetal position, almost in an instant drifting into the theatre of childish dreams that sleep offered.

Molly crept silently across the living room and checked the cassette recorder she had left earlier to record the sounds of the empty house. The cassette had rewound itself which meant that it had done what she had intended it to and had recorded ninety minutes of probably nothing.

She picked the equipment up and carried it to the kitchen where she placed it upon the work surface and pressed the playback button, as she set about the chore of slicing the ham and bread, making ready the family meal.

The house fronted onto the main road that connected Castlefields to its neighbouring village of Answorth and it was no surprise to Molly that the slow, drone-like noise of passing cars could be heard coming from the single speaker.

The low pitched sound would be repeated over and over and she wondered why the usually quiet road had endured so much traffic. Usually this would only be seen when the town's rugby league club were playing a home game and the away team's supporters would flood the streets with the vibrant colours of their scarves and flags.

The constant drone began to irritate Molly and she reached over and pressed the fast forward button which would scan the audio recording whilst sounding the playback at speed.

"She has no right to take the child." The knife fell from Molly's grip and clattered noisily across the kitchens floor, butter glistening on the brown carpet. She stood in total horror, shocked at the elderly voice that had reverberated from the speaker.

"It's always the same for the boy: do this, do that". Again, the sound of an old woman's voice echoed around the small room. The blood drained from Molly and she felt light-headed and faint as she desperately fumbled to press the 'stop' button on the machine.

As silence once again settled around her she desperately tried to fight back the panic and fear that had washed over her like some huge tidal wave rising from the oceans' depths. The whole of her body tingled and it felt like hot pins were being inserted into every fingertip by many unseen hands of torture.

Molly stared at the cassette recorder in disbelief. Rational thinking slowly ebbed its way into her mind and she began to doubt what she had heard. The old woman's voice had been distinct but maybe she had been mistaken. She tried every direction her mind would allow to reason and to think of the rational alternatives to what she had heard.

The house was old after all, she thought. The windows had long gone past the day they should have been replaced and the shrunken wood of their frames allowed every noise from the road outside to enter as if the glass had been removed.

As her breathing began to level to that of normality she slowly reached out and with fingers trembling she pressed the 'rewind' button and after several seconds again pressed playback. Molly listened with trepidation. Again the slow droning of passing motor vehicles disturbed the silence as the speaker played back a piece of the past. This time there was no voice or words spoken just the constant low pitched grumble barely audible then a little louder and then barely audible again until the noise was lost only to be repeated seconds later.

Confused, Molly again pressed the 'fast-forward' button "….the same for the boy: do this, do that." The same voice broke the silence. In shock, Molly's finger snatched away from the button and the voice was once again replaced by the low heavy sound that she had interpreted as passing traffic. Panic now rose within her and she ran from the room into the narrow passage that separated the kitchen from the living room and opened onto the staircase. She mustered her strength and shouted out to Roger to come downstairs immediately.

Hearing the fear in her voice he wasted no time and leapt from the bed and rushed downstairs expecting the house to be engulfed in flames.

Molly held out the recording equipment and simply said to Roger that he should listen. Confused at her obvious panic and upset he asked no questions and pressed the playback button. Yet again the low rumbling of what sounded like passing motor cars resounded from the single speaker and he looked at her and shrugged his shoulders in question. With trembling hands she reached out and pressed the 'fast-forward' button.

"She has no right to take the child." As if his hands had been scalded by some sudden searing heat, Roger dropped the recorder onto the floor, its batteries spilling out onto the carpet in impact.

Eyes widened in disbelief at what he had just heard, he stared aghast at Molly and as if to remove any trace of the ghostly voice forever, he raised his slipper-clad foot up to his knees before sending it crashing down on the fragile plastic recorder.

Limping and cursing as he made his way to the living room Roger simply told Molly that the fragments of plastic would need clearing from the carpet before Billy cut his feet on the shattered remnants. As he heaved himself onto the sofa he reminded her that he would be watching television while she finished preparing the meal.

Billy stretched and yawned - disturbed by the sound - and wearily sat upright, rubbing his eyes as if altering the focus on a set of binoculars in order to gain a better view of his surroundings.

"What was that noise, daddy?" he asked, in the slurred voice of the half-woken.

"Nothing to worry about, son," was the monotone reply, "Just clumsy old me dropping that silly cassette recorder."

Without further question the pair accepted the plated sandwiches that Molly offered them in outstretched hands as she entered the room.

Chewing the bread in unison like some rehearsed orchestra, father and son sat side by side, all concentration now focused on the antics of the brightly coloured Tom and Jerry playing out their latest duel of wisdom, each wishing to outsmart the other in a never-ending battle of wits.

Over the coming days Molly tried desperately to raise the subject with Roger of what had happened that early evening. Like generations of local miners before him his mind had become entrenched with rational and explanation. Ghostly capers were the thing of written pages and Hollywood film sets and had no place in the grime and reality of the working man's existence.

But, she would argue, just how could the speeded up traffic noise be transformed clearly into the unmistakable sound an elderly lady's voice, speaking about a child?

Feeling that his manhood was being threatened and that he could not explain the sudden intrusion into his family's life he finally announced the answer.

"Radio waves," he declared with a grin. "That's it, radio waves." With his new-found explanation Roger took to centre stage and the words flowed as if he were reciting some speech to congratulate the happy couple on their wedding day. Radio waves, he expanded, were all around. Everything now was controlled by these invisible lines of energy that were being pulsated from the high-powered transmitters into the modern day homes of the world.

Now believing every word that seemed to flow from him without thought Roger expanded on the rationale that had to be.

The cassette recorder also doubled as a receiver to the invisible waves that gave us the news bulletins and sounds of our favourite music twenty-four hours a day. The voice had simply been that. A radio station had overlapped its allotted frequency and the transmission had spilled over and had been picked up by the recording apparatus. Simple, the answer was there. A rogue voice being transmitted and had been recorded within the confines of the empty house.

With his new-found confidence Roger went onto explain that the reason for the need to speed the recording to hear the words was that the signal had been weak and delayed in its reception on the cheap apparatus that had received it.

So why then the apparent shock and desire to stamp the cassette recorder out of existence with such force that it had resulted in Roger spending the following day away from work nursing a swollen toe, Molly had asked in quick reply. Again the master of answers, not to be beaten, he shrugged off the fact that shock had overcome him and simply retorted that he had momentarily lost his grip; seeing the batteries burst forth in impact, he had lost his composure and frustration had taken over, resulting in the shattered remains that she had to clean away.

Molly knew all too well that the fight was lost and to press the showman into further explanations of what she had previously encountered were futile, and would result in mockery and further disbelief for days to come.

Instead, the obedient housewife agreed with the rationale that the wise one had delivered, smiled and simply asked what time Roger would like his treat of smoked mackerel fillets and bread.

Days turned into weeks and the household gradually returned to normality. Molly would tend to all things that were associated with the family home and the welfare of its inhabitants and Roger would eke out an existence deep underground.

Often distracted from his parental responsibilities he did at least sometimes take up his role of fatherhood and educating his eventual heir to the throne that he commanded like only a father could.

Coal mining ran deep through Roger's veins as it had done so within countless family generations before him.

It was said that his own grandfather had been forced to walk his family on foot some two-hundred miles to escape the depravity and despair that mass unemployed had wreaked across his native county in the great depression of England's 1920s.

Heavy industry of all kinds was worst hit with the rising competition of world trade and the ancient coal mines were closed down as profits fell and the owners sought out more ludicrous ways to continue their wealthy incomes whilst riding the backs of the poor.

Yorkshire was seen as the London in Puss in Boots' story but this time the cobbled streets were not lined with gold as the pages foretold but with the newly-won coals from the earth below.

Roger's grandfather had taken his family by foot to seek out the new-found riches. What he had found to his detriment was only further exploitation by the ruling classes - exploitation that once again found him working towards an early grave for the want of profit.

Coal mining not only ran through the blood of his toils but it also ran through his thoughts of play.

Roger's idea of fun time was mine time and Billy revelled in the catacombs that his father created for him in the darkened living room of an evening. Bed blankets would be stretched between the furniture to create the coal face of imagination and piles of black, rolled-up stockings would take on the role of newly-cut coals that Billy gathered on crouched knees, careful not to touch the cotton roof of nature above him as he set about his task of loading the coals onto his favourite plastic truck; which, with one tug on the string that had been attached to its front, Roger would haul away and reap the profits of the unfortunate labourer hidden away beneath the canopy of soft bed linen.

Molly would despair at the sight of her freshly-pressed bed sheets being crumpled in childish play and would scorn the pair on her return from visiting her mother and Milan.

Unperturbed, the game would continue whenever she left father and son alone and despite her repeated scorn she would smile to herself with the contentment that this was the togetherness and love that united the family as one.

*   *   *   *

Chapter Eight – Over the Rooftops

Roger had either been lucky or unlucky and could never decide which it was of the pair he had been.

Always a natural to his subterranean surroundings, he had proved his worth at his ability to undertake and master in his own right whatever task he had been asked to do as an underground worker. At the age of just fourteen he had entered a world that he could never have imagined despite living and breathing the essence of king coal from his first waking breath as he emerged from the comfort and security of the loving womb.

At fourteen he had answered to the call of duty that the newly government controlled coal mines needed to replenish the lost generation that World War Two had snatched cruelly away. Migrant workers - displaced persons unable to return to their native homelands - had stemmed the immediate need for fresh mining stock to continue the pedigree but now more local resources could be harvested amongst the young workforce in waiting.

The eager young Roger took on the challenge that made him a man and reported for work. Dismayed at first that he would not be plummeted down towards the earth's core on his first day of service he accepted that all good things come to those who wait.

His first task had been menial to say the least. Like him, the tiny ponies had been born into a lifetime beneath the world that they could never have known. They had been bred over countless generations for their stout strength and willingness to obey the orders from their master. Although standing at just over a metre in height they made up for this in the strength needed to pull the laden steel tubs along the countless miles of underground rail lines wherever the diesel-powered locomotive could not venture.

Once descended into the depths they would only again be lifted to the warmth of the summer's sun during the two weeks holiday that the mine was closed for production in the month of August. Now blinded by the perpetual darkness that they continually resided in they would frolic in the pastures of fresh grasses and hay, unaware of the colours and scents that now surrounded their impaired sight and senses.

Before their lifelong imprisonment could begin they had to be learned the basics and this had been Roger's task. Not to be hostile to the confines of the harness was the first lesson and he soon found to his detriment and pain that the square, blunt teeth could inflict damage and pain from the four legged rebel in his charge.

Roger's abilities soon shone out to those that were in charge of natural selection to pick out the strong amongst the weak and before long he found himself undertaking the many tasks needed underground to keep the profits of coal flowing.

At the age of eighteen he had joined the elite of the highest paid of the underground labourers. He had become a true collier who would be respected amongst the whole workforce for his ability and knowledge to beat back nature herself and to cut away the coals from her belly that would keep the cogs of a proud nation turning for yet another day.

Roger had decided to take on the challenge whether or not his choice had been the unlucky or lucky side of the coin that had been offered.

The chance of becoming the earner of higher wages beckoned him and had taken away his decision before he realised he had time to really think things through in total earnest.

A Colliery Deputy he would become. The added financial burden of family life had swayed his decision as he signed away his own destiny in the only scrawled signature that he had ever known from the poorest of educations offered by the state.

The Deputy was the overseer of the men under his charge and many of the older generations that had worked under the brutal reigns of the private coal masters still saw the deputy as the whip handler that would count out the strokes of pain on those not carrying the full burden of their place in society, unlike the more submissive ones around them.

Despite his misgivings, Roger felt that he had made the right decision. Financially the family had been struggling to hold their heads above water and the boost to his income would be greatly accepted. Times had changed even in the grim backwaters of Castlefields and the younger generations opened their eyes for the first time and were not as socialised as he had been to follow the stereotypical path of their parents.

Hush Puppy and Adidas had replaced the crude, handmade footwear of his own childhood and he wanted his own son now to stand proud amidst the playground throng. Fashion did not come cheap and the added income would ensure that young Billy was kept abreast of the never-ending changing times of today.

    At first, Molly felt saddened when he had announced that he would have to work the regular night shift for the following twelve weeks. Part of his deputy training involved the handling of explosives which were widely used to blast way the hardest of rock that blocked man's pursuit of coal and the riches that it offered.

Shot firing, as it was known, was a dangerous job. To self-induce an explosion in a gas filled environment had been deemed the profession of the lunatic in Victorian days but with the advances of technology it was simply now seen as the profession of the insane and possibly dim-witted.

The shot firer worked the hours of night when fewer men were deployed underground. Roger was to spend ninety days with these men of few words learning the age old tricks of their trade that earned them the respect of their fellow workers. Their skill and precision at blasting away the exact amount of rock in order that tunnelling could continue at speed determined whether or not the miners received bonus payments to their wages for efficiency and production.

Molly saw the benefits of not having to share the bed and looked forward to the nights when she could stretch out in her own comfort without the restrictions and guttural sounds of snoring that her husband omitted.

Her own tired-induced sadness of shorter daylight hours lifted and she now felt compelled to play the part of actress, showing true remorse to lift her husband's feelings of regret of being away from the matrimonial bed in the darkened hours.

The constant snoring and shifting had left her feeling frayed and unable to keep up with the antics of the playful Billy and she saw now the release from the fatigue that she had felt from her never-ending burdens.

Now was the promised sanctuary of silence that only her own company offered and she would make the most of the coming months with relish.

Darkened nights passed as Molly fell into the routine of being left alone with her son, as the shortened days of autumn were replaced by the darker, colder days of winter.

The embers of the burning coals would reach out their fiery red heat as she lay entombed in her own solitude. Billy was above her battling out his own dreams of frolic and Roger was beneath her fighting out his own battle that would in turn warm the nation's hearth with the fuels of his endeavours.

Tuesday evenings offered poor entertainment for the viewer on television. Constant repeats of bygone shows, screened to fill in the endless gap of fresh talent, were broadcast to the nation by the television companies in the hope that these would recapture the audience that had been captivated to the frolics and mayhem of stage heroes long past their sell by date. The humour of the variety shows with their long forgotten post-war punch lines no longer cast their magical spell on Molly as they had once captivated audiences with the freshness of the age in which they had been created.

Never the most ardent of television addicts, she preferred the music of the day. The choice was never confined to what the broadcaster decided to air and it was the individual that could determine whatever sounds were omitted from the fashionable record players that now took centre stage in many households.

Despite the added responsibilities and restraints that marriage and being a mother presented, Molly retained the inner feelings of youth and recklessness that she felt, with sadness, were slowly ebbing their way past her. The hallucinogenic tones of rock bands like Hawkwind and Steve Hillage kept this feeling alive and she relished and grasped this precious need close to her heart.

Pink Floyd had recently released yet another hugely successful album and it was the rich tones of Dave Gilmour that offered her reassurance against all uncertainties as he beckoned that they were merely lost souls swimming around in a fish bowl year after year.

Lost within the carefully written words of the song, Molly's mind drifted away from her surroundings, lost in the tranquillity of a summer long since passed. The song of the lark filled the air as she looked up into the marshmallow clouds that scattered the beauty of blueness of the heavens above her.

The bubbling serenity of the stream splashed its own verse into the concert that nature had to offer and here she found the inner peace of what she truly desired. The innocence of youth once again beckoned as she picked out the buzzing of the bee as it searched for the sweetness of nature's sugar that the fragrant flowers offered in return for impregnation and fertility to ensure their own existence in times to come.

The lark lessened her song as the gentle breeze quickened its pace across the swaying fields of colour. The bumbling bee took refuge amongst the hedgerows as the white puffs of the artist's summery clouds darkened to announce that a storm was now brewing and the moment was to be lost.

Dave Gilmour's voice reached out; however, he was now asking the listener if they could tell the difference between heaven and hell, the difference of a green field to that of a steel rail and the reassurance of a smile through a darkened veil.

Molly opened her eyes to the coldness that she felt creeping its way over her as the clouds darkened overhead.

Pink Floyd had sung their last and now the record player was redundant within its own silence. Darkening clouds of the summer's day faded from her conscious sight as the coldness continued its icy path across her wakening senses.

The room in which she lay looked now unfamiliar to her as her sight slowly focused in the dimness that the evening offered.

The furniture was different and out of place. Even the sofa felt different as it offered its support beneath her. Slowly, her eyes picked out the strangeness that surrounded her. The room was the same, there was no doubt. The layout corresponded to the one that she had decorated and furnished but the similarities ended there.

She had been transported from the summer's day of bumbling bees and singing larks to some long lost film set of a bygone age. Her own modern and fashionable furniture of mahogany-effect woods of the distant east were replaced by the drab and lifeless relics only now to be found in the junk stores that offered quantity rather than quality. The vinyl silk sheen of magnolia that offered the faintest of reflection upon the brightly painted walls dimmed to the flatness of matte and buff conformity that she was not accustomed.

Her rising heartbeat synchronised itself to the regular and hypnotic rhythm of the ticking of a clock that she had never known. The clock of beautiful sounding Westminster chimes that she had only ever heard whilst watching television screenings of reproduced bygone days.

The heated red embers of the fiery hearth offered out no warmth against the tightening chill and only added to the coldness that had overcome her.

The aroma of freshly baked bread was absorbed into her senses as she scanned the scene before her in an attempt to understand what was happening.

Ice itself gripped her tightly by the arm and her gaze was snatched away to the source of the discomfort and confusion that she felt rising within her.

With great effort Molly forced her eyes to focus, her brain now desperate to piece together the puzzle that was unfolding. A jigsaw of pieces that her mind simply could not comprehend nor draw away the reality of the moment from the illusion that was set out before her.

Blurriness of vision and confusion were slowly replaced by reality once more and her attention was snatched to the coldness of the pressure that she felt being exerted

on her arm by an unseen pressure that was alien to her natural senses.

Billy stood before her, his hand resting as if to offer her reassurance upon her arm. As their eyes locked she felt drawn into the blackness of his stare, the very blackness of emptiness itself. The ice cold grip she felt on her arm intensified and she let out a scream of fear and pain. In mimicked response, Billy's own mouth opened to mirror her horror-filled gesture, but this time no sound was omitted.

Instead of the scream of surprise and fright came the flowing of a thickened substance akin to the mud fights of playground days lost. The mud-like discharge flowed down across his lips and dripped heavily onto the carpeted floor before him. The stench of rot and decay was unbearable and Molly fought desperately to fight back the vomit that was beginning to rise upwards from within her gut in readiness for the flight or fight adrenalin-fuelled mechanism that only deep fear ignited.

The scream reverberated into the very fabric of her surroundings and Molly heaved herself upwards from the prone position that she had been sleeping. The age old inborn instinct of survive or die pulsed through her veins, to feed the organs of nature's own induced amphetamine and bring about the primitive need to survive against all odds, and clarity slowly returned to her.

The coldness of the room lifted as the gentle heat from the red embers fought back against the coldness that had overcome her and her vision settled once again on the scene that was set before her. She was alone in the room once again and there was no stinking stain of filth on the carpet. The same stain that she had seen with her own eyes only moments before being spewed from her son's mouth. The furniture in the room was now familiar to her as being that of her own and not the dated collection of bygone relics that had surrounded her, as she had been woken by the ice cold grip of the nightmarish vision of Billy and his impenetrable black stare as their gazes had locked.

As the adrenalin once again withdrew, Molly felt the charged energy within her subside leaving her feeling weak and nauseous. Breathing heavily she sat back and tried to gain the composure of calmness in order that she could think clearly enough to be able to separate the fact of what she had experienced from the fiction of what had never been.

Only the slightest aroma of freshly-baked bread hung in the air to remind her of the fear that had overcome her moments before. Even this aroma slowly dispersed to be replaced by the remnants of the sweet sandalwood incense stick that she had burnt earlier to relax her mood.

The nightmarish vision of Billy had disturbed her deeply when he had stood before her, darkened empty eyes staring back into her own as putrid, thickened black liquid had spilled from his mouth.

The realisation hit her like a bullet on impact from some hidden assassin's carefully aimed discharge.

Usually Billy would annoy her to distraction with his constant and never endless running around the bedroom above her as he acted out countless dog fights between the victorious Spitfire and the ever defeated Messerschmitt as they waged war in the blue skies above the white chalk cliffs of Dover.

Model aircraft were the rage amongst the boys of Billy's age and he relished in their beauty and appeal. Tonight, however, there was no fight of survival between the Royal Air Force and the invading Luftwaffe and the usually creaking floorboards overhead were silent.

Already deeply perturbed by her own experience Molly leapt to her feet and ascended the staircase with the speed and urgency of a well-tuned athlete nearing the final goal of the finishing line. Usually careful to avoid the annoying groan of displeasure that the drying out timbers gave underfoot she bounded the steps with urgency and haste. Each step announced its own eerie creak taken directly from some forgotten horror movie but she sped on regardless.

Without hesitation or fear of creating noise she flung open the door and was instantly numbed by the icy blast that seemed to crash into her from every direction. The natural instincts of survival and protection within her again overwhelmed her and she stepped forward into the awaiting uncertainty. In the dimness her eyes slowly focused on the bed to her left. Her eyes focused and accustomed themselves and the sleeping form of Billy could be made out amidst the contours of cotton blankets and a duck feather pillow.

A movement immediately in front of her raised her already heightened feelings of panic and fear, and her shallow, exhaled breaths were exaggerated by the visual vapour that they produced in the chill of the room.

The light cotton curtains danced their dance to the cold breeze that the opened window had allowed entry to, equalising the temperatures outside to those of within.

Rationale had always been Roger's favourite word and Molly remembered this as she smiled and pulled down on the wooden frame to seal out the coldness of the darkened street below.

Usually she embraced the comfort and luxury that the matrimonial bed offered. With Roger deep underground she could sprawl out until comfort was found without hindrance of restricted movement or the annoyance of the natural sound of his snore. Roger was a master at this fine art and Alison would constantly warn her that this would be worsened as age crept forth. Milan, she would proudly announce, kept the devil himself from slumber with the noises that he omitted during the darkest of hours.

Instead, maybe more for her own comfort rather than the disturbed silence that Roger would create on his return from the depths, Molly eased her way under the sheets beside her sleeping son.

Billy's own subconscious was awoken by the movement at his side and the deepness of his sleep rose from the darkest depths of nothingness.

With surprising ease he found himself lifted from the horizontal position of sleep to the vertical stance of wakefulness. Although still darkened by the shadows of the night his vision cut through the blackness as if illuminated by the power of a hundred torches.

The scene before his vision had been set. He was asleep but standing before himself as his bodily form remained comforted in the arms of Molly.

Billy's eyes met those of his own. This time there was no mirrored images of looking into reflections and photographs. This time the reflection only offered back the shielded eyelids that sleep and death mirrored back to the observer.

He felt himself rising above the sleeping sight before him and was drawn through the closed window where he had earlier held the plastic model airplanes, intrigued how the gentle breeze had turned their propellers ready for take off.

The street below felt warm as the summer's rays baked their temperature to dispute man;s forecast of the day for showers of rain.

Billy looked down at the scene that was set before his eyes.

Beneath him lay the path of adventure. So green now with its ripened nettle heads ready for the knight to slay as he galloped forth in constant victory versus the foe that could never win against the power of the striking willow.

With speed, Billy's sight travelled onwards over the uniformity of the grey slate roofs of the town's housing. Laughter and fun could be heard coming from the small gardens that separated each house from that of its neighbour, and children could be seen enjoying moments of fun and merriment in games beneath the warming of the sun's rays.

The thundering sound of the locomotive caught his attention as he passed overhead. The heat generated from its diesel power rose and Billy felt himself being shaken like an unfortunate aeroplane caught up in the fright of turbulence. The engine snaked slowly away as it hauled its precious cargo of coals to the nearby power station where the solid matter would be transformed into invisible power that would illuminate the landscape below when darkness once again settled.

Ever onwards he was driven until the drab slate roofs gave way to an oasis of fertility that nature held onto amidst the dirt and grime that Castlefields had produced.

The allotment gardens sprawled out beneath him. Each patch gave away its own colours depending on the vegetable that was being grown and the surface from above resembled that of a patchwork quilt illustrated in some magical children's fairytale book of magic and mystery.

The unmistaken sight of Milan could be seen amidst the greenery as he worked effortlessly tending the soil that he laboured with pride.

Stripped to the waist he walked along the neatly laid rows of cabbages seeking out the ever intrusive weed. Alison was sat nearby in the shade that one of the wooden sheds offered. Unlike the heat from the locomotive that made him rise like an autumn leaf in the wind, the scene beneath him pulled him gently downwards like the attraction between magnet and steel. Resistance was futile as the pull grew stronger and Billy gave into that of which he had no control.

Aromas with which he was familiar filled his nostrils as he was drawn slowly downwards. Freshly cut mint, the starchiness of the potato and the pungent smell of ripe tomatoes invaded his senses as he neared ground level amidst the greenery. Cabbage-white butterflies filled his vision as they circled their powdery flight around him.

As if touched by an inner sense of knowing, Milan stopped his laborious chopping with the wooden handled hoe and looked above him. Billy reached out from above desperately hoping for the touch that would offer reassurance.

"Billy!" The voice echoed out from a distance yet uncharted.

As if grasped by powerful unseen hands he felt himself being pulled at great speed upwards. The greenery that he had almost touched fell sharply beneath him as his vision was blurred by the sheer speed of which he felt himself being pulled backwards.

The path of adventure became a tunnel of confusion as colours formed a kaleidoscope of light and the speed increased even more, making him feel nauseous. Streets that he had known all of his life became as one - as if seen from some high powered rollercoaster ride that had reached its exhilarating climax of excitement and fear for the adrenalin-pumped passenger. He felt himself being jolted from left to right as corners were turned without any respite being offered from the unforgiving grasp that had gripped him only moments before.

Billy rose from the bed as if he were the victim of some high speed crash that had caught him unawares in his sleep. The nurse at his bedside dropped the book that had absorbed her attention as she sat beside the sleeping boy that she had been deployed earlier to monitor.

With the tenderness in which she had been trained she calmed away the panic and gently eased Billy down until his head rested on the pillow beneath him.

The pungent odours of the mint and tomato were now replaced with the sterile stench of bleach as Billy opened his eyes to the whiteness of the hospital ward in which he now lay.

Molly held Billy's hand with the clasp of love and protection as she gently explained to him what had happened. She had been sleeping soundly when she felt the movement at her side. At first she thought that she had been dreaming as she was rocked back and forth on the soft mattress beneath her. The pain from the first blow to her shoulder jolted her senses and dragged her from the depths of slumber.

Billy was flaying his arms around and it was immediately obvious that something was seriously wrong. In reassurance she put her own arms around him in an attempt to steady his panic at what she first thought had been caused by the fear of some unseen nightmare.

However she tried she was unable to wake Billy from whatever horror had taken hold of him and deep rooted panic thundered into her as she desperately fumbled the three digit number for the emergency services on the telephone that took pride of place on the bedside cabinet.

Thankfully, the ambulance had arrived within minutes and the trained medics reassured her that Billy would be well taken care of in their expert hands. The short drive to the local infirmary some two miles away seemed like an eternity for Molly as she had clutched her now-sleeping son's hand tightly. The constant bleep from the monitoring equipment only added to her fear and anxiety as she carefully listened to the pitch of his heartbeat.

The waiting doctors examined their young patient carefully before agreeing on the conclusion that Billy had suffered an epileptic seizure and they would carry out a series of medical tests to try and determine what had triggered this.

Roger had been alerted that his son had been rushed to hospital whilst he had been learning the finer points of working with explosives deep underground. A locomotive had been despatched to collect him from his place of work four miles from the shaft bottom and he had been driven directly to the hospital in the minibus that belonged to the colliery.

He had sat hand in hand with Molly as they waited in desperation for the prognosis to be concluded by the team of specialised neurosurgeons deployed to determine the reasons behind the violent seizure that Billy had suffered.

In Roger's haste to reach the hospital he had neither washed nor changed his clothing and the reflection that greeted him as he looked into the darkened window was that of a stranger he had not seen before. Usually the refection that greeted him was that of neatness and cleanliness but tonight the image before him was that of dirt and hopelessness that he had never before seen in himself.

The coal blackened face was filled with the expression of fear and weakness and a far cry from the confidence that usually greeted him in the mirror. The tattered grey vest and torn shorts only added to the misery that he now looked at and he felt for the very first time in his life regretful for what he had become. The realisation hit him hard and only added to his feelings of sadness and worry. He was not the confident joker after all. Here before him was the reflection of truth and lowliness; a common working man that laboured to earn enough money to offer his family the bare necessities to sustain a reasonably comfortable existence amidst the harshness in which they had been born.

Roger felt the first tear run its course slowly down his blackened cheek and he pulled Molly closer to him for comfort. In response, she placed her arm around him and her own tears welled as they held each other tightly and cried the pain that only parents can for their loved ones in times of crisis and deep worry.

The specialised team had subjected Billy to an Electroencephalogram, which had meant that dozens of electrodes had been placed around his scalp to determine brain activity. They had found that for some unknown reason brain activity had been heightened above what was considered to be normal but could not determine the cause behind this exaggerated activity. Epilepsy was unlikely but not ruled out but the likely reason was that Billy had sank into a nightmare so frightening that his body, feeling acute danger, had simply gone into shock - creating a seizure of utter panic.

* * * *

Chapter Nine – The Wind of Change

Molly gently stroked Billy's hand as she coaxed him to recall what he could remember before he had lost consciousness.

Billy said that he had been awoken by Molly as she had clambered into bed beside him. Feeling reassured that she was now at his side he had submitted to the tide of sleep that washed over him. As sleep overcame him he recounted that he had heard a noise which seemed to come from the centre of his own head and had filled his body with the feeling of an intensified electrical charge. This had frightened him and he had fought desperately to force himself awake. As the noise increased he had found himself unable to move. The noise seemed to induce a paralysis that he had been unable to fight against. Billy told Molly that the noise within him had scared him to the point that he had simply given in to the fight which had only seemed to make the feeling worse.

Billy remembered that the dreadful noise and unpleasant feeling that had tingled throughout his body had suddenly stopped, and he had then been overcome with a new sensation of happiness and love. He recalled that even as he had looked down at the sight of himself sleeping he had felt neither fear nor panic and the experience had felt completely natural. Excitedly, he went on to say that he had dreamt he had become a bird and had flown high above the town's rooftops, into the warm sunshine to visit his grandparents, before the sound of Molly calling him had caused him to wake with a startled jump.

Molly stared out in utter disbelief. Since her teenage years of library membership she had been an avid reader of anything that touched on the unexplained phenomena where science could not produce a rational explanation. From the mysteries of unidentified flying objects, the impossibly marked out straight lines on the planes of Nazca in Peru, to the witness sightings from the shores of Loch Ness of some prehistoric beast that had continued to live when all other species of its time had perished.

She recalled a book that she had read which gave the accounts of people that had claimed to have out-of-body experiences.

Molly recalled one account in particular from the book. The writer had claimed to have experienced dreams of being able to fly. He had described how he had simply swooped through his bedroom window and flown above the trees of the neighbourhood where he lived. He described the feeling of flight – saying that it had been effortless, needing no exertion to propel himself forward at unusual speed, and that the usually drab colours of his natural surroundings took on more vibrant and vivid tones. Immediately prior to this experience of flight, the author described a feeling of paralysis that had crept over him. This had been accompanied by a dreadful noise which was both disturbing and frightening whenever this had manifested itself.

Immediately Molly had identified and connected together the accounts from the book's author to the recollections from Billy immediately prior to being admitted to hospital - the feeling of flight above the rooftops and the vivid colours that he had witnessed as he had travelled effortlessly above his very own path of adventure. The feeling of paralysis immediately before he had felt himself being raised into the air and the violent pull backwards into his own body all echoed the author's writing. This had not simply been a seizure, she concluded with fearful realisation, but had been the direct result of some unknown paranormal activity.

Quietly, Roger eased himself into the chair beside her, careful not to wake the now resting Billy. He had returned home to wash away the filth and grime that had earlier covered him as he had rushed from the mine to the hospital.

Slowly, expecting ridicule from the master of rational thinking, Molly relayed her fears as their son slept soundly from the mild sedative that the nurse had recently administered.

Surprisingly, Roger listened in silence as she recounted other instances that she had been unable to explain.

She recalled how Billy had always sought out and preferred the company of imaginary friends to those of flesh and blood from an early age and how she had kept her concerns from Roger for fear of ridicule.

Molly remembered the day, when at two years old she had left Billy to his own devices as she set about the ritual of completing the weekly laundry; armed with the crayon set and paper that his grandparents had bought for him the day before she had left him to his own devices in his playpen as she busied herself in the kitchen.

Expecting a picture of only chaotic lines she had been disturbed and shocked by the artistic scene of a flower-adorned scene that greeted her, as she checked on Billy before hanging out the freshly-washed laundry to dry.

Although the lines held the crudeness from the blunt tips of the cheap crayons there had been an ingrained detail to the picture that could have only come from skill and knowledge which would have to have been acquired from practice. There was no doubt in her mind that the work set out before her had not been that of a child.

Fearful of what the colourful paper represented she took it from the floor and placed it onto the glowing embers of the fireplace. Immediately it ignited and within seconds only the blackened remnants of what once had been remained.

For the rest of that day she had attempted to coax her artistic child to reproduce the masterpiece that had been created, but this resulted in confused trails of colours that his childish hand produced.

The nights that she had been awoken to the murmurings of an elderly woman's voice and on inspection to its whereabouts within the darkened confines of the house had always found Billy awake and amused with something that had never been visible to her.

Molly recounted the recording which clearly replayed spoken words that resounded only when playback was trebled in speed.

Surprisingly, no ridicule was offered as Roger listened to her concerns. Even more surprisingly was his admittance that, yes, he agreed that something was far from right within the house that they had purchased as happy go lucky teenagers without a care in the world.

She was surprised if not somewhat shocked at Roger's acceptance that something indeed was unexplainable within the matrimonial home. Quietly, he went on to explain more about his own fears that he had never relayed to anyone about his own experiences when alone in the house.

He remembered one incident in particular when he had returned at dawn from work and had been drawn to a movement at the window of the bedroom which they had decorated as a nursery for Billy. Alison would often keep her daughter company by staying the night whenever Roger had worked the night shift and he had assumed that the silhouetted figure had been her checking on her beloved grandson. Roger had waved a friendly good morning greeting as he continued up the path that led to the kitchen door. In reply, the figure raised an arm and waved back in response.

Fearful of waking his sleeping family, he had carefully climbed the staircase and eased himself into bed beside Molly.

Fatigued from hard manual labour he had drifted into a deep sleep only to be awoken in the afternoon to the aromas of cooking announcing that his meal was ready.

He had been surprised to find Molly and Billy alone in the living room as he entered and enquired as to the whereabouts of Alison. Roger had felt deeply unsettled to learn that Alison had not visited the evening before and that she had certainly not stayed the night.

Roger knew deep down in his heart that he had not been mistaken. The female form that he had greeted with a cheery wave had been real and not just a figment of his tired imagination. He also knew deep down that if he were to relay his fears to Molly then this would fuel her own concerns that something that could not be rationally explained was present and active around them. Despite the inner feelings of fear rising within himself that he had directly looked into what he could not explain, he forced himself to remain silent about the exchanged wave of greetings hours before.

As if to fortify his inner feelings of bravery and manhood he gulped down the scalding hot coffee that he had collected from the vending machine on the corridor outside the children's ward.

Clasping Molly's hand even more tightly he recounted another experience in the house whilst he had been alone.

Billy had been particularly troublesome and had drove Molly to distraction with his strange behaviour that unseen people were around him and she had decided to spend the evening with Milan and Alison. At least then, she had thought, when he awoke in laughter during the early hours she would have the added help to comfort him once again to sleep and gain much needed rest.

Roger had been forced to labour even harder than usual during the night as the coal face had suffered a collapse and the cavity needed constant supporting with hastily cut timbers to avoid further delay in the production of coal.

Wearily, he had arrived home exhausted and had clambered onto the bed without the energy to even remove his clothing.

As his eyelids succumbed to the much-needed sleep that quickly washed over him he had been startled into immediate wakefulness by the heavy and hurried footsteps sounding from the wooden staircase immediately outside the closed door to the bedroom in which he was resting. The footsteps had appeared to stop as they neared the landing that separated the bedroom from the adjoining bathroom and he began to curse himself for imagining what had simply not been there.

Smiling to himself he had turned on his side and clutched the feathered duvet close to his chest to ward off the chill that he felt within the room.

This time the noise had not been a figment of his imagination or over-tiredness as the door was shaken violently within its wooden frame. He had turned in haste and fear to see the wooden barrier shake as if being violently pushed back and forth.

Roger admitted for the first time that he had felt fright like he had never before felt in his life and Molly responded by reaching out and drawing him close in a loving embrace of reassurance.

Realising that no ridicule was to be offered, he continued. The shaking of the door had lasted for maybe thirty seconds before silence had once again been restored and Roger remembered the sheer fear that had crashed over him.

Like the child of days long since gone he had drawn the duvet across his face as if to become invisible from prying eyes.

The minutes had slowly ticked away in the hushed quietness that had descended once again in the stillness of the darkened dawn. Bravery and fearlessness ebbed its way back through his veins and began to build upon his confidence as he slowly pulled away the covering that had offered him the magic of childish invisibility. The door now lay still in its frame and his mind had raced to seek out the rationale that it had always sought whenever he had been faced with the impossible.

Clutching at the offered straws that he had been presented, Roger concluded that the wind from outside has simply entered the house through gaps in its aged and shrunken wooden window frames. Trapped within the walled confines the breeze had searched for escape and had simply fought briefly against the wooden barrier of the door before finding a more penetrable route for its release.

As ever Roger thought that he was the master of solving the puzzle and again he had smiled at his own stupidity that had created his fear within. With new-found confidence he had eased himself from the bed and made his way to the narrow window that looked out onto the road below.

Although darkness met his gaze the scattered street lamps had offered out their orange glow enough for him to pick out the still forms of the young tree saplings that his adjoining neighbour had planted recently to form a future boundary to the immaculate garden he had created. The young trees were small and fragile and their string-like branches had been completely devoid of any movement that even the slightest of breezes would create. Even the discarded sheet of newspaper from someone's feast of fish and chips from the evening before lay lifeless on the pavement below.

Roger had felt the chill once again rise within as he slowly realised that no amount of his rationale could explain what he had witnessed and he hurried to turn on the light switch, forcing the darkened shadows back into the corners of the room from which they had emerged.

He had remained in the illuminated bedroom until the rising sun ebbed slowly away at the natural shadows that the night had created. He had known that to tell Molly what he had experienced would be extremely unwise and would seal the realisation that something paranormal at times was present in the house and this had a direct connection to their son's presence.

Like the recording of the woman's voice he had dismissed, there had been no rational explanation that would secure the phenomena within the realms of normality.

Man and wife had sat silent within their own thoughts until Billy slowly stirred from the sedative-induced slumber that had helped to ward off whatever terrors had instilled enough fear into him to cause the seizure which had taken over his body.

They had sat comforting Billy until the doctors had done their afternoon ward rounds. Drawing the curtained partition that gave privacy away from the other bed users they examined Billy and asked how he now felt.

They explained to Roger and Molly that their son appeared to be stable enough to be allowed home. Although epilepsy could not be ruled out they had thought this unlikely, so no medication was needed unless he suffered further seizures.

Whilst Billy had been getting changed into his clothes in readiness for the short journey home, his parents had agreed that at least for the immediate week ahead they would stay with Milan and Alison.

The ordeal had deeply frightened them and they both felt that a return to the house could result in avoidable stress for Billy which could slow down his recuperation from what he had already endured.

When Alison had met Milan, shortly after he had arrived in England, they had purchased a larger than average house at a bargain price during times of a national recession that had settled on most of the post-war countries.

Alison and Milan were delighted at the decision and welcomed them with open arms. They adored Billy with all of their hearts and had been fearful for his welfare when they had received Molly's distressed telephone call from the hospital waiting room.

Evenings now were not spent alone; whilst Roger laboured deep beneath them, Molly revelled in the happiness that they would all sit together in the large kitchen that acted also as a living room.

Daytime hours were spent helping Alison around the house cleaning and polishing the countless brass ornaments that she had been collecting for over twenty years.

Milan and Billy were inseparable. It never ceased to amaze Molly that the same bond she felt for the man had now been passed onto her son.

Dark winter nights were spent sitting by the coal fuelled stove that acted both as oven and heating for the entire house.

The chequered battleground of the chess board once again took centre stage and countless victories were fought with Billy always the victor of the day.

Weary from the countless battles Milan would become the storyteller that had enthralled Molly when she too had been young.

Billy would sit beside him as he drank his beloved whiskey that seemed to fuel the words of magic that he spoke.

He would always tell of a land of beauty and mystery. A place that would enchant the soul with its mountains and forests. A place of dark forests that were kept alive with countless swirling rivers and majestic waterfalls that reverberated their crashing sounds for miles around.

He would speak of a hidden city that lay deep beneath the imposing feature that gave the appearance of a huge, forest-covered pyramid. The city had once been home to the king of the lands and had been so sacred that even an invading army had not dared to travel the slopes that had been built to protect the most highest of majesties.

Milan would go on to explain to his now-captured audience that the sacred city was protected by two layers of defence. The first layer was that of the earth that man had toiled for hundreds of years to collect and transport from the mountains that stretched as far as the eye could see in all directions. Over the centuries this layer was slowing being washed away from the storms that had plagued the landscape. The second layer had been made in the form of a thin shell and it was this layer which was the final protective barrier that allowed the magical city to exist unnoticed through the annals of time.

The storyteller would continue, that if this thin layer of final protection were to be broken then hardship and misery would fall onto the people of the lands for hundreds of miles around.

The stories were countless and still held Molly transfixed to the words as they were spoken.

She would regress to her own childhood and the form of Billy as he sat beside Milan would be transformed into her own. Memories of her own childhood would be relived before her and she would constantly be transported back to a time when fun and mirth overshadowed everything else.

During those evenings of happiness and contentment she would often feel the tears well up and would make her excuses to visit the bathroom before anyone noticed.

Days gradually turned into weeks and any hopes of the family returning to their own home were dashed when Billy had become severely distressed when Roger had suggested that it was time to leave their temporary lodgings.

Fearing that the panic that set into Billy could induce another seizure the couple sat and discussed the options available to them.

The answer had been simple. Across the street from Milan and Alison's home a house had been placed on the market for sale. This would be the ideal solution. Not only would it give Billy a fresh start in a place that held no nightmarish memories, but would also be beneficial to Molly as she would not have far to travel to check on the welfare of her parents. Gradually the years had begun to take their toll and Molly found the need to visit them more and more frequently to offer her help if it were needed.

Roger made an offer to the owners of the house and was surprised the following day when this had been accepted. Two weeks later he had also received an offer for their own house and despite being five hundred pounds short of what they hoped they decided to accept without delay.

Legal teams on both sides of the transactions speedily finalised the sales and purchases, and within weeks Roger walked into the kitchen proudly shaking a set of keys which would herald a new beginning for the whole family.

Excitedly, they had arranged furniture and hung new curtains and before long the house felt truly like a home.

Billy quickly came out of the withdrawn state he had sank into during his early years and seemed happier than he had ever been in his whole life.

Days of playing alone in his bedroom with friends that were invisible to all but him were gone and he spent his time now outside, amongst the other children in the street.

Milan and Alison had prepared one of the empty bedrooms in their own house and had told Billy that this was his own piece of sanctuary and that he was welcome to stay there whenever he had wanted.

Happily he had taken up the chance to be in the company of the man that he adored so much and he would sleep at the respective houses on alternate days.

Months rolled into years and the horrors that had plagued the family during the short time they had lived in their first home fell behind them and became clouded within the mists of their memory.

The passing of time slowly ebbed on as it had done so since the very first light that had heralded the dawn of a new age.

Billy evolved into the playful, happy go lucky child that any parents could wish for and laughter now echoed out within the walls of the family home.

As the bond between Milan and Billy strengthened so too did that of father and son. Roger became more relaxed and the tensions that had appeared to surround him eased away as each day passed in his new surroundings.

No longer did Molly feel the need to be reserved whenever in her husband's presence and she also felt that a new lease of life had crept its way slowly over the horizon.

Moving from the house had seemed to lift a huge weight of oppression from above their heads and now it felt that the plug had finally been pulled, releasing whatever tensions that had forced back the happiness and pleasures necessary for any family to survive and remain together in harmony.

Being so close to Milan's magical allotment garden made even the longest days of summer fulfilled with the feelings of being within a paradise lost.

Roger and Molly would find deep and satisfying pleasure in each other's company as they would spend evenings harvesting the carefully grown produce that Milan had tended since the frosts of spring.

Billy also revelled in this magical place of mystery and would proudly invite his new-found friends to share its ambience and tranquillity.

As the passing of the years gradually stole away Milan's once bear-like strength Billy became the muscle that was needed to continue. Weekends would be spent helping wherever he could and he found deep satisfaction giving back to the man what he had received in love during his early years.

Teenage years slowly beckoned and Billy, now armed with the emotions of reality, would often feel the sadness that inevitability brought with it.

The cracks of weakness became slowly visible to him whenever he was within the company of his grandparents.

Alison, the one time athlete of household chores had slowly succumbed to the debilitating rigours that arthritis offered to its chosen victims. Her once nimble and agile posture was slowly dimming like that of a candle that had burnt through the night, only to have its glow overshadowed by the rising sun. The spring in her step had slowly been replaced by the appearance of a limp that hindered her passage on the staircase.

Milan too was slowly being defeated by time. Never one to complain, it was obvious that the clock within his body had begun the final countdown that would eventually lead to its final failure.

Although he had suffered a broken back shortly after his arrival in England, he had fought back against all odds and had lived a seemingly healthy life. Whether or not it had been the dimming of resilience with age or the wound weakening, it was obvious that he too was becoming less and less agile with every ticking of the clock.

The coal dust that he had inhaled daily whilst working in the depths of the mine now began to play out its own harmonica-pitched tunes from deep within him as he slept soundly upon the sofa after ever-shortening hours of toil tending to the land.

The wheezing would resound until he finally woke and then the guttural coughs would begin until finally his tightened airway had been cleared.

Roger, although neither a knowledgeable or keen gardener would help out the best that he could in order to keep the allotment garden going.

Although limited with his own free time he would dig the earth side by side with Milan, ever careful that his own strength never overshadowed the man that he had always admired. Weakness of strength was one thing he always thought, but to damage the pride was another.

Molly too would give more and more of her time helping Alison with the daily rigours of never-ending housework. They would sit and talk over freshly made cups of tea and biscuits and she would always be deeply enthralled with her mother's stories of times gone by.

The long gone days of milking the teats in summer pastures green, the starched collars worn by the young girls born into service to shine the silver of the cutlery before the rich could feast on the labours of the poor. The sight of her father as she had innocently returned from her day of schooling as he lay upon the kitchen table. The shattered corpse that had lain pulverised from the tons of fallen rock that had snuffed out in an instant the life he had known.

Despite the collective happiness now felt as the family had forged together as one, the reality that slowly the unstoppable tide of time was beginning its path of erosion.

As always the waves would be unstoppable and would continue with their own path regardless.

King Canute, centuries before had tried to stop his own waves that crashed relentlessly upon the shore. He had failed, sat upon his jewel encrusted throne on the golden shore of his own defences against what was to be.

Realising his imminent defeat, he had withdrawn to higher ground, feet dripping from the wetness that the never-ending waves had continued in their haste to advance forth despite the highest of his commands.

* * * *

Chapter Ten - Do You Remember Me How We Used To be?

Molly spread the drab contents of the local newspaper before her, laying it flat on the cheap, pine reproduction breakfast table that had been bought several years before in order that the family could keep in line with the latest trends of their neighbours.

The pages of the local gossip reflected the grey emptiness that enveloped around her. Even the local news was dull, lacking the gossip and intrigue that was being flaunted daily within the tabloids of the national newspapers. The court reports and obituaries were the only items of interest and it never ceased to amaze Molly how people were drawn to the misery of others around them. Whether it be the death of some known local or the appearance before the town's magistrate for some demeanour - the intrigue was always there.

Molly's thoughts subsided away from the reality and gloom of the printed misery that lay before her on the table. With a smile, her thoughts took a backward step to the evening before. Billy had spent the night at Milan's, idling away the hours beating his ageing foe on the chequered battlefield of chess.

Roger had been in a surprisingly good mood and had reminded her of the young man that had stole her heart and lifted her spirits whenever they had stolen time together as the love struck teenagers that they had once been.

He had laughed as Molly had galloped on before him on the path of adventure, cutting the heads from her foes with one slice of the willow branch that she swung from left to right.

With the hug and kiss of real companionship they had slowly walked the short road that led to home and security.

The mood was set and continued once inside the family home. Today there were no distractions. No Billy to disturb the moment with his constant intrusions into the couple's private life. As their lips met in loving embrace Molly felt all of her emotions being drawn from her like the gentle pull from a magnet being gently lowered onto steel. Her mind dissolved into the kisses and warmth to which she was now being exposed and she felt that her very soul had been entered and filled with the warmth of love.

Roger took her hand and led her up the narrow staircase. Each step for Molly had become like that of walking upon softened marshmallows warmed softly by the gentle heat of passion.

Laid upon the matrimonial bed Molly gave into her feelings of resistance. Each kiss from Roger was met by Molly's own, as the chemistry that only true love can produce between two people that shared their lives together ebbed its way across them.

Although marriage had created some of the problems that would face all married couples at some stage of their togetherness it had also created a sense of loyalty and deep-rooted respect.

Deep down she knew that Roger would often put before him a shield of masculinity that offered very little to the onlooker, but which was very occasionally exposed and in need of the gentle love that breached the walls of his resistance.

He was the man of his times - the hard-working collier that would be expected to have no weakness.

Molly respected that this was how it had to be, but at times like this she knew that Roger did have a caring and loving side to him that he fought desperately to hide from those around. To reveal this softer side would be an announcement that he was not the man that he portrayed.

No longer the lustful teenagers that they had once been, the kisses would diminish and be replaced by the gentle strokes of adoration. The strokes in turn would evolve into an occasional tickle of fun that would have the recipient howling out in uncontrollable laughter. The barrage of tickles escalated and the couple found themselves in an open battle of frolic and laughter. Pillows became the chosen weapon of the day and adults became children once again as they rained countless soft blows on each other playfully.

Out of breath, the opposing sides once again came together as one; the determined enemies signing their own peace treaty, not with a pen and handshake but with the power and might of their touch. Smiles of happiness and togetherness now filled the battlefield that had been and the once brave warriors succumbed to the fatigue of battle and laughter.

Eventually their laboured breathing from the exertions of the pillow fight settled and they held each other in love and togetherness.

Here was the man that she had married, Molly thought to herself, as she looked into his resting face. Despite the cool bravado that he put forward, deep down Roger remained the swashbuckling hero that had stolen her heart amongst the tranquil grass meadows and woodlands surrounding the grime and uniformity of the place where she had been born.

She gently leaned towards him and placed the kiss of love upon his forehead as his breathing announced that now the warrior was being drawn into sleep and rest.

Turning in contentment, he lay on his side facing the window with his back to her as was his favoured position of sleep. Soon his shallow breathing deepened and then gave out to the guttural, irritating sound of deep sleep and restricted nasal passages.

Molly had constantly scolded Roger throughout their marriage that his snoring had kept her awake long into the darkest hours and left her feeling drained and tired throughout the never-ending day of the coming chores that motherhood presented.

Again the joker, he would repute her accusations with the simple logic that if he did indeed snore as bad as she constantly complained, how it was that it never disturbed him…..

Molly lay in the darkness and withdrew her thoughts from the annoying grunts of deep sleep and total relaxation that Roger bellowed out into the darkness and stillness now of the night.

Her lot, after all, was a good lot, despite her husband's downfalls and faults.

Despite these, Roger had always provided for his family's needs. What he had lacked in actual participation of family fun he had made up in whatever financial support and security that was needed to make the family unit flourish amidst the hard times that settled across the coal mining communities of their once proud nation.

The bitter, year-long strike against a barbaric government, hell bent on forcing the working classes to their knees, had been lost and now it was the once proud miner that would take the full weight of the government's revenge on what they saw as opposition to their right wing policies.

Militant in his beliefs to stand up and be counted whenever he felt that his fellow worker was being dealt an unfair hand in the game of life, Roger would always be the first one to take stance against the threat to the worker's pride and it now saddened Molly that, at times, he would have to swallow the pride that ran through his blood and accept the way of the defeated.

She turned gently over onto her side, careful not to rouse her husband from his much-earned slumber. In the darkness she wrapped her arm across him and placed her head upon his chest. The rhythm of his beating heart reassured her, like it did with a foetus deep inside the womb, that all was well and protection was at hand, and soon her own eyes flickered away the last glimpses of sight and her steady breathing amplified to join the man beside her in peaceful sleep.

Molly's dreams that night were the dreams of happiness and contentment.

Billy had been a demanding baby and craved every bit of attention during the hours that he was awake. Even sleep failed to quench his demands for motherly companionship and at times she had speculated that he had some kind of in-built radar system which would alert his dream-filled thoughts with the knowledge that he had been deserted. In his sleep he would let out the gentle sobs of babies to alert their long suffering mothers that the child was aware of their absence and needed the gentle reassurance of safety that they were not alone.

As man and wife lay together in the warmth and comfort of slumber, Molly saw herself sitting within her own theatre of dreams and was drawn to watch out happier times of her adult life, which were all too easily forgotten in times of misery and sadness.

With the never-ending chores that being in charge of a baby's life beckoned towards the inexperienced mother, so too had the challenges of a boy forced into premature manhood with the arrival of family responsibilities.

Roger had soon learned, as countless others had before, that boyhood had left him with those first cries of offspring from the womb. He had reaped the pleasures of the woman and now he should accept the responsibility that would continue for the rest of his life.

With the responsibility so too came the need for financial security and whilst Molly had laboured relentlessly to make the family home comfortable, Roger had also laboured to provide the financial income that was needed simply to feed the mouths that he loved.

Overtime became a necessity to survive and he would find himself working almost double the allotted hours of the working week.

Pressures of early family life had played a heavy role in their first years of marriage and days would often be ended with quarrel and resentment, neither side giving in to the other and accepting that these troubled times of their relationship would pass as the burden of immaturity lessened its grip with age and knowledge.

Molly smiled now with the warmth of remembrance as she watched her theatre of dreams play out the warmer, more pleasant chapters of family life.

Billy had begun his school years at the gentle age of five and it was then that the old spark of togetherness had been rekindled within her marriage to Roger.

With more time to spare from the ritualistic, never-ending duties of motherhood, Molly found time to add again the spice that had brought man and wife together in those crazy days of love and lust.

Billy tired from his day of schooling and having to wake early for the day's busy schedule, settled into the routine of being put to bed earlier than he had done so before the rigours of being woken early. This gave Molly the time to put the needed effort into her relationship in order for it to not only survive but to flourish and prosper.

She remembered one such evening in particular that had set the pace of happiness for the years that were to follow.

Always the one to experiment, Molly had planned to seduce her husband when he returned from his labour in the early evening with the new-found tastes of the Asian culture that were taking the nation by storm. Exotic tastes from faraway places had slowly found themselves being popular by the younger generations of the drab and dreary mining communities of northern England.

Ready-made curries that could be heated in their containers were now readily available in the supermarkets and freezers of the more modern local shops.

With new found vigour of wanting to reignite the passion between man and wife Molly had taken the concept of exotic cuisine further and had obtained an authentic recipe for chicken korma from one of the weekly magazines that she read.

Molly had instantly been attracted to the rich and colourful photograph of the Indian that leapt at the reader from the glossy pages spread out before her as she sipped sweet tea, sitting at the small, pinewood table that had yet to be used for the purpose of family dining.

The inviting picture focused the reader to scan across to the dish's description, which claimed that the recipe was a classic and authentic Indian dish favoured for its creamy and mild taste. Chicken korma, it went on to say, was indicative of the Moghul cooking of Northern India which was renowned for its sweet curries, butter dishes and delicate flavours.

Molly knew all too well that the way to a man's heart was through his stomach and excitedly spent the time that she had that afternoon scanning the local stores and market place for the required herbs and spices. Although fresh herbs had not been available, she had managed to obtain dried packets that she thought would work quite well. Besides, she realised, if you had never eaten a chicken korma before, then if it was not made to utter perfection you would never know.

With the aid of the occasional glass of white wine she set about mixing the ingredients together as the recipe instructed.

As the fresh chicken breasts bathed in their creamy marinade she gently read Billy his favourite bedtime story of Hansel and Gretel.

As her words softly explained, "Look, father! We're rich now. You'll never have to chop wood again," Billy's eyes had closed in relaxation and comfort that only childhood sleep offered.

He was now in the magical realm of forests and mountains. Where mornings of autumn mist settled gently across the valleys that rose with forests of pine trees, cushioning away the noises of the bubbling spring waters ebbing up from underground caves to feed the fertile land with its needed nutrients.

A magical place, which she recalled with warmth and regret for its passing from her own childhood, the golden fruit and the dragon slayer of Milan's mysterious lands she would never know.

Careful to avoid the boards that let out their creak of despair, Molly silently descended the staircase leaving Billy in the paradise that the spoken pages had offered out in their promise of tranquillity and peace.

The chicken korma's sweet aroma bathed the small kitchen with the richly-scented taste of the unexplored and never known. Excited at the new fragrance she set the table to perfection, as she had learned from the schooling that had taught women to be women and men to be men. Boys would make ashtrays out of wood and the girls would learn to sew and cook in readiness for their future lives of simple housewife drudgery.

She lit candles to finish the masterpiece that she had created when the door opened. Roger gazed in surprise at the scene that was set out before him. His wide eyes exaggerated by the mascara like lining of his lashes that was the trademark of a coal miner. This was due to the never-ending settling of the fine black dust which would later take away their health, and finally their lives, as the dust permeated deep into the lungs, forcing the natural taking of breath to become a laboured and deadly chore.

The smile of the charmer returned as Roger closed the door behind him and looked across at the scene set out in his welcome.

The gentle aroma of something not known, the candlelight and the gentle rhythm of Neil Young's enchanting 'After the Gold Rush' centred the stage of the rich atmosphere that welcomed the dark-eyed man home from the depths.

The loving charmer had finally come home, prompted maybe a little by the promise of the east that was set out before him.

His gentle kiss sealed the clasp of love. Not the touching lips of passion, but the soft kiss of true appreciation placed gently upon Molly's forehead, confirming the loving tone of the night.

Drawn from the magic, Roger asked about Billy. Billy was deep in sleep with Hansel and Gretel in stories of old, she reassured, as they held each other so tight that it felt they would suffocate not only each other, but the whole room with their love.

Ignoring the sweetly scented food of mystery, Roger opened the door that led into the small garden of grass that they proudly enjoyed as their little piece of nature against the grime that surrounded them.

Roger pointed to the stars. He traced The Plough with his fingertips as if some magical wand would light up the connecting lines of each pinnacle of light to form the true shape of the constellation.

Saturn and Mars he also pointed out as he gently pulled Molly to lie on the damp grass beside him.

Together they counted the stars that were set out before their vision. The pinpricks of light that he informed her were mysteries of life itself.

Imagine, he softly spoke as he held her hand tight yet lovingly, that somewhere above them on one of those pinpricks of light, a couple in love could be laid out on their own dampened grass, looking out at the scene that lay before them wondering if they were the only Molly and Roger in the universe that were so very much in love.

Yes, the charmer had returned, she thought, as she closed her eyes and sank into the love that she felt was being offered. This was how it should be between man and wife; love for the moment was here on the dampened grass looking high into the sky that held its own mysteries which may never unfold to reveal all.

The magic of the moment was simple. Love could not be bought and it was this simple act of togetherness that opened the show in Molly's own theatre of dreams.

The show progressed and acted out the following day of what once had been.

Molly woke to the sound of a blackbird's shriek, dismayed that his own peace and serenity had been breached by a passing tom cat going about his ritualistic hunting of all things furred or feathered. His cackling call alerted others of his kind to the danger that was within their midst and would continue until the sly cat had passed without harm being done.

Molly rolled onto her side and gently placed her arm around Roger's strong shoulders, careful not to wake him from his own slumber.

The warmth of love still enveloped her from the night before and she asked herself what had happened in her marriage to take that feeling away for so long.

Had it simply been the pressures of parenthood and long working hours needed to finance the extra mouth, that had pulled them apart like the opened curtains whose true beauty would only be revealed when joined together as one - when the day was done and their union would ward away the darkness of night?

Molly sank into the heart-stopping love that she now felt. The warm kisses had flowed like that of champagne celebrating a momentous day of some victory of the victors. The cork had been broken to unleash an energy that had taken her by complete surprise.

The love, she now realised, had never dwindled - it had simply lain dormant like the volcano of Roman times, to rise up again, taking the unwitting victims of Pompeii by complete and utter surprise. Love had always been there, only it had become disguised and sewn into the fabric of everyday life, a life that was weighted down with the need and want of the lowly working classes.

Next morning, Molly rose with the feeling that a thousand flutter byes (of Milan's words) were bursting to break free from the confines of her inner self. She was the teenage girl again under the magical spell cast by her first love.

Billy noticed the change in her as he sat eating his favourite strawberry jam on toast whilst reading the latest escapades of Desperate Dan forcing down yet another huge helping of his beloved cow pie.

With the true innocence that only a child can possess, he asked Molly if she had read the brightly-illustrated comic before he had awoke and was this why she was so happy.

Molly smiled as she rubbed the top of his head with affection and simply said that she was happy because she loved him and his father so much. She suggested he should go upstairs and get dressed as they were all going to the local park to make the most of the morning sunshine before Roger left again for yet another afternoon deep underground.

The magic of the previous evening continued as they took turns pushing the laughing Billy on the squeaking swing that Molly had sat on as a child whilst her own mother and Milan had pushed her during the summer days of long ago.

A game of tag followed, and the squeal of Billy's laughter resounded all around as Roger faked his inadequate capabilities of being able to catch the side-stepping child as the three of them ran in a frenzy of fun and joy. Adult and child came together as one to form the unbreakable bond of family union and Molly found herself overcome by sheer joy at something so simple that she had missed so much - true happiness that she had missed for so long with the burdens of everyday life and its constant demands.

As they threw the stale scraps of bread to the eagerly waiting ducks that had taken up home on the small round boating lake, she wished with all her heart that this day would last forever. That the simple act of family togetherness could bring about so much joy amazed her. They were, after all, simple people with nothing to announce their prosperity in a money-driven society which preached that only the wealthy could afford the fun times of life. Money could never buy the happiness that she now felt as the three of them walked hand in hand through the drab uniformity of the streets in the place she knew as home and security. Money could never buy the laughter that had filled her heart with joy as Roger had intentionally slipped to allow his son to escape in their game of tag. Money could not buy the laughter either from when the stale bread had fallen on the unwitting duck's head, startling it to take refuge in a vertical dive beneath the water's surface, thinking that predatory attack was imminent.

The same happiness had continued when the trio had returned home. Roger had taken the dusty acoustic guitar from the cupboard, tuned its strings and proceeded to play out his favourite tune of 'Hurdy Gurdy Man', made famous by Britain's answer to Bob Dylan. As always, Billy was transfixed to the sound of the steel strings being brought together in harmony and tune as each chord followed the next. Billy knew the words and father and son sang in harmony together until the tray of freshly made sandwiches were set out before them. They were placed on the brightly coloured rug that protected the carpet from stray embers in front of the fireplace that added the warmth throughout the winter months.

The slide show in Molly's own theatre of dreams flickered on as it moved to the next episode of happiness that was being screened.

Her eyes opened to the dappling of the summer's sun as it cast its silhouette from the leafy sycamore tree that stood alienated against the brickwork and concrete of the street outside. A relic now from the ancient times of Castlefields' existence, the tree held fast with the stubbornness that it should live out its days regardless of the changes that now surrounded its splendour.

Beside her, Roger lay snoring in restful sleep. The leaves of the old tree outside were superimposed across his face in gentle shadows of grey and gave him the appearance of having a laurel crown from some black and white Hollywood movie depicting the Greek Gods of a civilisation lost in the annals of time.

Carefully, she reached over and gently placed her own lips upon his. Not with the kiss of love she gently bore down pressure until the two came together as one. As if resurrected from the curse of a poisoned apple from the pages of a children's classic, Roger stirred with her touch and opened his eyes. With the speed of a striking cobra he spun to his side and forced Molly, face down onto the duck feather filled pillow that had offered her comfort through the darkened hours of night.

Feigning struggle against her assailant Molly gave into the attack and both man and wife gave into the laughter that followed.

Seizing the moment Molly asked Roger if they could spend the day together to enjoy the dying days of summer before the dampness of autumn took its hold on the nature that surrounded them.

Surprisingly, Roger agreed, on the condition that she run like the wind downstairs and make him a breakfast of fried eggs and bacon. After all, he said, if man was to rise up to the energies needed to keep a woman happy, then man needed the sustenance to feed the energy that would be required.

* * * *

Chapter Eleven – The Partisan

Castlefields had suffered from the effects of large scale coal mining since the first deep shafts had been sunk in 1865.

The coal owners had simply bought the land and could do with it how they pleased.

There had been no green environmentalists to argue the fight against what was right and what was wrong for the planet and the quality of life for its inhabitants.

Coal was king and coal created wealth. Only wealth and prosperity mattered for the elite that ruled and the coal would be won at all costs.

The waste of washing away the worthless dirt and grime from the purity of their product had been easy. Land adjacent to the shafts would be purchased and the rock and dust would simply be piled there to be forgotten.

One hundred and thirty years later the result had been a man-made mountain of blackness that overshadowed the whole town. The whole landscape had become changed from the one that natural geology had chartered to create the lands. Black mountains of sulphur-filled debris were now the landmarks that alerted newcomers that they were in the realms of old king coal.

Over the years nature had tried to recapture what she had lost to the greed of mankind and had created small pockets of oases across the defeated landscape.

Grasses grew wherever they could in isolated colonies amongst this lunar landscape that had been created amidst the debris. As the grasses lived, died and then lived again their natural nutrients had been absorbed to offer life to other plants brave enough to step into the footprints that mankind had forcibly left behind.

The blackberry was one of the few species that had stepped up to the new-found challenge of having to survive in the hostile and poisonous environment that man had created in his quest for wealth.

Molly had always enjoyed the short walk to the perimeter of the man-made mountain of coal waste that could now be seen on the horizon for miles. In summer the huge mound of waste carried with it the dullest tones of grey highlighted by the greenery of the growing crops of wheat and barley that the tenant farmers grew to eke out their own financial existence, rather than having to brave the depths of the town's centrepiece of coal production.

Today the walk was especially poignant to her as the aroma of burning straw filled the air all around, permeating everything that came in contact with the smoke filled breeze of the late summer's day.

After another successful harvest the local farmers were now burning the leftover stalks of their crops which the harvesting machines had left behind. This took her back to her own childhood as she was drawn to the image of Milan, stood, naked from the waist up, carefully tending to the many fires that now announced that the harvest was over and the coolness of autumn dampness was now beckoning.

Each year he would offer to the farmer his services of burning the fields in exchange for a tractor load of pig manure with which he would make fertile his own soil on the allotment that had become his life.

She revelled in her own childhood reminiscing as she walked hand in hand with Roger nearing the place that would offer them the finest fruits of nature's basket.

The summer had been particularly hot and dry and had gone on record as being one of drought proportions. Water rationing had been instigated by the government and anyone found to be using water to excess would be hauled before the courts and penalised financially.

The blackberry, however, had thrived in the extended heat of the long hot days and now her plump, purple fruits echoed out their presence amongst the hedgerows that formed the connecting line of rural and industrial coming togetherness as one, as if to disguise the difference of man's own ignorance to his surroundings to that of the scene that had been set out long before his reckless intervention.

Like excited schoolchildren faced with a never-ending scene of treats, the pair set about pulling the fruits from their natural restraints and soon the plastic shopping bag bulged with the profits of their endeavours.

Molly had promised Billy the sweetest tasting pie on his return from his day of schooling but she had never anticipated that the crop would be so bountiful.

Born-again children, the pair of berry pickers had effortlessly become and they eagerly ate the plumpest and ripest of their finds. Hands, already stained the brightest of purple, were now joined by tongues of similar colouring.

Each mocking gestured towards the other was reminiscent of some faraway school yard taunt of old.

The tongues were drawn out in merriment and mirth, and man and wife had once again entered the innocent fun realms of their early days that had been lost in natural maturity with the gentle passing of years.

Molly felt an unpleasant, soft, watery thud upon her temple and fell to her knees in defeat.

The sniper had found his mark and as she lowered her palm it revealed the rich, red, coagulated, seed-filled jelly that had smeared her face on impact.

The bastard, she thought, with a grin. He had surprised her with his cunning but she would live again to fight the day of the ultimate victor. After all, she held the bag of fruity ammunition that had started the fun laden war of childishness.

In retaliation she scooped out a handful of the juice-filled berries and waited for her moment that would take her hidden assailant by surprise.

Roger had crouched on the opposite side of the thick wall of spikes that the blackberry grew in an attempt to dissuade the taking of her fruits bearing the seeds that would continue the plant's existence year after year.

Molly was impatient and assumed that attack would not happen - and even if it did she would miss her mark and the juice-filled berry would be lost in the coarse grass at his feet. After all, he thought to himself, she was a woman and it was common knowledge that women simply were not designed to throw objects. Men, on the other hand, were. This had evolved from the hunter-gatherer, where it would be the man that left the comfort of the cave, armed with sharpened stones to hurl at his unsuspecting prey which he would then drag back with pride to the waiting woman who would then carve and cook the fresh meat for the hungry family.

Slowly, he rose; despite having reassured himself that Molly was incapable of precision aiming his natural instinct still warned him to take care. As he peered over the leafy canopy of the bush Molly was nowhere to be seen. Maybe he thought she had taken haste and fled to safety, fearing that another barrage of accurately aimed fruit was imminent from the master sharpshooter.

With his new-found confidence of victory Roger stood and surveyed the grassy ground in front of him as he picked another berry in readiness for when his prey was spotted.

He was now the sniper of those war films he loved to watch. The blackened spoil heap of colliery waste immediately in front of him now took on the appearance of some distant mountain range deep inside enemy territory. He was the chosen one who had been selected to take on the might of the opposition single-handed. His heroic deeds would win over the war and would free the people from the oppression that they had endured under the forced rule of their attackers.

The heroic partisan absorbed the very fabric of his surroundings, melting away unseen into the environment like a stalking lion as he picked out a lone gazelle.

Movement to his left caught his attention and he slowly turned, lifting his arm in readiness to take aim. The empty and tattered old crisp packet came to rest once again in the long grass, shielded from the gentle breeze that had lifted it momentarily from its place of rest.

Seizing the moment Molly leapt from her place of hiding on the opposite side of the blackberry bush and released her own handful of sticky sweet fruits towards the startled Roger.

Like a relentless machine gun, berry after berry sought out their target as each one became crushed on impact, turning Roger's face and shoulders purple as the juices were released.

Surprised, he fell back and tripped against the lower branches, landing on his back, partly hidden by the long grass. Showing no pity Molly seized another handful of berries from the bag and released them with a scream of excitement and joy before turning and running towards the gentle slope that formed the outer perimeter of the huge spoil heap dominating the landscape.

The realisation of defeat settled on Roger as he gathered his composure and wiped away the worst of the sticky berries from his face. He could hear the delighted shrieks of joy from Molly as she ran to gain distance from the retaliation she knew would follow.

Roger, she knew, was a proud man and defeat would not be readily accepted.

More like the gazelle than the hunting lion he jumped to his feet and crossed the open ground before the slope with speed. Not daring to look behind her for fear of falling she pushed even harder to keep the distance between the hunted and the hunter.

She may have taken the sniper by complete surprise and won the battle but as she heard the heavy footsteps drawing ever closer she knew that she had not won the war.

Roger pounced and took her by surprise. His arms wrapped around her and the weight from his body forced her to the soft ground. She desperately tried to fight off her attacker but soon realised that resistance was futile and that he had the advantage of strength which quickly overcame her feeble efforts or any chance of warding off the forced submission.

With the conquered prey tightly in his grasp the punisher began the punishment. His hands, still sticky from the berries that he had moments before wiped away from his own features, daubed the face below him. Molly's struggles only exaggerated Roger's hold on her and the couple laughed like hapless children playing out their favourite game.

Their lips met as one and Molly could taste the sweetness from the juice that now covered both their faces. With renewed strength, like that of a teenager that she now felt she had regressed into, with the frolics and laughter of fun Molly heaved herself upwards and dislodged Roger's weight so that he slid sidewards. The momentum of his sudden shift and his tight grip around her brought Molly from the floor and onto his chest and aided by the gentle slope, that moments before the couple had ascended, the gentle roll gathered in pace, sending the pair tumbling down the grassy slope.

Dazed by the light-headed dizziness that the fifty metre roll had caused, the pair lay in a heap of laughter as they came to rest, lost in the longer grass that the level ground offered.

Their clothing was smeared purple from the burst bag of blackberries that Molly had held onto despite their moments of mayhem and madness, and like two weary trench warfare veterans they walked arm in arm back along the route they had taken hours earlier.

Fearing Billy would be without the cherished and much-loved sweet pie that he had been promised, fresh blackberries were purchased from the high street greengrocer's shop whose sales assistant looked at the purple stained couple with intrigue and interest.

The coals crackled in the warming glow of the hearth sending fire reddened sparks upward and out of sight, swallowed by the pull of the chimney above.

"Eat it all now, Billy." Molly spoke softly with love in her voice that only a mother could offer.

"Local blackberries are hard to find."

Roger looked over the newspaper that he was reading and grinned sheepishly.

"Yes son, and hard work to collect too."

Another cascade of glowing sparks was released as the coals settled and dropped within the heat of the fire.

"Family life," Molly thought to herself, "Is a happy life."

* * * *

Chapter Twelve - Pit Heads and Cobble Stones

It was still dark when the booming sound of the colliery siren echoed its call to the town's men for them to wake and make their weary way to their place of work. Billy hated the dreaded sound that would stir him from his slumber each morning. This would be followed by the heavy sound of the miners' footsteps, as they slowly made their way to the colliery's gates, laughing and joking as ever, despite facing the harshness that was to await them, deep in the dank bowels of the earth.

As the footsteps faded into the darkness he gathered his slumber filled thoughts and reached for the cigarette that he had taken from his mother's handbag the night before as she was distracted by a visiting neighbour. Wearily climbing from the comfort and warmth of his bed he tiptoed across the room and opened the window. Leaning out he struck a match on the rough brickwork and deeply inhaled the thick smoke. Struggling, he fought back against his body's natural mechanism to reject the invading nicotine-filled smog and stifled the cough before it took hold, to avoid waking his sleeping mother in the next room.

As Billy's eyes accustomed themselves he scanned, as he always did, the scene that was set out before him.

Castlefields was a dreary place to live, he thought, as he did so every morning. Here, coal was still king, despite the continued call from environmentalists for the need for cleaner energy. Everything in the town revolved around the colliery which was its bustling centrepiece.

The colliery had been the brainchild of Lord Boxwood, a nineteenth century entrepreneur who had made his fortune in the cotton trade. His thriving mills to the west were hungry for a cheap energy source and it was a natural progression that he sunk mine shafts on land that was readily available.

With the rich coal seams came the workforce that was needed and a never-ending influx of people desperate to find work soon began to arrive. The need to house the workers resulted in what Billy now saw in his early morning nicotine-fuelled gaze. A parade of streets and houses stood in uniform, as though orchestrated in some military barracks. This was not the housing of some luxurious tycoon to beckon new tenants into the fold, but rather more akin to the predator enticing its prey into the lair of capitalism at its finest.

Looking down with almost sadness the cigarette had reached its life's end and Billy carefully aimed the glowing remains at the ominous hawthorn tree which dominated the garden's perimeter below. Finger, striking with the speed of a firing pin on a rifle, the glowing ember fell short of its mark and landed, disappointingly, with nothing more than a shallow plume of smoke, onto the uncut grass that formed the family garden.

With the dying ember Billy's thoughts returned to him again as if they had never been away. Sinking back into reality he gazed down at the cracked face of the alarm clock that had ticked its own heartbeat through the dark hours whilst he slept.

Five a.m. the taunting arms beckoned, as if mockingly to say, "Ey, Billy, we don't forget you." As if mimicking the clockwork intrusion, the sound of 'Old Red' could be heard.

Old Red was the meanest cockerel Billy had ever known. He recalled as a child the bird had pecked and harassed him at every opportunity and that it was, if animals can be capable of it, a jealous thing. Old Red was granddad's prize cockerel, Billy was granddad's prize grandchild and the competition still flowed daily to earn the points of righteousness in granddad's presence. Billy knew deep down he was the ultimate winner but grimaced with loathing whenever the bird announced the morning's chorus. Maybe, he smiled menacingly, just one clean shot from the air rifle would settle the score once and for all.

Deep down he knew that the assassination of Red was not the answer. With or without the darned chicken he would still be awoken by the colliery siren, he would still listen to the damned as they made their weary way to the colliery gates and, worse still, that first cigarette would still shock his chest into the fits of rebellion that might wake his mother, Molly, from her well-earned, restful slumber.

Wearily he reached out and closed the window to ward off the damp, cold air that enveloped him in the stillness of the morning.

Hurriedly, Billy picked up the discarded clothes that he had thrown onto the bedroom carpet the evening before; he dressed and made his way downstairs.

Thankfully, he thought, dad had stoked the fire with fresh coal before he had left for work and Billy reached down to open the flap that allowed more air to fuel the orange flames.

Thursdays were always looked forward to with relish by Billy. Along with Sundays the two days offered respite from the early morning job he had taken delivering milk to the town's sleepy inhabitants.

Like many boys it was deemed customary to find employment at an early age in readiness for the day that they would leave the comfort of the classroom to find themselves plunged into the bowels of the earth, following family traditions of countless generations, winning the coals that would fuel the nation's homes and industry.

Although delivering milk meant having to wake at four a.m. the positive side was that, apart from school, the rest of the day was free to do as he pleased. Doing as he pleased was a pastime close to Billy's heart. He was a free spirit in a place that beckoned rigid compliance to ways that had been set in stone since the first mine shafts had been sunk into the virginal earth.

Castlefields was, like most northern mining towns, a close knit community. Here, everyone knew each others' families, and most families were related to each other in some way, either by blood or by marriage.

Billy hated the confines this closeness brought with it. If you were to break wind at ten a.m. the issue would be discussed at eleven a.m. on the coal face, deep underground, and father's greeting on entering the family home at the end of his day's work would be: "Why didn't you say 'excuse me'?"

Deep down he was the rebel, the rebel with a cause. Billy liked to stand out from the dreary crowd of conformists. The early eighties had seen a revival of the wild days of the 1960s and he enjoyed the spirit of bygone times.

He was known for his immaculate dress sense and dreams of adventure. In the confines of the bedroom he would indulge in the sounds that had created a teenage revolution twenty years previous. The Kinks, The Who and the upbeat tempo of Jamaican Ska bands would be played out on the old, single speaker record player that his aunt had kindly given him.

With the speaker pressed to his ear Billy would close his eyes and drift into the solace and freedom that the music inspired. Castlefields would disappear and he would visualise himself in the bustling streets of London. The summer's striking rays would dazzle against the brilliant chrome of the Lambretta that he rode and the local girls' attention would be drawn to him like the magnetic pull of the spinning planet.

All too soon he would be plunged back into the depths of dreariness by the invading calls from Molly, his mother. The music was driving her insane and could he please turn the volume down? London again was gone and the never-ending sounds of heavy industry would be heard, reminding everyone where their very place in life was sealed.

Wrenched back into the arms of reality Billy looked out of the kitchen window, hot coffee burning his throat. It was five-thirty a.m. according to the kitchen clock, seemingly proud of its own punctuality in the realms of time. Today was his day; school was closed this week for half term holiday. No school meant the freedom he sought so much and the desire to do as he pleased.

The plan for today was set. The reason for his early rise was simple. Today he would forage into the local woods with a friend to seek out fresh examples for the beloved birds' egg collection he held with pride within a drawer at the side of his bed. Once found, any new species of bird's egg would be carefully taken home where a small hole would be drilled into the delicate shell and a small glass pipe, slightly smaller than the hole, would be inserted and delicate breaths would be blown through the pipe, forcing the yolk out. Once emptied, the precious egg would then be placed in the flour-lined drawer and labelled, a treasure to show to others of Billy's apparent expertise in seeking out and recording the breeding habits of the local feathered friends.

Billy closed and locked the door quietly, posting the key through the letterbox. Castlefields remained deep in age old traditions and it was still expected that only on reaching the age of twenty-one years would you be permitted free range of the family home and be allowed to hold your own key.

As usual the ever punctual Jowett was waiting at the bottom of the street. Although Jowett had been a good friend of Billy's since they met two years ago at high school he was still considered by Billy as an oddball due to some of his behaviour.

Sometimes, well, a lot of the time, Billy thought Jowett's mouth moved a little too freely for his own good and not all of his voiced opinions were approvingly accepted. Regardless of this he was reliable in every way. If it had been agreed to meet at a certain time and place, he would always be there. If tempers rose, it would be his fists and heart for the fight that could be counted and relied upon in those times of need.

As usual Jowett offered out his outstretched hand as Billy approached. This was not the age old handshake of a gentleman's greeting, but merely the offering between two close friends of the lit cigarette butt he had smoked as he waited for Billy's arrival.

"Looking a little rough this morning, Jowett." Billy passed the compliment with a wry smile. "Maybe mammy not got out of bed to brush your hair this morning…"

"Very funny," was the quick reply, followed by a customary slap on the back in mock aggression.

The usual banter followed the cigarette offering. This light-hearted conversation was a customary thing in the closely-knit mining communities. Although its aim was to ridicule the other, it was always done, and received, in good humour. The custom would progress, as Billy was to find, on the coal faces deep underground where the weary colliers would find solace in the constant dark humour of comradeship.

With a spring in their step the two gave up the humorous greeting and headed down Castlefields Lane, the main thoroughfare through the drab town of terraced houses and grocery shops, towards their chosen destination where they would seek out any precious birds' eggs that they had not yet added to their prized collection.

Despite having its roots firmly set in heavy industry the small town was encircled by open countryside.

The grey slopes of the colliery waste heap were surrounded by fertile agricultural fields. These, in turn, were interspersed with small pockets of woodland which found the nutrients for their own survival in the bubbling brooks and streams that crisscrossed the fresh open spaces producing crops of wheat and barley.

It had never ceased to amaze Billy just how different the landscape could be, depending on which direction was to be looked. Before him lay a place of beauty and paradise, the ripening crops of the deepest of yellows would dance their dance of grace to the tempo of the warming breeze whilst the scattered woodlands would offer peace and comfort from the sun's rays. With a simple turn the vision would completely change. The crops of cereal would be replaced by the greyness of the towering heap of colliery spoil; the towering trees were replaced by the steel latticed forms of the colliery winding headgear that sent the men deep beneath the earth's surface and brought the newly-won coals into the sunshine that they had last felt millions of years before when they had been the vegetation that stretched out to the horizon's past.

These were the greatest days of Billy's life without him ever realising. Carefree, and without a worry in the world he thrived on his own innocence and that of the others around him.

He truly was the free spirit that could be carried by the gentle summer's breeze to any place he wanted to travel.

The heroes would echo out their chorus, ringing out their voiced charms to the believer.

The 1960s revival was in full swing, fuelled by the screening of the classic film Quadrophenia.

The film had played out the life of Jimmy, a typical youth caught up in the excitement of London's kaleidoscope of music and newly emerging fashions. The teenagers had liberated themselves from the trappings that had previously forced them into becoming mirror images of their parents before them.

It depicted a time when the chains of restriction had been broken and the hapless teenagers had formed their own individuality for the very first time.

Billy lived out his own Quadrophenia. He would pay particular attention to his appearance and this would eventually make him stand out from the crowd of faces that had lined the cobbled streets of Castlefields since the first soil had been cut in search of the rich coal seams deep below.

The ever-proud Milan would beam out his smile of pride whenever he saw his immaculately dressed grandson; dark suit and black tie pressed as ever to perfection.

He had constantly stressed, as the child had grown, that he should always be the leader of those within his company and should never become the simple follower of others. It was now obvious to the ageing man that his words of wisdom had not fallen on deaf ears and his spirit was lifted each and every time he witnessed Billy captivate everyone around him with his presence.

The cool breeze found its way through the narrow opening of the window and brushed against Billy's cheek like the gentle kiss from the girl of his dreams.

"Billy," she called out to him, the softness of her voice reaching out and drawing him closer to her.

He turned slowly in response and put his arm around her to draw her closer to his touch. Instead of the softness of her shoulders Billy could not understand the hard, flat surface that met his fingertips. Confused, he felt for reassurance but again his touch was met with a cold and solid form that lay before him.

"Billy, for the last time - are you awake?" This time the voice was unmistakable as being that of Molly as she called up from the hall at the bottom of the stairwell.

"Blake is waiting and it's not fair that you are still in bed when you arranged for him to call."

Slowly he rose from his slumber and focused on the wall immediately in front of him. Realisation that he had been dreaming dawned on him as he felt the patterned wallpaper that lay beneath his touch.

Smiling at his stupidity he rubbed away the sleep from his unfocused eyes and wearily pulled himself to his feet.

"Shit," he said to himself, as he peered at the plastic alarm clock on the wooden cabinet beside him. 12.25 p.m. its hands called out to him in mocking silence.

"Shit!" he retorted again as he fumbled for the t-shirt and jeans that he had discarded the night before on the carpet beneath his feet.

Billy was now the proud owner of a set of state of the art stereo headphones that allowed him to listen to his favourite music without disturbing anyone else in the house. No more was there the constant banging on the wall from within the adjoining bedroom of his parents as The Specials sang out 'Gangsters' and 'Ghost Town'. No more were The Kinks forced to give up their melody of a 'Sunny afternoon' to anyone's annoyance at having their much-needed rest and sleep disturbed in the early hours past midnight.

The drawback to Billy's personal pleasure was like that of today. He would lose track of time and would fight against the sleep that darkness offered only then to wake deep into the new day of tomorrow.

Blake sat patiently waiting as Billy entered the small kitchen.

"Me and your mam were in two minds whether or not to call the undertaker," he wittingly announced with a shrewd smile.

"Very chuffing funny, comedian," Billy replied. "Not my fault I was asked to stay back for an after-show party at Stringfellow's nightclub, was it?"

Molly beckoned Billy to take a seat at the farmhouse-style breakfast table as she poured the boys some coffee.

Drinking the hot, sugarless coffee, Billy craved the nicotine that the day's first cigarette would offer him. He had been a secret smoker ever since he had started high school some three years previously. Without much in the way of resistance he had foolishly given in to the peer pressure of those around him and had quickly become addicted to the readily available 'coffin nails' as they were commonly known.

Scrupulous shopkeepers, eager to make money rather than keep within the law, had exploited the local schoolchildren by splitting packets of cigarettes and selling them individually. To make the transaction more appealing they would also include a single match in with the extortionate price, in order that the apprentice smoker could want for nothing else to kick-start their new-found habit of self-induced death.

"Sorry, mam, have to dash," Billy announced as he poured the remnants from his cup into the kitchen sink and placed the now empty vessel onto the already piled up stack of plates in the plastic bowl.

Before Molly could answer from the living room where she now sat the two boys were already making their way down the concrete path, heading for the town's main street.

Once out of view, Blake produced a packet of cigarettes from his jacket pocket and passed Billy one. The pair puffed away in unison, careful not to allow prying eyes through the net curtains of the houses to catch sight of the cigarettes they held, hidden in their hands. The town's gossips were able to relay messages faster than the telephone and if anyone was to witness their misdemeanour then this would be passed on to their parents or respective families within the hour.

Blake knew all too well what the consequences of this would be. Last month he had witnessed his own father forcing his older sister to eat the remaining cigarettes from the packet he had found in her jacket.

He had grimaced as she had been violently sick afterwards and would swear that since then her skin had taken on a greenish tint. It was this apparent greenish tint that Blake feared the most from being found out that he had followed the family tradition of nicotine addiction. The harshness of the leather belt across his buttocks he could tolerate, but to have the skin tone of Martian descent, he could not.

The two boys hurried to their destination without becoming engrossed in the continual 'hellos' that were offered to them along the route which would take them to where they wanted to be.

Castlefields was in the throes of a rebirth that was to cast away its old Victorian values and appearance.

Old Lord Boxwood had long since departed and as his decaying bones were trodden down with the relentless passing of time so too were his ideals of creating the perfect dwellings for his working classes.

It was now the turn of the demolition gangs that would tear down the very fabric that he had created in his quest for power and wealth.

The uniformity of the long terrace of back-to-back housing had long since served their purpose of offering shelter to the simple folk who had wanted for nothing else.

Tin bathtubs placed in the kitchens with water warmed from the open coal fire had once been deemed a luxury to those who had never known any different.

Six people sharing the same restricted bed space, hugging closely together to fight off the winter's draughts that would creep through the ill-fitting window frames, turning their collective breaths of sleep into steam that would fog out the view from the windows when they would finally rise with the calling of the distant rooster.

Echoes of this not-too-distant era were now slowly being removed with the bulldozer that would erase personal history of times past forever.

Demolition of the old always brought about the playground of the young and it was this playground that the pair now descended upon.

The occupants of the dilapidated houses had been offered, without argument against, alternative accommodation within the relatively new housing estates the local authorities had created, to offer luxury and prosperity amongst the deprived working classes.

Whole rows of the rundown houses now lay empty of occupants and the once thriving terraces were now silent. With the people gone it seemed the very heart and soul had been ripped out of what had once been generations of families calling the drab brick structures home.

History had once been made in these very streets. One hundred years ago the now abandoned and deserted cobbled walkways had told a very different story to the one they now portrayed.

Lord Boxwood had forced upon his workforce a reduction in wages in an attempt to even out his profits as the worldwide price of coal fell. Infuriated, the miners had immediately removed their labour and had blockaded the colliery entrance to dissuade other workers who had been drafted in from neighbouring towns to be used as substitute workers.

Feeling that his control was being threatened, the lord had used his family connections and had been offered the help of the local infantry brigade to quell the rising unrest.

Unfortunately for both Lord Boxwood and the striking miners, the decision to draw in troops as a show of almighty strength had been a bad one and ended in disaster.

The infantry brigade had only recently returned after suffering a catastrophic defeat overseas in the Far East.

Still smarting from what could have been total annihilation, had it not been for the apparent apathy shown to them by their victors, the British army had, for the first time, suffered defeat in foreign lands that it now fled in tatters and shame. Maybe it was more propaganda than mercy that had allowed the survivors of the rout to return home and tell their story.

The usually peaceful miners had felt deeply betrayed by their lord and master and as the morning wore on their unrest grew as more troops were ferried in from the nearby army barracks.

Sporadic fires were lit along the town's main street leading up to the colliery and a group of the more militant of the miners formed a frontier across the railway line in an effort to stop the steam train from leaving the station and collect more reinforcements of infantry men.

The riot act was duly read out to the swelling crowd by a local magistrate and this had only added to the feeling of animosity between the opposing sides.

The bravest, or rather the more foolish, of the men facing the line of khaki-clad infantrymen jeered out the noise of the magistrate's voice as he had desperately tried to read out the words from the paper scroll that he held aloft before him.

In desperation and stupidity the very man that had been sent to quell the rising unrest withdrew from his lost announcement, amidst the rising shouts and whistles and had ordered the troops to advance towards the unarmed crowd that stood before them.

Panic had immediately pulsed through the defiant miners and they had scattered immediately at the sight of the solid wall of uniforms and fixed bayonets walking in total discipline towards them.

Unfortunately, panic had also ebbed its way through the advancing lines of soldiers. Long before the days of maintaining the role of peacekeepers in foreign lands plagued by civil war and unrest, these men had simply been trained to kill the opposition at all cost.

As the fleeing miners scattered towards the safety of the houses where they had been born and bred the first shots were fired. In desperation, the officers had tried to quell the rising excitement and bloodlust that pulsed through the ranks of men that had supposedly been under their control and jurisdiction.

The sharp retorts of gunfire had only added to the panic that had now set in on both sides and the figures of authority who had been viewing the whole episode unfurl before them held their gloved hands over their faces, in an attempt to mask away the reality of what had taken place.

No sooner had the shooting started, its deathly echoes subsided. Whether or not it had been the desperate officers who had finally gained control of their men, or the men that had been jolted to their senses to the horror that they had committed, only history would perhaps tell.

In those fateful seconds the damage had been set forever. Four innocent men had been taken cruelly away from the families that needed them desperately for their own survival. Eleven men had been rendered disabled for the rest of their lives, forcing them to take on lower paid work underground, plunging their poverty stricken families further down the shaft of depravation. Countless others had been left to tell the story.

The day that the working man was shot into submission by the ruling classes to feed the masters' deprived lust for power and wealth.

These were the empty streets where Billy now stood.

Knowing the history that had seeped into the brickwork of the now empty rows of dilapidated houses he felt a distinct chill rise up over his spine.

"Fuck, Blake, just feel this place now," Billy whispered, as he stared along the vacant windows and took in the eerie silence that seemed to permeate everything that the eye viewed.

"Feel it?" Blake replied, "Smells like most of the idiots left without flushing their toilets!"

Billy sniffed tentatively, excrement he did not do and the very odour had always made him wretch uncontrollably.

"That's not shit, Blake, that's the smell of emptiness and abandonment that the houses give out, now that they have been deserted."

Blake looked at Billy with the widened, exaggerated eyes of astonishment.

"Weirdo," he grinned and pushed Billy in mock aggression onto the paved path that rose up from the cobbled street.

"Come on, follow me and I'll show you abandoned," he mocked as he sidestepped, avoiding the push of retaliation that followed.

* * * *

Chapter Thirteen – The Genie and the Smoke

The old wooden door creaked against its frame of restraint as Blake pushed against it. With desertion and abandonment came the damp coldness that seeped its way into old woodwork, forcing it to swell.

"Look, Billy," he announced as the door slowly opened.

Amidst the emptiness of the streets outside lay a treasure trove of family life that had once been and now was gone forever.

Before him lay the Mary Celeste that he had read about from a book loaned from the town's library. The book told of a drifting ship that had been boarded only to find that it was devoid of human life.

Meals had been set at the table in the galley and the simmering pan of broth gave out its aroma of welcome to its now intrigued guests.

The mystery of the abandoned ship was now set out before Billy's vision. The drawn curtains added to the mystery as his eyesight accustomed itself to the darkness that descended as he stepped forward into the living room. Slowly, the darkened shapes around him fused into the unmistakable contours of furniture. The settee of corduroy brown dominated the room, positioned before the empty fireplace that would have warmed a thousand hearts during the passing of time.

It was as if the occupants had simply said 'farewell'; closing the door as they had left for the final time.

"It's party time!" Blake's voice cut through the silence startling Billy to his senses.

The old door again gave way with its groan of redundancy as figures walked in from the dazzling light outside.

Richard and David continued with the cheer as they announced their arrival, with outstretched hands holding in each a bottle of cider, bought from unscrupulous shopkeepers who had no interest in their age, only that of the profit that they would gain.

As the door was once again seated into the surround that had been made to ward away the draughts of winter, Billy's eyes focused on the fifth occupant of the room.

Victoria now stood before him in all of her natural beauty. The dimness of the room's lighting only added to her charm and appeal and the same feeling of deep excitement washed over Billy as it had done so the very first time the two had met.

The two had formed a close bond of friendship that was now slowly progressing to the next level. They had stolen kisses away from the view of others whenever they had the chance to be alone and Billy felt that he was slowly falling in love.

With the door firmly shut the party began.

As always, Billy beckoned Victoria to sit beside him, away from the crazy antics whenever his friends took on the company of alcohol.

Richard and David maintained the role of circus clowns as they play-acted their roles of idiocy. A natural duo they were not, as their attempts to re-enact the comedians of times past fell onto deaf ears and the expected claps of laughter were replaced by the groans of constant dismay from the limited audience sat before them.

Just like a magician at the end of his act of never-ending wander, Blake produced the final curtain call that would leave the audience feeling numb from the show that never was.

Cannabis had eventually found a ready-made market in the working class youth of the northern mining towns.

It had been a slow road for the cultivated herbal high which had begun its journey amongst the hippy communities of the late 1960s but now it had finally made its presence known amidst the cobbles and terraced housing of simple folk.

Blake had been the teenagers' pioneer and had somehow crossed paths with a small-time dealer who operated the backstreets of the nearby city of Glebes.

The five revellers had drawn together their weekly allowances that their parents had given them and had collectively financed a small piece of the heavily scented, soap-like substance.

Blake, now the connoisseur of all things herbal and forbidden, passed around the crudely-made joint to the eager participants before him.

Richard and David, not smokers by choice, coughed in unison as they each inhaled the pungent smoke from the offered tube of fun.

Despite the harsh discomfort and protest, their lungs made apparent with the husky cough against the smoky invader; they were not to be outdone and deeply inhaled the fumes.

Blake, Victoria and Billy were far more refined and sat at peace, slowly drawing in the rich vapours in turn as they sank into their own thoughts, their inner senses heightening despite the utter feeling of relaxation that was slowly taking over them.

Billy settled himself into the marshmallow softness that the old sofa offered to him as it had done before for many years to countless weary sitters in the room.

As the minutes slowly ticked his mind began to oscillate and each eye seemed to take on movements around him at a different pace. He felt as if he were seated in some deserted cinema from a past long gone as he watched two different screenings of the same show. One screen gave the viewer the dulcet tones of autumn gold and the other broadcast the sepia memories of yesteryear.

A sensation of inner tingling entered through his fingertips and slowly washed over his whole body. The feeling was not unpleasant and Billy fought off his inner instincts of resistance until the warming effect had taken over his entire self.

He felt as if he were slipping in and out of reality at a rapid rate and both became intertwined as the natural chemicals unlocked the hidden doors deep within his mind.

Movement of those around him appeared to play out in both slow motion and exaggerated speed at the same time, and he became increasingly confused as to which of his eyes was relaying the truth and which was being distorted as the drug seeped deeper into his brain.

Laughter rose from nowhere within Billy as if he had just been privy to some punchline from the finest comedian. Like some highly contagious disease, unexplained mirth spread around the room and everyone had become infected as the blue smoke spread about its hallucogenic laughter.

The slightest of giggles would accelerate into side-splitting mayhem as the five jokers revelled in their new-found genie of the magical smoke.

As the shadows reached out to claim what was rightfully theirs the sensation too withdrew from Billy and he slowly glided back into the true clutches of reality.

The double cinema screens came together and only broadcast the one scene of reality that was now being played out before Billy's eyes.

The dulcet, golden tones of autumn merged as one with the sepias as Billy's rationale took control once again.

The plastic tumblers of cheap, fizzy cider flowed and the strained jokes and punchlines of attempted humour slowly became hilarious.

Outside, the shadows descended onto the deserted street as the sun dipped low behind the man-made horizon of the colliery spoil heap.

Only the ever-resourceful Molly had thought in hindsight that the inevitable darkness would spoil the fun of the evening. She lit two candles that she took from the small leather handbag which hung loosely from her shoulder and placed them onto the empty fireplace that had warmed a thousand hearts before its now sad demise of abandonment.

The shadows slowly crept back across the carpet and walls as the twin points of dull light grew in strength, thwarting their darkened advance and sending them recoiling to the depths they had only moments before ascended.

Blake again passed around the cannabis joint that he had rolled and each took their turn inhaling the bitter-sweet smoke from the rolled tube of wafer thin paper.

The laughter amidst the tiny theatre subsided as the light-blue haze of tranquillity settled across its seated audience.

The duo of never-ending mirth, the artists Richard and David, sunk slowly away from the laughter of centre stage and took to the wings that the small room offered.

The initial high had slowly subsided and now it was the turn of the darkened shadows of hallucogenic fun that slowly crawled across the tired carpet beneath the revellers' feet.

Victoria's breathing settled warmly upon Billy's chest as he reached out his hand to couple her inviting and loving embrace of friendship. Exaggerated by the tranquilising effects of the deeply-inhaled herbal smoke, Billy sank into the deepest of sleep.

From some faraway place he heard the distant goodbyes that Blake, Richard and David announced as they departed the place of comfort where Billy was now immersed.

Slowly the candles diminished their offering of light and retreated against the blackness that was always to be the victor.

Victoria nestled her head on his chest gently for comfort and the movement drew him from the slumber that had settled into him.

The room appeared lighter than it had, despite the candles having burned down to nothing. Not only did it appear more illuminated but it also felt warmer, the musty damp smell of desertion had been replaced by a feeling of love and care.

Billy felt confused as he carefully scanned the room. The drab interior that he had only hours before entered into now felt very different.

The room had now taken on the atmosphere of a place that was welcoming and inviting. The simple clutter of everyday living filled his vision. Ornaments of china figurines lined the tiled fireplace in front of him and wooden framed prints adorned walls at his side.

Billy felt movement at his side and fear rose within him as his senses heightened.

Adrenaline pulsed into his bloodstream as he felt his heartbeat quicken and fill his chest with a pressure that felt uncomfortable. Like the child of old he closed his eyes against the fear that he felt, in the hope that closure would bring about invisibility.

Slowly, Billy opened his eyes and looked to his side where the movement had come from. To his heartfelt relief Victoria lay in deep sleep, nestled closely upon his chest for comfort. Her breathing was deep and rhythmic which reassured him that she remained in deep sleep at his side.

The creaking of the inner door to his left immediately snatched Billy from his thoughts and he instinctively turned towards the source of the intrusive sound that had broken the silence.

Fear spread across him like the wild fires spread across the driest of mountain plains, whipped into frenzy by the raging wind as their eyes locked together.

The boy looked at him momentarily with the deepest of stares capable of penetrating the soul, before casting his eyes away to Billy's right. Like the cat that had finally found the cream the smile across the young boy's face widened as his stare passed over Billy and settled upon the carpet immediately in front of the fireplace that now gave out warmth from red hot coals that glowed within its hearth.

Now mesmerised with the scene that was being played out before him, Billy watched with intrigue.

Despite the initial stare towards Billy, the boy entered the room as if he were alone. He appeared totally unaware that anyone was seated on the sofa before him as he bent down and picked up a toy car from the floor and held it close to his chest as if fearing that it would be taken from his grasp.

Billy closed his eyes and reopened them in the hope that the illusion would be gone and once again he would be surrounded by the emptiness of what had been only moments before.

Nothing had changed and the boy remained before him.

Billy looked carefully towards the boy that now stood with his back to him, facing the glowing coals of the fire that now warmed the room.

The child appeared very real as he stood in the room. Billy's mind raced in desperation for an explanation that would lessen the fear within him.

He remembered the cannabis-induced feeling of high that had swept over him earlier as Blake had passed around the communal joint for everyone to experience its magical effects.

He also remembered reading about the effects that cannabis can induce and how they could differ enormously between individuals.

Billy smiled as the realisation washed over him that he was not witnessing some paranormal activity of a day within the house's history from long ago, but was experiencing the hallucogenic effects from the drug that continued to act upon his mind.

The smile on his lips broadened into a grin as Billy slowly realised that what had filled him with so much fear that his body had been overcome with a feeling of absolute paralysis had been a mere figment of his drug-fuelled imagination.

Uncontrollable laughter flowed from him and he remembered that this too was a recorded effect from the chemicals now opening hidden doorways deep within his brain. Victoria stirred at his side as the laughter within him rose and he patted her shoulders with the touch of reassurance that indeed all was well.

The boy of Billy's imagination turned quickly as if something had startled him and he stood facing Billy with his own look of horror spreading across his face.

Now enjoying the moment of unreality, Billy leant forwards and without warning gave out a childish, "Boo!"

The boy recoiled in horror, sending the toy car clattering to the ground before turning and running out of sight through the door that he had entered minutes before.

Billy now whooped with laughter causing Victoria to rise with a startled jolt into a prone position at his side. The warmth within the room withdrew and the fire within the hearth was gone. Emptiness again settled and the musty odour of dereliction and desertion once again filled the room.

"Billy, what's wrong?" Victoria asked as she placed her arm around him as much for her own comfort than his.

"You won't believe it," he replied, still chucking to himself, "I thought I'd seen a ghost but realised it was simply a hallucination!" His chuckling continued.

"What are you talking about?" she beckoned, still only half awake.

"Here, look." He pulled himself to his feet and took a step towards the empty fireplace.

"It was a small boy and he came running through the door there and stood here just in front of us." Billy placed his foot down onto the old carpet. Immediately he lifted it again as he felt something hard beneath is shoe.

Intrigued Billy looked down towards his feet.

Fear and panic hit him with the force of a runaway coal train, almost sending him crashing backwards onto the sofa.

The toy car that the child had sent crashing to the ground lay at Billy's feet. Instinct, brought on by sheer terror, took hold of him as he struggled to control the scream that made its way from deep inside him and slowly forced its way between his clenched lips.

Grabbing Victoria by the hand he pulled her violently as he sped towards the door to his right that led out onto the cobbled street outside. Startled, she too felt the fear that ran from Billy and the pair ran, side by side, past the deserted houses that had once been the heart of a community. Only when he reached the relative safety of the street lighting that gave illumination to the town's main street did Billy slow down and eventually stop. His chest hurt as he gasped for much-needed oxygen to feed his over-exerted muscles and lungs.

The pair walked slowly towards the brick shelter of the bus stop and slumped in unison against the rough coarseness of its inner wall.

That night Victoria tossed and turned as she desperately fought back the sleep that repeatedly attempted to overcome her as dawn approached.

The deep-rooted fear within Billy as he described what he had seen disturbed her. Each time he recounted his recollections of what he had witnessed whilst she slept at his side, she felt an icy chill run from within her, forcing the fine blonde hairs at the nape of her neck to rise, as if to defend herself from unforeseen demons that lay in wait for their moment to come.

Billy had sworn Victoria to keep whatever had happened that night a closely guarded secret from everyone, especially Blake.

Blake, the never-ending joker, would never allow Billy to forget the night that he had been so frightened he had dragged poor Victoria down the deserted streets at the mere sight of a small boy. He would relay the story to all that cared to listen about the night that Billy had wasted his chance of finally being alone with the beautiful Victoria and that maybe, just maybe, this had been the real reason behind Billy's deep-rooted fear.

The fear within Billy remained and despite questioning himself continually and repeatedly going over and over what he had seen and experienced that night the answer was always the same. The boy had been an apparition of a day long since past and had been as real to Billy's vision as had the glowing embers within the hearth that filled the room with warmth. He had been invited to view a snapshot that had re-emerged from the annals of history to play out again before the unwitting observer.

He had become a regular of the town's library and had scoured the meagre shelves for any information on cannabis and its use.

Despite its limited offerings the library did give out some information that he found helpful.

Billy read with interest that the ancient Chinese would use the seeds of the cannabis plant in rituals where they would attempt to conjure up the spirits of dead loved ones. They had believed that the trance-like state that the drug induced allowed them to leave their physical bodies and cross over into the spirit world. The book went on to describe how other ancient tribes believed that the hallucinogenic effects of the smoke when inhaled allowed their long dead forefathers to cross over from the spiritual realm into that of the living.

Whatever the explanation, the experience had shaken Billy but thankfully Victoria was true to her word and no one was to learn about what had happened that evening.

Billy avoided the old streets as if they had been swept by some deadly plague and he would always make up some excuse if ever Blake and the others invited him to join them for an evening of fun and merriment.

It came as a great relief the afternoon he heard that a bulldozer and demolition teams had made their move. Within days the buildings were gone and only rubble remained. Within a few weeks the rubble had gone too and the only evidence that a once thriving community had resided where the empty space now stood were the old sepia photographs of bygone days adorning the library walls.

* * * *

Chapter Fourteen – Spirit of the Age

Victoria stood before the beautiful flowerbeds that lay before her. The colourful reds and yellows rose out from amongst the lush greenery of vegetation, and she felt that she had indeed found a paradise lost.

She had arrived earlier than arranged and looked down the hill of meadow grass expectantly waiting for Billy's approach.

The hill overlooking the edges of the town had been their special place for over a year, soon after their relationship had begun to take on a loving, more meaningful connection that brought them together whenever they had the opportunity to be alone.

Whatever had happened to Billy, the night he awoke to the sound of his terror within the empty house, had brought them closer together.

He had withdrawn himself from the band of brothers that Blake, Jowett, Richard and David were to him. Billy gave them excuse after excuse as to why he would not visit the dilapidated streets of what once was.

Victoria smiled to herself as she fondly recalled those few weeks until the demolition crew had moved in to wipe away forever the source of Billy's fear.

Billy had withdrawn himself as the self-styled leader of the crowd and had sought her company out over that of his lifelong friends.

She had revelled at the new-found attention being bestowed upon her and rose to the challenge with unrestrained glee.

Soon the pair was widely known to be an item and would laugh off the childish taunts of jealousy from those that had yet to find love.

With the demolition of the streets of old, Billy had once again taken his rightful place amongst his friends. The leader returned to the pack but deep inside he had changed.

Billy would seek out the company of Victoria at every opportunity. He would bade his friends farewell long before the sun had spent its last rays and the pair would meet in secret, away from the prying eyes of gossip.

Victoria rose from the comfort of her thoughts to the warning cry of the carrion crow. It rose into the sky, alerting everyone of the intruder that had invaded its solitude. She turned towards the sound that had broken the silence. Straining, she peered over the long grass that cascaded down the gentle slope before her to the ancient footpath that snaked its way from the houses that filled the skyline.

Her heart skipped, missing a beat, as she focused on the unmistakable figure that climbed the old wooden stile. Excitement merged with panic as she lowered her head, careful not to be seen as Billy glanced upwards towards the place they had arranged to meet.

In her excitement, Victoria had arrived at their secret place early. She had given in easily to the old adage that a woman must keep the man waiting.

Now, she panicked. Billy also was early for their rendezvous and the thought of that sent her mind racing wildly.

Maybe he just could not wait, she thought to herself excitedly, spying cautiously at his appearance as he walked up the slope towards her.

Her heart fluttered, and she pushed her hands onto her chest, as if to quell the rising excitement within her.

"He's early too!" her words resounded within her as her heartbeat rose almost to breaking point.

Panic overcame the passion within her as she desperately tried to fight back her inner emotions.

"Billy really likes me!" The inner voice within her mind shouted out in overwhelming clarity.

"If not, why should he too come to our place early?"

She thought desperately to fight off the excitement that welled from within her.

In immature fun, she bent and scooped up the hardened seeds from the grass stalks beneath her. Her hand full, she rose from her lair of hiding. The assassin that she now became fired her deadly arsenal towards the target within her sights.

The seeds missed their mark and scattered amidst the long grass at his side. Feigning the mortal wound that never was he fell to the floor, eyes closed in simulated death against the brightness of the blue sky above.

Victoria rose from her place of hiding in feverish excitement and ran towards the prone figure that lay on the sun-baked ground before her.

Billy watched her approach and leapt up as she bent over his lifeless body. Startled, Victoria fell backwards into the tall grass that lined the footpaths' edges. Now the attacker became the attacked as Billy gently covered her body with his own. Laughter crashed over them as they rolled over and over, deeper into the pasture to be lost from the sight of all but the ardent of onlookers.

"Hey, you're early, how come?" Billy asked, inbetween breaths.

Victoria felt her heart beat even faster as Billy's warm breath settled upon her.

"Early?" she asked, trying desperately to suppress the warm blush that she felt spreading across her already reddened cheeks.

"I did not realise I was early until I got here and saw the church clock," she lied.

Billy saw through the lie and held her even more tightly in his arms as he leant over, momentarily looking into her eyes that radiated warmth and love. Slowly he moved closer to her until their lips met with the kiss of true love and togetherness. Heartbeats came together and forged one rhythmic beat that seemed to shatter the peace and tranquillity of the hill with the pulse of mirrored affection.

Victoria had settled into Billy's life as if it had been her destiny to do so. She had been welcomed with open arms by both Molly and Roger who were pleased that their son had found such a beautiful, sweet-natured girl to romance.

Milan had immediately bonded with her and had found a fresh audience within Victoria to which he could continue with his stories of mystery and magic.

However, Alison had slowly slipped into the cruel world of senile dementia and needed constant attention.

Victoria had stepped into the fold as if she were a natural carer to the needs of the elderly. She would visit daily and offer her help to Molly in the day to day running of the home, giving the ageing Milan the much-needed support that he deserved.

Billy felt indebted to the dark haired beauty. He reassured himself that she was the girl for him, and that he would love, honour, and protect her for the rest of his life.

Blake and Jowett lay like two snipers in waiting camouflaged in the long meadow grass.

They had followed Billy as he made his way through the town's streets, careful not be spotted as they stalked their prey with stealth and accuracy as if they were highly trained spies on a mission to protect national security.

Billy played down the love that he felt for Victoria, even to his closest of friends, but they had suspected differently.

The constant excuses of not wanting to hang out on their favourite street corners, the careful preening to always appear his best were just some of the telltale signs that their friend had other things on his mind.

Now the answer to their questions was revealed before them on the hill. Billy had always maintained that he felt nothing for Victoria, only the gratitude that she helped to nurse his ailing grandmother. They had continually tried to chip away at his resolve, but were always met with cast iron resistance whenever they placed Billy under their interrogation.

The answer now lay before them as they silently watched the two embrace in the kisses that only true love creates.

The game finally up, the pair rose from their place of hiding and walked the short distance up the hill towards the prone couple.

Lost in his own thoughts of passion, the newcomers took Billy by surprise as their shadows fell across him. Startled with the intrusion into his privacy, he pushed himself away from the embrace of Victoria and desperately tried to focus against the bright glare of the overhead sun.

"Got you, Billy!" came the unmistakable sound of Jowett's dulcet voice.

"Sorry lads, I'm staying in today." Blake mimicked as he leant over them, tapping Billy gently with his foot.

"You guys are unreal, you know that?" Billy responded quickly as he rose to his feet. "Set of perverts spying for a cheap thrill, that's all you are!"

Playfully, Billy placed his hands upon Blake's chest, and pushed him backwards, forcing him to lose his footing and fall into the cushioning grass.

Jowett laughed only the laugh that he was capable of. A combination of euphoria and lunacy as Blake rose and brushed the dust from his shirt.

"Take a look at that, Casanova," Blake winked as he passed Billy something that he had pulled from his pocket.

The small plastic bag contained what looked like dried out remains of some long dead plant. Billy knew from experience that this was not the usual offering of cannabis that Blake preferred; he thought of himself as some kind of expert whether it was drugs' natural state of dried out flowers and leaves, or its processed resin form that was distributed in soap-like blocks.

No, this was quite different to what Billy had seen before. The strands within the package were entirely dry and felt coarse to the touch, even through the protective sleeve of plastic that contained them.

"Liberty Caps," Blake whispered as he placed his arms around Billy's shoulders.

"Liberty Caps?" Billy responded with confusion. "What the fuck are Liberty caps?"

The master of all to be known now took on centre stage. He explained what the dried out remains were within the small plastic package that lay within Billy's palm.

The wizard of all things magical played to the audience before him. Blake explained that what the bag contained were the dried out remnants of mushrooms that held hallucinogenic properties. He claimed that he had purchased the bag the day before during one of his weekly visits to Glebes. He had been reliably informed by the seller that the dried out mushrooms held within their stalks the ability to alter the mind, enabling the consumer to enter the realms hidden away from the scope of normality.

Voice hushed, as if prying ears would eke out century-old answers to questions long since lost, Blake went on to explain that the dried out mushrooms had been at the very heart of the druid rituals and beliefs.

The white robed men of English mysticism and Stonehenge had in fact, used the very mushrooms he now held, to conjure up the spirits of not only loved ones, but those of their pagan Gods they revered.

Even the Celtic people, he elaborated, had held the mushroom in the highest esteem. Before battle, the warriors would devour the freshly cut stalks in the belief that they would momentarily enter the after life, and if they were to be killed in battle their final passage would be swifter and less traumatic.

Billy looked carefully at the plastic package in his hand. On closer inspection, he could make out the individual forms of toadstool shapes that appeared to be long past their sell by date.

As he gently shook the package, the dried out mass separated, and he could see the mummified mushrooms in their unique shape.

Despite being dried, Billy surmised that in life, the little mushrooms would have been small, maybe the size of his little finger nail. The dried out remnants indicated that the miniature fungi had taken on a teat-like form - pointed at their tips with a long, exaggerated, thin stalk - that wound, almost coil-like to raise the spore carrying body high above the pasture grasses that it preferred for its growth and prosperity.

With eagerness Blake snatched the plastic bag from Billy's scrutinising grasp.

"Watch, maestro, and learn from the true master of mysticism." The grin broadening across his face confirmed, in his eyes, that he, was the most knowledgeable of all things hallucinogenic within the small group.

Carefully, he poured the dried out husks onto his open palm, carefully shielding them from the gentle breeze that blew across the field below them.

He divided the small mound into three separate piles and discarded the empty wrapper upwards to be carried away by the wind.

The captive audience before him watched as he pinched one of the three small piles of near-dust between finger and thumb, placing the contents into his mouth, before drinking from the coke bottle that he produced from his jacket pocket. With an exaggerated swallowing motion, he jerked his head back and let out an enormous "Ahhhh," to indicate that the deed had been done and the forbidden fruit had once again been taken with relish.

Jowett, ever eager, rose to the challenge, and held out his hand to take the offering. He repeated the ceremony as the master had before him. Despite his bravado, he struggled to swallow the coarse stalks, and was forced to take a second drink from the offered bottle before his airways were finally cleared.

Billy was less enthusiastic and kept his hands at his side.

Victoria looked at him with the plea of disapproval in her eyes that Blake immediately recognised.

"Come on, Casanova, what's it to be?" Blake's sarcasm was evidently ridiculing.

"Little Miss Lonely Heart, or the band of brothers?"

Billy felt the blood flow to his face and desperately tried to fight off the blush that would reveal his embarrassment.

Although his feelings for the girl at his side had risen to heights he had never before experienced, he knew that to back away from the challenge, would result in loss of dignity and contempt for months to come.

With an inward sigh of frustration he gave in to the peer pressure and held out his hand to take what Blake offered him.

Victoria turned and looked at him with dismay.

"Fuck you Billy Hall!" she whispered as she turned. "Play with your little friends and their idiotic games - I'm history!"

With this she stepped onto the packed earth footpath and walked, with purpose, towards the line of houses in the near distance below.

"Got yourself a fiery one there, lad." Blake retorted as he transferred the contents of his own palm to that of Billy's.

Not to be outdone, and to avoid further embarrassment, he accepted what was offered and placed the contents into his mouth. His first reaction was to retch as the deep flavour of soil filled his palate.

As a small child, Billy had joined the other children as they had played games of cooking. Heaped piles of watery mud had been fashioned into circular moulds and then left in the summer's sun to bake. Emptying the baked mud pies out of their containers and seeing the product of their endeavours had been enough for all but Billy. He had been the foolish one to taste the masterpiece of the grandest cook and had vomited profusely for the rest of the day, forcing an early exit from primary school.

The taste now within Billy's mouth conjured the memories from that day and he desperately fought back the urge to eject the unpleasant taste from his mouth.

Desperate he gulped down the bitter liquid from the coke bottle and grimaced as the straw-like texture slowly slid down his throat into the depths of his gut.

"Ahhh." Billy let out the mimicked action of his reckless friends as the nauseating taste crossed beyond his taste glands and took its steady course to reach his bloodstream.

The brothers three settled themselves for the unexpected as they lay hidden from view amidst the meadow grass away from the prying eyes of any travellers upon the footpath.

Jowett passed round a cigarette. Each in turn inhaled its nicotine-fuelled vapours, waiting to experience the hallucinogenic effects that had been promised to Blake yesterday on the street corner in the nearby city.

The sun slowly dipped in its passage and the sky took on hues of fiery red as the first of the laughter rose from within Blake.

"Okay comedian, share the joke." Billy announced without taking his eyes from the cloud directly overhead.

Jowett joined in the laughter as if the silent joke had been told telepathically and for reasons that Billy could not rationalise the laughter spread into him.

Stretched out on their backs the three comedians lay, unable to suppress the uncontrollable laughter that had possessed them. They laughed together, until they felt that their sides would break from the exertion.

The sound of a car approaching caught Billy's attention amidst the confusion and he strained to decipher from where the noise came. The hill on which they had no access roads and confusion bore into him.

Slowly the realisation hit him. They had been observed entering the field to the side of the footpath by the resident farmer, and he was now charging his way towards them in an old Land Rover he often used to chase unwanted visitors from the land he tended. Worse still, Billy thought to himself, old man Betsy was notorious for carrying a loaded shotgun. He gave little thought against firing its scatter shot in the direction of unwanted visitors who had been foolhardy enough to flatten his crops.

Countless stories had been told of generations of teenagers that had spent uncomfortable, and painful evenings having lead shot removed from their backs and thighs as they had dared to encroach on the crazy old farmer's land.

Not wanting to spread panic Billy rose from his place of rest and scanned his immediate surroundings to determine where the motorised sound was coming from. Nothing in the fields around him gave any indication of a mechanical intrusion but yet the motorised sound prevailed and became louder. Confused, he scanned the horizon for the source of the sound, but the meadows beneath him were void of anything other than the skylarks that sang their song overhead.

The mechanical sound of a nearby engine remained and seemed to be coming from the direction to Billy's left. Turning, he caught sight of a car that was being driven along Castlefield's Lane some two miles away in the distance. The engine sounded as if it were metres away and filled his head with its deep rumble.

Panic rose within Billy; he felt nauseous and light headed. At his side Blake and Jowett continued with their laughter, oblivious to the fact that Billy had moved from his position.

As the engine noise slowly faded into the far distance away from sight, another sound caught his attention, making him turn to his right. The town's colliery spread out before him, the spoked wheels of the headgear turning as they wound up the hard earned coals from deep beneath. The heavy sound of footsteps echoed all around as Billy watched the scene set out before him. Ant-like figures walked their way across the concrete space towards the collection of brick buildings.

"They never stood a chance," came a voice, carried by the cooling breeze as it drifted upward to fill Billy's head.

"Poor buggers," came a distant reply.

Panic now added to panic as Billy tried in desperation to understand what was happening. The car had been too distant for Billy to have heard its engine as it drove away from him - way into the distance; now voices resounded within Billy's head as clear as if they were being spoken by the laughing twins at his side.

Billy shook his head in disbelief and looked again at the scene in the distance below. As if by magic, the men he had seen and heard moments before, vanished and the colliery appeared void of any movement, other than the spinning wheels aloft of the steel winding gear.

The air in front of him seemed to ripple and revolve around him, he felt a sharp pain rise within his stomach, as if he was to vomit. Waves of nausea washed over him as he fell to his knees, steadying himself against the disorientated dizziness that filled his mind.

As soon as it had spread into him, the sickly feeling withdrew and the warm breeze also settled; the ripples of colour withdrawing into the distance and then out of sight.

Slowly, Billy stood from his kneeling position. The experience had unsettled him deeply, he regretted being foolish enough to listen to the disputably wise words of Blake.

Laughter sounded again at his side; he turned to watch as his two friends lay on their backs, fits of merriment engulfing them as they pointed skywards, amused at whatever it was only their eyes could see.

"Blake; Jowett!" Billy's voice broke through their laughter.

"Listen!" he continued, "I want to go; I don't feel too good…"

As if the invading voice was another part of the joint illusion they were experiencing, Blake's and Jowett's giggles intensified, and the pair's pointed fingers were now aimed at Billy.

"Come on, guys, listen!" Again his desperate voice only seemed to fuel the fires of entertainment that were burning out of control within them as they rolled crazily from side to side, flattening the meadow grass as if it had been subject to some mysterious crop circle manifestation.

Realising that his pleas were falling on deaf ears, Billy turned and stepped onto the earth footpath that snaked its way down the gentle slope towards town.

"Fuck you!" he called, as he walked slowly away.

The laughter gradually diminished as he distanced himself with each step that took him closer to the houses that formed a brick red barrier before him.

Movement above the slate-grey rooftops caught his attention as the carrion crow flapped its wings to gain height, propelling itself forward in the cooling air as the sun cast its shadows across the buildings beneath it.

The colours caught Billy's attention as each flap of the crow's wing beat out a gentle plume of colour that was slowly absorbed into the air as it flew. Purple dissolved into powdery blue as the crow made its way steadily overhead towards him in its own quest to break from the restraints that the rooftops held.

Overwhelmed by the light-headed feeling overtaking him, he took rest, leaning heavily against a wooden post that supported the fine wire mesh that acted as an impediment to the sheep that were herded in the field opposite.

The crow, going about his business flapped his song within the cooling air and took to the sky that he knew so well.

Colour filled Billy's sight as the skyline before him took on the dulcet tones of yellow. With each gentle flay of the feathery wing that the crow offered came another make-believe colour.

He heard his own delayed footsteps as they thudded down the path, as if he was a worn out traveller seeking a place of refuge and rest after hiking throughout the day.

The colours that spread across the sky rotated, as if mixed in one huge kaleidoscope, changing from delicate yellow ochre to the brightest of magenta appearing as if the entire sky had been absorbed into one huge light show from some rock concert.

As the crow flew into the distance the pulsing tones of colour slowly faded to be replaced by the natural shades of the coming dusk.

As normality once again comforted , Billy left his place of rest and hurriedly walked closer towards the houses that lay before him.

With each step he left the unreal world he had briefly encountered behind him.

Voices could be heard as he slowly drew closer and relief rose within him as he caught sight of people as they hurried about their business before nightfall.

Aromas of cooking filled his nostrils as he entered the side street that would take him out onto the town's main street. The deeper he walked through the houses that rose up on both sides of him, the stronger the smells of cooking became.

The rich smell of boiled cabbage and cooking meat washed over him in a crashing wave and again the feeling of nausea rose within him. The stench became unbearable and Billy felt the burning sensation of bile as it bore its way upwards from within his gut.

Unable to subdue the rising sickness within him he bent down and held onto the rough brickwork of the wall to his right for support. Vomit erupted from his open mouth and spread on the pavement before him. Billy gasped in air as he retched until his sides ached and he began to feel faint with his own exertions.

The scarlet centipedes scattered across the pavement, seeking their own refuge as they freed themselves from the gluttonous liquid from which they had been born.

Billy stared in both disbelief and horror as he rose in shock and stood looking down, desperately trying to comprehend what was happening. As his eyes focused the writhing form of many legged bodies became still and he was faced with the half digested remnants of carrots and mashed potatoes which he had earlier consumed for his lunch.

"Fuck, what is happening to me?" he asked himself aloud as he wiped away the bile from his mouth and pushed himself from the wall that had offered him support.

The aromas had all but drawn back and the town before him appeared like it would have done on any chosen day of the week.

The automatic timing switches had completed their ordered duty and the shadows of dusk were being ebbed back into the recesses by the glowing orange illumination of the street lighting.

The vomit beneath his feet was void of any movement and Billy breathed a sigh of utter relief as this realisation sunk into him.

Whatever he had seen and heard was merely a figment of his imagination, exaggerated by the chemical effects held within the magic mushrooms that he had foolishly taken.

The gentle smell of cooking once again returned and the monotones of passing cars brought about the normality that Billy craved.

Stepping forward, Billy entered the main street. The humdrum sound of passing traffic passed slowly by as Billy gained his composure.

Everything now appeared normal before him as he walked, avoiding the uneven paved surfaces of the pavement that could result in the unwary traveller tripping and taking a fall.

He realised that to go home would be a foolish thing to do until he was sure that the mushrooms had worked their course and were out of his system.

His parents would be enraged with him if they found out that he had used any drug and even worse, he would have to face the wrath of Milan.

He decided that he would seek out Victoria and hope that the apology he offered would be accepted and she would show pity for his sufferings.

He rounded the corner that led him onto the high street and walked hurriedly past the Working Men's Club where he knew Roger would be present.

Billy felt the inner heat within him rise and wiped away beads of sweat that glistened on his forehead.

Despite the coolness of the air around him his body temperature rose and Billy felt as if he was going to faint.

He stopped and leant against the rough brickwork of the wall. The sweat now ran its course onto his eyebrows and down along his cheeks. He raised his sleeved wrist onto his face to wipe away the irritation.

Unable to stem his rising temperature, Billy hurriedly clawed at the sweater that clung to him, drenched with the perspiration that flowed from his pores.

Standing upright, he desperately tried to control his breathing, stemming the rising panic that was racing through him.

"Billy!" Roger's voice startled him and he instinctively spun round to face his father.

The force pushed into him before he could completely turn and Billy fought to keep his balance and avoid being knocked onto the uneven pavement at his side.

Ice cold water that had hit him with unbelievable force crashed over him and then as quickly as it appeared it was gone.

Not a trace of it was left as Billy examined the dry concrete that sprawled beneath him.

Fear gripped him in its icy grasp once again as he realised that even the sound of Roger's voice had been an illusion created deep within his own mind to trick and confuse him in this hallucinogenic world he had entered earlier with his band of brothers, on top of the grass-covered hill overlooking the town beneath.

Adrenaline was discharged into his bloodstream as he turned and ran. Victoria's house lay about half a mile away, nestled neatly among one of the modern housing estates that had replaced the old after the demolitions crews had finished their work.

Cars slowly rumbled past the athlete in full flight and Billy stared in disbelief and horror as the turning wheels towered above him, the glistening chrome wheel trims brightly illuminated by the thousands of pulsating fiery sparks that echoed out the entire range of the summer's rainbow.

"Billy!" Roger's voice echoed again from somewhere behind him and he instinctively stopped and turned to acknowledge his father's call.

A wave of filthy water rose up in a deep swell above him and seemed to hang in the air before crashing down onto him with a deafening roar. This time Billy was unable to steady himself from its force and was sent backwards, hitting the pavement with a sickening thud that sent fingers of pain pulsing up along his spine and across his shoulders.

Thick water entered his mouth and he retched at the foul taste that oozed across his tongue and entered his windpipe, forcing back the spent air that he desperately tried to exhale.

Darkness crept across his vision and he struggled in vain against the overwhelming strength and power that had overcome him. Billy felt his life being drained from him and an eerie feeling of comfort and reassurance replaced the fear that had overtaken him.

A light appeared before him, filling his entire sight with its beckoning glow. The weight that had only moments earlier descended upon him and mercilessly crushed him into ground, slowly lifted as the orange glow intensified, forcing back the darkness and the shadows bathing him in its vibrant glow.

Noises began to drift over him, carried by the gentle breeze that cooled the beads of perspiration from his forehead. Voices in conversation beckoned to his left and the high pitched tone of a car's horn startled him to his senses.

"Ey, drunk, its wake up time!" shouted a driver mockingly as he passed slowly, nosily peering out from the car's open window to take a better look.

The glow of the light intensified and he so desperately wanted to be absorbed into its welcoming glow.

Again, the sound of a car horn broke through his thoughts and the blurriness of his vision sharpened into focus.

Above him, cradled high upon its concrete support, the street lamp cast down its light that would keep the darkness of night at bay until the moon had run its cosmic course and was replaced by the rising sun.

Confused, he pulled himself to his feet and felt at his clothing that had been drenched as he had been knocked to the ground by the sheer force of the wall of water.

Dry. Everything around him was dry with not even a hint of moisture.

"Fucking mushrooms!" He turned and ran along the pavement once again, turning the corner to his left that he knew would lead to the small estate where Victoria lived.

"Billy!" Roger's voice echoed from behind him. This time Billy did not stop and look. He knew that whatever it was that he had experienced was a figment of his drug induced imagination and he continued without hesitation. There was no wall of water to follow as he sprinted along the street that would lead him to the safety and companionship of the girl that he had grown to love with all of his heart.

Without losing momentum he ran, only to pause at the ornamental numbers that adorned the doors of the houses that he speedily ran past in haste to reach his final destination.

23, 25, 27. This was it; number 27, Moor Row. Fumbling wildly at the catch that secured the small wooden gate he felt something touch his neck. Instinctively he raised his hand and felt something hard to his touch protruding from the side of where his Adam's apple lay at the front of his throat.

A snake-like branch pushed out wildly, breaking free of the palmed hand that Billy pressed against it in an effort to stem back its unnatural growth. Sheer terror now gripped him as he felt his neck being slowly crushed as the tree-like form encircled his throat and began to cut off the air supply that he so desperately needed. The coarseness of the bark dug into his fingers as he fought for his life, trying to break free from the deathly restraint that had spawned from his own being.

Lack of oxygen slowly lessened his resolve to fight and he felt himself being overcome by weakness. As he fell in what seemed like exaggerated slow motion to the grassed ornamental garden beneath his feet, he remembered how ironic it had become.

He had read a book about Britain's last executioner and had wondered, ever since the last page had been turned, what it would feel like to be hanged.

As consciousness slowly left him Billy smiled to himself. At least now the question had been answered, he thought, as the impeding blackness swallowed him out of existence.

The sterile stench of bleach clawed at his nostrils as he fought against the restraints that were attempting to squeeze the very live from within him.

As Billy struggled against the overwhelming strength that had captured him in its restraints the sound of a gentle ticking crept from the shadows, forcing his attacker slowly back.

Tick-tock, tick-tock, filled the darkness around him and he strained to identify from where it came.

With his body bound tightly, he slowly turned his head to the right and peered into the blackness before him. A clock shone with pride upon a wall, its chrome picking out the merest of light and reflecting this back to the onlooker beneath.

The warm feeling of reassurance spread through Billy as he realised that all was not lost to him. Time was the essence of mankind and the ultimate difference between life and death.

As laughter rose from within him, the shining timepiece seemed to move against the restraints that had sited it above him.

Magically, springs sprung out at its sides and chrome outstretched hands morphed at their ends, waving as the high tensile steel settled. Springs again sprang their dance and formed legs to be capped by silver-white boots that kicked and thrashed in an effort to become connected to the ground below.

Billy strained against the leafed branch that held him horizontal in a position of helplessless as the clock magically sprouted a head. In horror and disbelief he watched powerlessly as the clock pushed with all its might against the wall that held it aloft. Loose plaster slowly fell to the ground as it rocked from side to side and the unmistakable form of a grin spread across its face. With one final heave the clock pushed itself from the wall and bounced on the bed immediately to Billy's left, its weight sinking into the mattress.

His scream echoed against the four walls of the hospital room as the clock jumped onto his hand and he struggled in desperation against the restraints that held him.

"Billy, it's me," Victoria's voice cut through the terror that had engulfed him as he felt the warmth of her hand as it nestled into his palm.

"Baby, everything's gonna be okay,." The reassurance in her voice calmed him as he opened his eyes to the light that was all around.

The clock on the wall above him broadcast that it was 9.20 a.m. and sunlight filtered through the small window behind him.

A nurse leaned over and detached the straps that restrained him to the steel bed and lowered down the sides that resembled those of a baby's crib.

"Good morning, Jimmy Hendrix," she said with a smile, as she gently held his wrist between finger and thumb.

Victoria explained that her father had been alerted by heavy knocking on the door and had found him, semi-conscious on the small lawn that fronted the house. He had already been told by his daughter what the boys had been up to and had experience of the effects of hallucinogenic drugs from his own teenage years in the 1960s.

He also knew both Roger and Milan well enough to know that if they were to find out what their golden boy had done the discipline handed down would be harsh and unforgiving.

Instead he had played out a gamble and telephoned Molly to ask if it was alright for Billy to spend the night with them as they had ordered an Indian takeaway.

With the deceit secured he had then driven the psychotic Billy to the local hospital where his condition had been monitored throughout the night. As the waking nightmares reached their peak he had been restrained by leather straps in order that his thrashing caused him no harm.

The gentle ticking of the steel clock counted out the rhythm of time but now there were no horrors to unfurl as Billy watched its hands slowly move across its circular face.

Victoria stayed at his side until he was discharged later in the day, and as they walked hand in hand along his very own path of adventure he knew deep down that she was the girl that he would be with until he breathed in his final breath.

The blackbird watched as the loving couple passed beneath, singing out a chorus of love and hope that their future aspired to bring.

* * * *

Chapter Fifteen – When Spirits Break Free

Dappled rays of sunlight settled upon his face as he woke. Sparrows perched upon the rooftops, chirping their morning chorus of 'hello to the world' - announcing the dawn of yet another new day.

Billy had slept little during the night. The nightmares had cascaded through his mind relentlessly and he now lay on the bed exhausted.

It had been the same scene each night since he had experienced the horrifying effects the day he had foolishly bowed to peer pressure and swallowed the harmless-looking, dried out mushrooms.

Each night he would lay in bed and attempt to fight off the sleep that his body so desperately needed.

Each night he would lose the battle and feel the comforting blanket of slumber wash over his mind as his eyelids closed.

The noise seemed to come from deep within his brain and would always start as if it was a whisper of reassurance, breaking down the barriers of resistance.

With the barriers down, the noise would intensify and reverberate as if an electrical surge was being discharged from deep within him. Billy would fight against the strengthening grip that he would feel being cast around him with little success and, as the noise intensified he would find his mind slowly becoming detached from his body. Although he would open his eyes and see the darkness of the room around him he would be unable to move. Paralysis held his struggles at bay and he would lay fearfully still on the bed, unable to move his head to ascertain from which direction the murmuring of hushed voices came from.

The whispering voices would always be the same, coming from the darkness all around him.

Although he was never able to pick out any of the words spoken he had always been sure that they were aimed at him. It was as if the hushed tones were mocking and ridiculing him as he lay full of fear, defenceless from their onslaught on the bed.

It was not the whispered voices that caused the fear within but the feeling of vulnerability and hopelessness as he lay exposed to whatever it was that had crept from the shadows and stalked him in his fragile slumber.

Last night had been particularly stressful for Billy. Whilst he had lay paralysed and defenceless he had felt a weight lower down on the mattress at his side as if someone had sat upon the bed.

The voice that broke through the darkness was hushed as if the speaker was fearful that others within the house would hear what was being spoken to the defenceless target of their energy.

"Billy!" the voiced hissed at his side. "Show no fear, for you have allowed us the final freedom that we have awaited for so long."

The voice sounded so distant and yet so near, seemingly echoing as if confined to the darkness from where it came.

"You opened the door for us, Billy, and allowed us to break free from our restraints."

In desperation he tried to break free from his own shackles that held him rigid to the bed beneath him.

Experience told him that to try and move his limbs would be fruitless and the only way of breaking free would be to move his eyes from side to side and then to carry the momentum of movement down across his body. Slowly but surely, the movements would course their way throughout his body and at last he would feel his limbs as they slowly rocked from side to side.

Once again the driver behind the wheel, Billy had finally broken free from whatever it had been that had taken him in its steel grasp. The release had been far from gentle and the force from his exertions had sent him crashing from the edge of the bed onto the carpeted floor with a thud that he feared would have woken his parents.

Struggling, in an attempt to control his laboured breathing, he had lay where he had landed, carefully listening into the darkness for any sound that would alert him that his struggles had drawn the sleeping from their slumber.

Billy had spent the rest of the dark hours wrestling back the sleep that attempted to once again take its hold, exposing once more the unseen forces that dwelled within the darkest of its nightly shadows.

As the crescent moon paled and dipped in its silent, timeless pass over the resting planet below Billy struggled in his efforts to stay awake and would feel himself slipping away to be consumed by the natural need for sleep.

The fight would be a tug-of-war battle with both sides gaining and then losing ground to the other until finally all resistance was lost and the gentle sounds of snoring gradually rose from within him, the slight vibrations in the air letting out a rhyme that only the shadows would embrace with their dance until the dappling rays of sunlight forced them back into the corners and cavities from which they had emerged.

Billy struggled with the toast that Molly had placed before him, choosing yet another cup of black coffee to fulfil his appetite.

Roger had left two hours earlier to visit his deceased friend's parents and to help them with their weekly shopping.

Peter's parents had never truly recovered from having their son cruelly taken away from them and it seemed they would never fully come to terms with their loss. Molly had always felt tears well in her eyes each and every time Roger spoke about his dead friend and would remember Billy's innocent words as Peter had briskly walked past them when they had rested on the bench, taking in a moment of relaxation from their walk through the bustling town.

Peter's ageing parents had remained lonely, not only for the coming Christmas but ever since Mother Nature had retaliated so cruelly for what had been taken from her.

Wiping the moisture from her eyes Molly began to clear the small kitchen table where Billy sat, lost deeply in his own thoughts.

"Billy, try and eat a little." Her voice broke through the silence that had descended as both had become lost within their own thoughts.

"Billy, are you listening?" This time, her voice rose to capture the attention that had evaded her on her first request.

Billy's lost thoughts were quickly drawn back to him as he desperately tried to take in the air that his body needed and panicked at the realisation that he could neither breathe in nor out. As the panic within him grew, he instinctively rose to his feet, sending the table before him tipping forwards causing the china bowl and coffee cup to fall, their impact smashing them and sending razor-edged shards in all directions across the carpet, many of them lost in its thick woollen weave.

Molly let out a scream that reverberated around the walls of the small kitchen, only to add to the chaos that had manifested itself from nowhere.

The scream added to Billy's fear as he tried in vain to take in even the slightest of breaths that would brush away the darkness now emerging from the outer perimeters of his vision. He staggered backwards, coming to an abrupt stop, restrained from further retreat as body and wall came together in a collision that brick and mortar would win outright.

The force of the impact sent Billy reeling forwards and he fell to his knees, blackness now winning the battle against the light that threatened its supremacy.

Fear and panic subsided within him and slowly gave way to acceptance as he felt a warm wave of tenderness and happiness wash across his senses. Summer days of fun raced their paths across his thoughts. Childish laughs once again rang out their song across the yellow-ripened wheat, as he saw himself leap headlong into the blanket of straw beneath him. The green, warm waters of the pond called out their tune, inviting all away from the bloodthirsty gnats that buzzed their intrusion, seeking out blood from their unwitting host as the sun reached towards its zenith of the day. A fishing float dipped beneath the shimmering water's surface to announce that the prey had indeed succumbed to the bait that had been cast.

"No, Billy!" A voice rasped into his ear, startling him from the cushion that had once been the life he had lost forever in the passing of time.

Cold air filled his lungs with a ferocity that he instinctively drew back against, forcing him from the prone position that he had landed, up onto his knees.

"Back, back, boy, it is not the time!" the voice within his head ordered, and an icy chill of air blasted into his lungs, forcing out the dark coffee that he had only moments before consumed.

The thickened liquid spewed out from within him, slowly cascading down onto his chin, dripping its gluttonous path onto the woollen weave beneath his knees.

Molly's panic broke through the silence as she desperately performed what she had remembered of the Heimlich manoeuvre which she had seen on a recent medical documentary on television. Her feeble efforts of raining life-saving slaps across Billy's back were more annoying to him than anything else and he pushed himself free from her grasp. He grabbed onto the work surface, using his upper body strength to pull himself upwards onto his feet.

Molly, her breathing laboured from the panic that had taken over her rational thinking, leant wearily at Billy's side.

She wiped the remnants of the dripping coffee from his chin, using the stretched fabric of her sleeve as a makeshift cloth.

Embarrassed by the motherly affection that was being offered to him, Billy pushed her hand from his face and stepped forwards, opening the door to take in the morning breeze that gently met him as he stepped outside.

"Just went down the wrong hole, mam; I'm okay," he called out, without turning to face Molly. "Besides," a laugh was forced through the irritation that continued to burn into his throat, "You'd make a lousy nurse!"

Satisfied now that all was well and she no longer had a crisis of life and death on her hands, Molly wrung out the damp cloth that she now held in her hands and began to wipe away the damp patches of coffee permeating the fabric of the carpet beneath her feet. After all, she mused, a tidy home is a happy home.

Victoria waited impatiently for the familiar sound of Billy's footsteps as she sat on the low brick wall immediately in front of the doctor's surgery.

The imposing structure of Saint Gile's church cast its forbidding shadow over the houses before her and she hoped that Billy would arrive before the funeral cortege bid its path of sad farewell and came to its final resting place on the road before her.

The monotonous tolling of the single iron bell had begun moments before to strike out its sad announcement to all that yet another departed soul was about to be praised in death as it had been so in life.

Victoria hated funerals and would shiver with fear and panic whenever she heard the sound of the town's bell echoing its song to remind the living of what was to finally come.

As her own panic began to rise within her, Billy rounded the corner to her left and cheerily waved. Excitement quickly overcame fear as she pushed herself forwards away from the brickwork where she had sat for the last twenty-five minutes waiting for his arrival. She placed her arms around him in a greeting of both love and friendship.

Billy had hated and feared doctors since childhood. His clouded memories of the time that he had spent in hospital as a child always rose within him whenever he came face to face with the medical profession.

Distortions would relay their cruel part as he would remember the seizure that he had suffered and how the doctors had fastened electrical wires onto his head to punish him for the inconvenience he had caused.

What had been a simple and routine medical procedure to determine why a child should suddenly fall into something akin to epilepsy, to the child through the passing of time had been remembered as being an appointment with horror.

Victoria, however, had tirelessly prompted him to overcome the fear within him and seek medical advice.

Despite his growing maturity and manhood Billy still found himself unable to communicate entirely with his parents. The day to day tasks of 'hello and how are you' were still continents away from the finer, more personal aspects of conversation that Billy needed to share but simply could not.

It had been Victoria that had nursed him back from the brink of disaster when he had needed someone following the disastrous attempt he had made into uncovering the world of hallucinogenic drugs. She had kept the secret safe from the closest ones around him and had sat patiently listening to details of the night terrors that now stalked him in his sleep.

She had finally persuaded him to seek medical help in order that he face the fears that had plagued him ever since he had innocently opened the door to another world; a world that only existed in the far reaches of his mind, chemically induced when he had swallowed the potent mushrooms with his friends.

The waiting room offered little comfort to the already distressed that sat on the wooden benches aligned in neat, clinical rows facing the reception desk. Billy smiled to himself as Victoria, like the mother hen, ushered him towards a vacant seat and gestured for him to sit.

The doctors' surgery had always amused him as he surveyed the sickly occupants sat looking at the clock positioned high up on the magnolia painted wall.

The first restrained cough would signal the macabre Mexican wave and chest emissions would reverberate around the confined room until finally coming full circle to the embarrassed announcer of sickness.

Billy wondered to himself if the same thing would be repeated if he were to break wind. Would there be a chorus of followers releasing their own inner pressures as with the cough, or would he stand out from the crowd of misery who would silently stare their disapproval creating their own wave with their whispered sighs of disgust?

Victoria passed him one of the dog-eared magazines she had taken from the pinewood table that took centre stage between the reception desk and the seating area.

As with the majority of things in Castlefields the magazine was out of date and lost to the modern world of today's readers.

"President Reagan is shot in the chest by would-be assassin John Hinkley," the headline boldly announced to the reader. Billy was drawn to the story that had been written; Ronald Reagan had been, after all, a great cowboy hero. He had seen the dynamic gunslinger in action on the silver screen as a child and now wondered how such an amateur had pitted his wits and beat him to the draw of weapons. Maybe, Billy mused, Ronald had not been as quick as he had remembered and should be placed now behind the likes of the Duke and Eastwood. No, Mr Reagan had indeed fallen short of the magnificent gunslingers lining the annals of true merit and awe within his mind of listed heroes.

The cheaply veneered pinewood door immediately to Billy's left slowly opened. An elderly man that emerged turned his head and their stares locked as he gingerly closed the door, careful not to breach the silence that the waiting room held.

His limp was immediately apparent as he took his first step, almost dragging his right foot behind him, as he slowly made his way towards the exit door that opened directly onto the seating area.

As he approached the seated area where Billy sat, the aroma was displaced from that of sterile bleach and disinfectant to that of summer days long since gone. The sweet odour of an over-ripe tomato, mingled with the bitter smell of tobacco burnt from the oaken pot of a well seasoned smoking pipe, filled the air around him.

As the man drew pitifully close, his advance slowed by the dreadful incapacity that had taken away the rightful use of a leg he had once commanded, he raised slightly the trilby hat silhouetting half of his face in darkness.

"Your turn, son, the doctor awaits you."

Billy rose without further prompting. He had never been a patient patient and hated any form of waiting.

He rose, careful not to arouse suspicion amongst the damned that sat before him and stepped silently towards the door that offered medical intervention and answers to the questions that he so desperately sought.

The chrome handle offered only rigid resistance as he pushed down to disengage the lock that honoured its closed secrets to all.

Confused, Billy exerted more pressure onto the rogue lever but still the resistance prevailed and offered no middle ground of either give or take.

Like a fuse wire lit by unseen hands the first of the cautiously hidden coughs ignited the next until a chain reaction took hold within the room. Billy's breaking of the silence as he wrestled with the uncooperative door had released the pressures of suppression that the other patients had not dared to be the first to release.

The coughs and splutters of the sickly resounded around the confined sterile room as the wave of sickness crashed into him. The bitter-sweet odour of crushed tomatoes and tobacco permeated thickly into his nostrils and filled his lungs with a sensation they could not endure.

Confusion and panic pounded into him as he released the handle that now felt icy cold and offered the same sensation of chilly tingles he had felt as a child after compacting fresh snow with his bare hands. The sensation of tiny pins being inserted into his fingertips rose upwards as if in a desperate race of pain and agony, towards his shoulders and chest.

"Billy!" The gentlest of voices beckoned to him from nowhere and everywhere.

"BILLY!" This time the voice was more focused from the tunnel that had taken over his vision. The warmth of the touch upon his shoulders magically dispelled the icy fingers that had silently crept upwards as if reaching out to take the body as their own.

The chorus of coughs subsided once again into the silence that was expected from such a place and Billy felt the stares of a multitude of eyes burning their way into him as he slowly turned to the audience that he had created.

"Billy, my love, that's the store cupboard." Victoria's voice only seemed to add to the embarrassment that washed over him as he felt his face redden.

"But that man...." The words came out hurriedly. "He came out of here and told me that I was the next one to see the doctor."

"There was no man, Billy, maybe you were mistaken."

She motioned for him to look out across the waiting area to the empty space that lay between them and the room's only exit door.

Eyes of the seated damned glanced quickly downwards to gaze at the floor beneath them, to avoid those of Billy as he scanned across them in a desperate effort to determine where the elderly man had gone.

The first of the restrained coughs broke through the unnatural silence that had befallen the packed room of sickness. As if a fuse paper had been lit by an invisible flame, the single cough was transferred from patient to patient and echoed from every corner of the room.

The panic within Billy rose as if permeating from the worn carpet beneath his feet.

He struggled to control his breathing which seemed to accelerate as if it were racing at great speed towards some unseen finishing line where the final winner would be determined.

Victoria placed her arms around him in an intimate gesture of both love and reassurance, slowly guiding him back towards the exit doorway, near to where they had been sat.

Preying eyes looked up from their places of hiding, now that the target of their curiosity had turned from them when being led quietly away.

Slowly the muted coughs transformed into the faintest of whispers as the seated audience now revelled in the spectacle that had been set out before them.

Lunacy had yet to be attached to simple illness as had the common cold and angina and the lunatic was still a sight to behold, a source of amusement to the onlooker that it attracted.

"Insane!" The low, whispered hiss reached out from the seated lines of normality.

"Totally lost it…" This time the hushed words reached out to him and blanketed his shoulders in a coldness that only added to the attack of deep anxiety that had swept over him.

"Billy Hall, the crazy one….." This time the whispered voice held malice and contempt as it reached out to embrace him in its mockery.

"Billy Hall - the madcap fool of the entire town!" The whisper had escalated into a voice of anger that pressed against his shoulder blades, almost pushing him forwards with its force and aggression, away from the caring hold of Victoria's gentle embrace.

Despite the fear and panic that had taken hold of him, Billy's natural inbuilt instinct was to meet aggression with aggression and he spun, breaking the clasp of love that had been set to comfort him.

"Billy Hall…" The whispered voices did not fear breaching the hushed silence from the sterile confines of the waiting area.

Billy desperately scanned the vacant faces that were uniformly laid out before him, to ascertain the source of the mockery that had ridiculed him seconds before in his time of need.

The open stares that met him with their greetings of morbidity and fear exaggerated the anxiety that had already taken its hold within.

He looked carefully into the gazes of desperation that met him from the rows of seated sickness and dismay waiting eagerly for their final verdict.

The cancer patient, he saw no hope for as she waited patiently with only death in her eyes.

The poor man with constant indigestion would be surprised with his own death later that day whilst walking wearily to the pharmacy to collect the medication prescribed to ease the flatulent induced pains that he suffered; the doctor would miss out on his diagnosis that he had examined a dying heart.

The teenage girl that sat quietly ushering her own muted giggles as she eagerly read the latest gossip from the glossy magazine resting upon her lap.

The once-proud mother beside her now sat solemn faced, embarrassed for anyone to know the reasons behind their visit to the medical centre.

Death itself would be the unborn child's name as the stroke of a pen would condemn the growing foetus to the death penalty, never to know life.

Billy only saw the misery and pain that was to fall on those around him as he looked deeply into the eyes of failed hope and despair.

"Billy Hall." The whispered voices once again cast their tendrils out to him.

"Billy Hall!" This time the whisper grew louder, breaking into the realm of clarity.

"Billy, wake up...!" Victoria's delicate voice touched him and dragged him slowly from the depths of slumber that had befallen him.

Slowly, his eyes regained focus and he once again found himself sat comfortably in the cheaply upholstered wooden seat that he had settled into beside the exit door of the medical centre.

The coughs and splutters of the sickly and damned broke into the silence and the final prodded finger to his ribcage from Victoria completely brought him to his senses.

"Billy Hall, please." There was an impatient tone in the receptionist's manner as she called out the next patient's name to see the waiting doctor.

Gingerly, he rose and walked down the aisle towards the door of diagnosis.

A weeping woman looked up at him as he passed, the whites of her eyes tainted slightly yellow as if touched by the smokers' hand.

Last night's curry was to blame for today's inconvenience, the middle-aged man explained to his neighbour in suffering, as he held away the pain from his chest with open palms.

Giggles from the girl, as she pointed out to her mother, the latest naked upper body shot of some steroid induced monster that belittled the natural contours of the working man.

Billy turned once again and looked out across the sea of sickness before knocking politely three times against the heavily grained doorway to knowledge, understanding and hopeful diagnosis.

"Come." A voice of utter authority beckoned from within as if giving out the final order to men in the trenches, to rise from abject safety and meet death in their finest hour.

Doctor Aincliffe sat rigid above the desk that was laid out before him.

Notebooks and journals were laid out in neatly organised rows, as with the seating arrangements beyond the door in the waiting room.

Billy immediately felt intimidated by the man that sat before him.

The spectacles that were designed to aid vision rested on his beak-like nose as if it were his aim and intention to look down at his subjects set out before him.

Here was the voice of authority to which Billy complied, with the simple hand gesture to sit on the wooden seat positioned before the great desk of knowledge.

The sweetest of aromatic odours permeated from the glowing wooden bowl as the doctor breathed in the flavours from the pipe that he had placed between his lips.

"Mr. Hall," His voice resounded as rich as the smoke that bellowed out from his lips. "I have your records before me, so now, pray tell me, whatever is the matter today, my friend?"

Billy explained the best he could the night terrors that bore into him as the shadows lengthened and darkness beckoned.

With the difficulty that embarrassment brought with it he went on to describe the non-existent people that he would often see - the people invisible to others around him.

The bitter-sweet aroma that rose from the smoking wooden bowl that was held tightly between the doctor's lips clawed at Billy and made him feel nauseous with each and every breath.

The rustling of the papers before him was interspersed with constant 'ahs' and 'yes' as Mr. Aincliffe listened with interest to the stories being told.

"Hallucinogenic mushrooms, my friend." The voice was that of authority and wisdom. "Foolish to dabble in what we simply do not understand."

His eyes were exaggerated as Billy peered through the bifocal lenses that only seemed to reinforce the knowledge and power that the holder held deep within his sight.

"What is happening to you, my dear boy, is that you are suffering Hallucinogen Persisting Perception Disorder."

Dr. Aincliffe recognised the look of confusion on the patient's face.

"Flashbacks, my dear fellow." Thick blue smoke bellowed out from his mouth and seemed to dance through the dappled rays of sunlight breaching the confines of the aluminium horizontal blinds that masked the single window from preying eyes of passers by on the street below.

"I saw a lot of this back in the 1960s when every damned local collier foolishly thought that they were Jimi Hendrix." The smile spread neatly across his face as he was temporarily transported back to the happier times of his youth.

The doctor explained with clarity that the brain produces a substance known as dopamine and tests had proved that this can increase to levels that effect the flow of information to areas of the brain which control memory and attention.

As he worded his professional diagnosis, the man of ultimate wisdom and knowledge scribbled on a sheet of paper that he had torn from the booklet he had taken from the drawer to his right.

"Chlorpromazine should do the trick, but the medication could take several weeks to fully stabilise whatever it is that's happening in that empty head of yours." The smile sat smugly on his face as he passed Billy the unreadable prescription sheet.

"I take it you will not be participating again in the ritual of poisoning your body again?"

Embarrassed, Billy could only shake his head as he rose from the wooden seat and turned towards the door immediately behind him.

The face that looked out from the oil-painted portrait encased in a frame of darkest oak sent shivers racing down his spine. The rugged features of the pictured man were exactly like those that Billy had looked into as he sat patiently within the waiting room. Even the slight offset of the trilby hat perched at an angle on the man's head was the same.

Doctor Hilary Aincliffe, 1901 – 1975, the engraved caption read on the brass plaque set into the wooden frame.

Billy turned slowly. "Excuse me, sir, who was this man?"

"That, my dear fellow, was my father," smoke again plumed out from the doctor's mouth as he replied, "A fine practitioner and founder member of this establishment." His pride was obvious upon his face.

"Now be a good fellow and summon the next patient in before you leave."

The summer was particularly scorching and the forecasters had announced that July had been the hottest on record since the drought of 1977. The local council that governed the district around Castlefields had warned of the possibility of installing communal water taps to replace the water feed that was being piped into individual homes, a drastic measure to combat the rapidly depleting stocks of a commodity so natural but yet so precious.

The vast man-made reservoirs which lay high up on the moorland to the west were reported to be at critical levels and it had also been stated that the decaying spire of an ancient church could be seen visibly breaking the surface. The church had been the hub of a doomed village that lay in the way of man's progress. Victorian engineers had ruthlessly relocated its inhabitants in order that the deep valley could be dammed and flooded to feed the industrial towns below with a readily available supply of fresh drinking water.

A group of passing ramblers, walking late into the balmy evening, had reported hearing the toll of the iron bell from deep beneath the water's surface announcing the impending doom that was set to befall if the sun did not falter and withdraw its grip on the land.

A group of amateur paranormal investigators had aptly set up camp on the reservoir's mud-baked perimeter, hoping to bear witness to the phenomena of the unexplained. As of yet however, no further tolling of coming doom had breached the shallow waters and the group of enthusiasts sat patiently day after day for something that perhaps would never actually come.

Milan, slowing with the inevitable age that creeps its way to all living things had begun to struggle in his quest to retain the vigour of youth that he once had known and cherished.

He had retired graciously from the rigours of coal mining at the age of sixty-five and had been content with spending the extra time tending his precious crops of fruit and vegetables in his beloved allotment garden.

Despite his freedom from the back-breaking labour that had blighted him ever since his arrival in England, Milan's prosperous retirement had not been the bed of roses that he had envisioned.

Stiffening joints and laboured breathing, the direct result of inhaling daily the fine coal dust that had plagued the underground catacombs, only exaggerated the cruel effects of the ageing process.

Slowly, and with the deepest feelings of regret, Milan had succumbed to the realisation that he was no longer the young, unbeaten man that could take on the entire world. He had been forced to release the grip that he had cast on the fertile earth within his very own place of paradise.

As the years slowly ebbed past, less of the soil had been cultivated, preferring instead to slowly allow nature to reclaim what had once been hers to nurture. Fences were retreated to contain what he was still capable of managing as his body slowed and the locally famous produce diminished in quantity and quality.

All was not lost, however, as Billy found that summer to his delight.

Milan had offered him a place of paradise and sanctuary away from the hustle bustle and grime of the sprawling terraced streets; a place where Billy and his friends could idle away the long, hot days without the interference of daily drudgery and mayhem that the busy industrial town offered to its bleak inhabitants.

A very corner of England's finest, Milan announced, as he had led Billy to the corner of utter tranquillity out of both sight and earshot of the neighbouring houses that separated rural from suburban.

Billy had been overwhelmed - he had been given his very own piece of ground that he could do with as he pleased, and soon, with the help of Jowett and Blake, a crudely erected fence announced to the traveller that they were now in Billy's own very little kingdom.

Milan, a woodworker by profession in his native country, had fashioned benches from salvaged wood that had been reclaimed from the colliery's stockpile of timber and machinery.

The old picnic table that had mysteriously fallen into Jowett's possession somehow overnight formed the crowning glory to Billy's new-found playground.

No longer now would the town's weary inhabitants have to lean out of bedroom windows as darkness fell to dismiss the playful teenagers from hanging around the public benches and street corners.

Blake's father, still a keen craftsman despite his many years, had skilfully fashioned an impressive-looking barbecue after acquiring an empty oil barrel and steel meshing from the apprentice blacksmith whom lived across the street.

To impress Milan that all was not lost in his offering, Billy had set to work on the tiny space that was not taken by the objects of fun. Although limited in his knowledge and lack of green fingers, the neatly laid out rows of lettuce, spring onions and sweet peppers seemed to thrive under his watchful eye.

All was now set for a summer of fun and long balmy evenings would be spent with the sound of laughter, fragrant, mouth-watering aromas of gently cooking meat and the thirst-quenching taste of ice cold beers.

The evening had been particularly good as Billy now stared with satisfaction at the glowing embers that hung on to life within the barbecue's drum.

Money had been pooled together over the previous week and beer had been duly purchased from unscrupulous shopkeepers that often turned a blind eye to the transaction of alcohol to the underage. After all, profit was profit, regardless of age.

The local butcher also revelled in the trade offered from his newest of customers and concocted marinades in order that they try out his recipes and offer their approval.

Music had flowed as smoothly as the food and drink, and a good time had been taken by all as the revellers had marvelled in the glowing reds that the dying sun had offered to the skies before bidding its final farewell for the day.

Victoria, the ever sensible one had made her excuses to leave first. An early start to the day beckoned her after promises from her mother that she would take her into the city to shop for clothes.

Blake had been the next to stumble away his departure. He had soon succumbed to the vast amounts of alcohol that he always felt was his need to drink at such gatherings and had clung to the earthen path, slowly crawling away into the direction of the street lamps that were visible above the hedge of hawthorn.

Jowett now lay soundly in the foetal position of utter rest on the wide wooden bench opposite to where Billy sat, his gentle breathing announcing that sleep had finally arrived.

The glowing embers drew Billy's thoughts from him and seemed to take on the life that his memories released.

The silhouette of the old greenhouse took him to the days when he would become Casey Jones, the steam train driver. His faithful fireman Milan would stoke the stove that would heat the water pipes, offering harmony to the ripening tomatoes, and little Casey would stare in wonderment as the thick, black smoke bellowed from the steel chimney above. The contours of the glass house would be transformed into the iron hull that hurtled down the tracks at breakneck speed as the coals sparked the deepest reds of fury, sending mighty power to the wheels below.

The clicking of the gate catch some ten metres to his left dragged Billy from his memories, and his vision, hampered by the glowing heat of the barbecue, strained to make out anything in the darkness beyond.

Shapes began to break through the blackness as two figures approached.

Slowly, the approaching couple entered into the dim light that the dying embers offered and Billy was immediately drawn to the slender legs that leapt out from the white mini skirt that at least reclaimed some modesty for the owner.

Quickly and quietly Billy tried to gain the attention of the intoxicated, sleeping Jowett to alert him to the oncoming beauty that was approaching, step by beautiful step. Slumber, however, had its own desires on the nestled form that it now cradled deeply within its gentle clutches.

The slender legs came into focus and were supported by white leather knee-length stiletto boots that reflected back the glowing coals of the dying barbecue as they drew nearer.

Blonde hair flowed carelessly down onto her shoulders as she slowly and silently made her way to the bench where Billy sat.

Her companion gently released his grip on the hand that he had held as they approached, sitting beside the sleeping Jowett. Not wishing to waste too much time on the newcomer's appearance, Billy turned to his immediate side as he felt pressure bear down on the aged timbers that forged the seat on which he sat.

As their eyes met he felt as if he were falling into the fiery depths of hell itself, even feeling the need to instantly reach out and grasp the heavy timbers beneath him to halt his breathtaking fall.

Embarrassed by his reaction, Billy struggled in desperation to regain his composure but the simple word of 'hello' seemed to blur and echo from within his open mouth.

The corner of the allotment garden backed on to a well-trodden footpath that was used as a shortcut to the nearby town of Wentshelf. The town, as well as being historic with its ruined castle was also renowned for its lively nightlife and abundance of bars. Local legend was that the town offered more drinking places per square mile than anywhere else in the country.

"Hello." Billy finally breached the silence as his flawless guest eased herself down beside him.

She responded with a simple smile that made his heart leap as if breaking from the restraints that held it within his chest.

"Been up town and come for a warm?" The question came from him instinctively as he tried to free the silence within her.

With a smile she acknowledged the question and for Billy this was enough to satisfy the curiosity that had risen within him.

Embarrassed that he had not taken his eyes off the girl since she had sat beside him, Billy looked sheepishly away, focusing his vision over the glowing embers to where her companion had seated himself next to the sleeping Jowett.

Obviously a man of few words - he failed to even acknowledge Billy's nod of greeting and simply stared at the girl opposite.

Dressed simply in a white shirt and black trousers there was something about the newcomer that made Billy shiver from within.

It was not the silence that unnerved him but the expressionless stare that his eyes offered as he seemed transfixed on his female companion. This was something more, Billy thought, than the simple look of love and admiration. The cold eyes were void of anything other than sight and gave out no hint of any thoughts and emotions that were held within.

It was not with embarrassment this time that Billy looked away, but fear.

Movement at his side drew him from the wave of despair washing over him and he turned his head to see the girl at his side slowly rise. As if a message had been sent telepathically, the man of no words also rose from the bench opposite.

His empty stare remained transfixed on his companion as the pair rose together with a uniformed precision that looked like it had been rehearsed and practiced.

As the couple stood in unison they leant slowly forwards and raised their arms out before them, as if taking in the warmth from the dying embers that illuminated their outstretch palms with the smouldering ochre glow.

Held in some slow-motion distortion of time Billy watched as if suddenly paralysed as their fingers forged together, the tips meeting over the barbecue before them. Slowly the hands pressed down onto steel meshing that had earlier been used to cook the meats.

It was the smell that dragged Billy from the grip of paralysis. It was similar to that of pork but sweeter and clawed at his nostrils almost making him retch. With horror he looked across at the source of the sickening odour and was filled with revulsion as he saw that the fingers pushed onto the heated metal were blistering from the rising heat.

Open panic now bore into him and Billy sprang from his seated position. Acting without thought he quickly picked up the wooden handled garden rake from the floor. Turning, he aimed the wooden shaft towards the couple with the intention of using it to pry them from their madness and intention of hideous self harm.

Turning to face the would-be assailant, the girl's stare bore into him and stopped him dead in his tracks. The deep blue colouring of her eyes had vanished and was replaced by an opaque whiteness that held neither emotion nor life.

Her mouth opened and the stench of death Billy had once experienced after finding a fox's rotting corpse enveloped him in its essence of corruption and decay.

"Don't worry, Billy!" The voice was deep and seemed to echo into the night.

"We've been dead a long time."

Fear hit into him as if he had been targeted by the assassin's bullet and he fought to control his balance, falling backwards against the bench behind him. The basic instinct of human survival took over as adrenaline was pumped at breakneck speed into arteries and vessels deep within him, and he found himself running as he had never run before. The carefully laid out rows of salad leaves offered no resistance as he trampled them underfoot. Even the metre high picket fence erected to privatise the place of fun was vaulted without problem as Billy ran regardless of obstacle, away from whatever had just taken place before his eyes.

Pushing his body to its very extremes he ran through the dimly lit streets, his vision focused only on what lay ahead as his heavy footsteps evoked a chorus of barks and growls from the rudely woken dogs that leapt from their kennels to show disdain towards the source of their awakenings.

Only when Billy was safely in the confines of his bedroom did he take stock of what had happened.

He remembered the doctor's smug words as he had made his professional diagnosis and again thought how insanely pathetic he had been to poison his mind with the hallucinogenic properties of the mushrooms, simply to impress his friends.

Sleep evaded Billy and he lay patiently for the warming rays of the sun to slowly illuminate the darkened recesses that the room offered.

He decided that in order to save embarrassment he would tell no-one of what he had experienced. After all, he mused, nobody would really believe the horror story that he had just experienced.

Jowett sleepily pulled his shirt tighter around his neck in an attempt to shield out the cold as the dying embers of the barbecue finally gave out their last warmth of comfort.

His head pounded from the effects of the alcohol he had consumed the previous evening and the inside of his mouth felt as if it had swabbed with abrasive paper.

He cursed Billy for leaving him to sleep off his drunkenness and imagined him now curled up snugly in the warmth and comfort of his own bed.

Wearily he eased himself up from the bench and pressed his clenched hands behind him into his lower back, in an effort to massage away the aches and pains that the rough wood had instilled.

As he slowly rose to his feet he felt something press hard against his lower leg. Bending, which exaggerated the pulse of discomfort from within his lumber region, Jowett picked up the -handled garden rake and stood it upright beside the bench.

"The joker!"he thought to himself, as he imagined Billy smiling at the thought of his friend tripping on the clumsy booby trap he had set before quietly leaving the allotment garden.

The old adage of never drinking again entered his thoughts as he slowly made his way from the seating area towards the wooden gate that fronted onto the footpath and beyond.

"Strange." he mumbled to himself as he looked closely at the distinct imprints of a stiletto heeled shoe trodden deeply into the earthen path beneath his feet.

" I could have sworn Victoria had been wearing running shoes last night."

Closing the gate behind him, Jowett turned right along the footpath, heading slowly towards the first of the houses that heralded the outer perimeter of the town slowing waking to the dawn of a new day.

* * * *

Chapter Sixteen – The Changing Times

The summer had drawn to a close gracefully and deep down within him he realised that the warm months would be regarded as being probably the best days of his life.

Despite the problems he had endured the positives had always outweighed the negatives, and he lay content underneath the thick, duck-feathered quilt that kept the cooling draughts at bay.

Old Red, the cockerel of his childhood, had long since gone and it was now only the baited alarm clock that would awaken those sleeping through the darkened hours of nightfall.

Even the town was changing, he thought with sadness. Slowly the demolition teams had began to move in to replace old with the new.

Modernisation was to be the way forward, the town councillors would preach, in order to attract the voters at the next election - and modernisation it was to be.

Whilst others revelled in new beginnings to come as each Victorian terrace of houses was being flattened and reduced to dust, Billy looked on with sadness.

As each reddened brick fell so too did the very fabric and soul of each and every person that had once known that place as home.

The memories, the lives, were being slowly torn apart and he felt this burden heavily within himself.

The ghosts of happy times, sad times, memorable times and those of Christmas past were all within places that now lay derelict and unwanted as the town planners to made their kill for profit.

Nostalgia and memory did not bid well on the financial market and it was now money that did the talking.

"Billy!" The distant shout echoed along the dust and rubble of the place that his thoughts had taken him.

"Billy, if you're not downstairs in two minutes, your breakfast will be inside next door's dog!"

Molly's voice was that of authority whenever his father was away from home. Billy reached with his foot from the bed to tap his acknowledgment on the wooden floorboards below.

The bacon that was contained tightly within the pre-sliced white bread, as if it were to escape at any moment, had been overcooked but at least the coffee was good.

"You're getting lazy, little Billy boy," Molly scolded as best she could.

"You know today's the biggest day of your life." Her eyebrows raised in comical gesture.

"After all," the pause was short and appeared well rehearsed, "Not all boys your age get an interview to work at the colliery." Her wink, he thought, was a little too over dramatic as she scooped the remainder of the mushrooms onto his plate.

Having followed the constant stream of school children before him with nothing in the way of offered hope he had quickly resigned himself to the fact that his place in life had been pre-recorded for him to follow - that his path had been chosen with his birth.

Old King Coal requested an army, and it was to this army he had been assigned as soon as the umbilical cord had been severed, breaking him free from the motherly constraints that held him from harm.

King Coal had waited until the child had matured and today was the day that the child had finally crossed the barrier of boy to man.

"Enter." The dulcet voice resounded from the closed door that Billy now stood before.

With a creak that could easily have been remedied with a droplet of oil, Billy nervously pushed forwards and stepped inside.

The acrid, bittersweet smell from the dying cigar that rested within the glass ashtray caught his breath, and immediately made his eyes water as he entered the confined space within.

Billy felt that he had been summoned to meet the queen herself as he stood rigidly to attention before the aged oak desk before him.

"Mr. Hall," - the Mr. sounding more, "Mester."

"Please sit." The voice was akin to the gentleman, Doctor Aincliffe.

"Can you read, boy?" The question resounded around the matt finished magnolia walls and seemed to pound back into the absorbent wood of the heavy desk that seemed to draw the line between utmost power and the already defeated.

"Yes sir, I can read," was all that he could muster against the overwhelming odds that he now felt against him.

A newspaper landed without grace before him and Billy tried in vain to focus his attention to what was happening.

"Headlines, son," the voice of authority and wisdom beckoned. "Read me the headlines."

Both surprised and confused, he stared down at the tattered, tea-stained offering that lay upon the polished oak surface.

"Headlines, sir?" he asked, as if unsure at the question.

"Yes, son," his reply was short and without compromise.

The bold text leapt out at him as Billy focused on the sporting headlines, and despite the deep feeling of intimidation that was rising within him he looked directly into the interrogator's eyes.

"Manchester United, two, Liverpool, one." The short lived feeling of bravado crept away as quickly as it had come and his gaze once again retreated to the safety that the newspaper offered.

"Excellent Mr. Hall." The reply seemed a little too well-rehearsed as the sacred tick of acceptance was sealed with ink from the fountain held tightly in the nicotine stained fingers of success or failure.

"Congratulations, son, you have succeeded passed the test." His grin was a little too pronounced to offer any encouragement.

"You will be summoned in due course to undertake a medical examination, my dear friend." Once again the acrid blue smoke bellowed from his mouth as he lit another cigar he had taken from the ornate wooden box sat with pride on the desk.

"Close the door behind you."

The ground underneath him seemed to vibrate as he walked away from the imposing Victorian office building that had seen better days of grandeur.

Sadly, over one hundred years of windswept filth had stained the bricks black as if the building had been constructed from the very coal to which it owed its prosperity.

Rounding the corner, away from the office block, Billy's attention was drawn to the group of men that were walking towards the flat roofed building that stood opposite.

Their faces were blackened from the sweat and coal dust they had obviously endured labouring the early morning away deep underground as the town slept.

Despite the hardships endured, the group of miners laughed and frolicked as they walked through the weathered wooden door that led into the drab building before them.

Curiosity always got the better of him and he looked around to make sure that he was not being watched by anyone passing.

Slowly, he opened the door. The sound of laughter echoed from within as he entered, careful to close the old wooden door behind him.

The room was brightly lit as the high mounted strip lighting hung from chains reflected from the whitewashed walls.

Aluminium lockers stacked two high ran in a neatly laid out row down the entire length of the building's interior.

The blackened, weary miners that he had followed closely were now stripping from the filthy and tattered clothing that had been their attire whilst winning out the coals.

Steam clawed at his nostrils as he walked slowly along the locked cabinets that safely stored the miners' clothing and personal possessions whilst they worked underground.

The men he had followed were now in various stages of undress as they readied themselves for the welcoming shower that would wash away the filth that their bodies had endured every day of their working lives after they too had passed the same process he had earlier passed, ensuring him a future place within their ranks.

Standing watching the men, Billy soaked up the atmosphere that the building offered out to its new-found spectator.

He knew in that instant that he had found the destiny that had always awaited him. That he had been born and raised to walk in the footsteps of the men before him.

He had always, as a child, been drawn to the sight of the colliery and had mimicked in play the work of the miner that he would eventually become.

Now, here he stood amongst the fabric and life that had offered breath to the town and its people, and he revelled in the inviting embrace that was offered to him.

The pungent odour of sweat fused together with the sweeter scents of soaps and detergents and Billy closed his eyes to take in the full essence of his surroundings.

Nostalgia swept over him and he imagined generations of men that had taken in the same bitter-sweet aromas that he now welcomed with pleasure and the deep rooted feeling of inner satisfaction.

In that one instance Billy felt he had finally become the man that had been expected of him since the day of his birth.

Lost in his own thoughts the heavy slap that landed across his shoulders startled him as if he had been scolded with boiling water. The blackened face grimaced into a toothless smile as an old man laughed and closed one eye in a gestured wink before pointing to the shower room at his side.

"Your turn soon, son." He had a hint of sarcasm within his voice as he turned and joined his comrades busily washing underneath the separate faucets within the communal bathing area.

Despite the filth and grime of the ageing buildings outside Billy was taken aback at the cleanliness that the interior of this particular building offered.

White tiled walls elegantly crafted and contoured without flaw gave evidence to the master craftsmen of old, as they had tried desperately to offer comfort and luxury to those that would only face hardship and pain as they worked below.

The men before him seemed lost without inhibition as they continued their laughter; each in turn washed the others' backs with soap-fuelled cloths and sponges.

Fearing now that his innocent spectatorship could be misinterpreted as being more sinister, he turned and retraced his footsteps towards the door through which he had first entered.

Contentment and excitement filled him as he closed the door behind him. The laughter from within silenced as the handle was turned.

The gentle warming rays of sunshine added to the happiness that he felt as he walked along the narrow roadway that opened itself to the main street which was the artery of the town.

Bernard, the colliery's security officer, had taken an instant interest to the teenager he had observed walking away only moments before.

Curiosity too had always been his weakness as he slowly opened the weather beaten door to the old shower block the youth had just exited.

Dampness and decay met him as he cautiously peered into the darkened interior, the flashlight in his hand cutting a path of vision into the blackness beyond.

Rusted water pipes and ceramic tiles, yellowed with age, met him as he slowly walked the battered and broken rows of empty lockers.

To his right, the sad spectre of the now-deserted shower area bore no hint of the laughter and mayhem it had once contained.

Now its sadness reached out; the rusted, leaking water pipes bearing only the droplets of water that stained the floor beneath the darkest of browns.

With a shiver that ran the length of his spine Bernard turned and walked quickly back through the entrance door.

The old locker rooms had always given him an inner chill and he waited impatiently for the long overdue date that had been promised for their modernisation and future use.

Strange, he thought, as the door was firmly closed. Just for one second he could have sworn he had sensed the combined odour of both sweat and soap.

Billy slept soundly that night. His inner excitement had remained within for the rest of the day after he had left the colliery, making him weary as darkness fell.

Like a caterpillar he too had evolved into something so different from what he had always been. Soon he would become a man and take his rightful place amongst those that he had been privileged to stand beside in the shower room.

"Your turn soon, son," the old miner had said.

With those four simple words Billy had been taken into the fold and had embraced the invite without resistance.

Now as he lay in the darkness of the night he dreamed the dream of the working man and not the dream of the child.

Laughter echoed out from within the steam as the old miner vigorously scrubbed at Billy's back, washing away the dirt and grime, the medal of worth amongst mining folk.

*   *   *   *

Chapter Seventeen – No Turning Away

Tears rolled down his cheeks, blurring his vision as he gently arranged the flowers in a glass vase that sat before the headstone.

It had been four years to the day since Milan had given up the fight - the greatest battle of his life - and had slipped quietly away, his body ravaged by the cruel cancer that had slowly worked its way through his body, taking him little by little until there had been simply nothing left to take.

Alison's demise had come less than twelve months prior, following a routine stay in hospital. The nurse who had been working the night shift had found Alison sprawled on the floor at the foot of the bed. X-rays had revealed her hip bone had been broken in the fall and required surgery. Despite the careful monitoring by the anaesthetist the strain had been too much for her already fragile body to endure and her heart had simply given out its last thrust as the surgeon worked.

Billy stood before the grave and wished with all his heart that he could step back in time and once again be reunited with the two people he so desperately missed. He wanted to show the man he had become to those whom mattered most. No longer the troublesome teenager they had known and adored but now the hardworking man with a pride of his own.

Selfishly, he cursed the earth beneath the feet and felt that he had been cheated out of what he had wanted the most. He had been carefully nurtured by his grandparents throughout his childhood and desperately wanted them to see the finished article that they had helped to mould.

Billy had finished his schooling with no particular honours other than those expected of the working classes. He had fared well but was by no means university material and would follow countless generations before him into the depths to win out the nation's prosperity and might.

The medical assessment had almost cut his mining career before it had the chance to start. The examiner had raised his eyebrows as he read Billy's medical history. He had been deeply disturbed by the recording of what could have been epileptic seizures on two occasions. Billy had reassured him that these had been isolated incidents and he had suffered no repeat attacks. Satisfied that he had yet another offering to give to the coal masters he placed his accepted stroke onto the papers before him.

With that one stroke Billy's fate was sealed and there would be no turning away.

He had taken to mining like a duck to water and revelled in the excitement that his new subterranean surroundings offered him.

Coal ran through his veins and he would marvel with awe whenever he passed through the Victorian workings that his ancestors had skilfully constructed, when the first coals had been drawn to the surface in 1865.

Despite the harsh conditions they had endured, working under the coal owners that demanded only profit and cared little for the workers beneath them, it was obvious that the men took pride in whatever they did.

He had inwardly mirrored the images that his forefathers had portrayed. The statutory-issued orange overalls would not be worn and he preferred the worn out clothing from his own wardrobe to wear as he laboured like those before him.

The fur coat had raised eyebrows to say the least when he paraded his new-found acquisition with pride after purchasing it from one of the local charity shops.

Taking down his name for deployment, "Ronnie Brain Dead," the Polish deputy looked Billy up and down and had simply wrote, "The Bolshevik" on the sheet of paper that would inform management of the men employed on that particular shift.

Despite his sometimes odd ways Billy had immediately been recognised by the powers that be as having an inbuilt ability to outwit Mother Nature and win out the coals from beneath her feet.

He had been selected, soon after starting his enforced career, to attend Technical College where he was to be taught the finer side of mining. One day each week for the next three years Billy would once again grace the classroom with his presence. Advanced first aid, testing for gas and general leadership skills had been on the curriculum in the working man's school and he had excelled in everything that had been placed before him.

The raindrops glistened, as if produced from the very finest of diamonds, as they settled and then gently wound their weary descent on the marble grave marker before him.

Billy was thankful for once to the laden clouds that passed overhead for the droplets they now released. To cry, after all, was a weakness that was not to be tolerated in the man's world that he had become part of. Crying and showing of emotion was for the women folk and mentally disturbed only.

Tears of grief now ran freely down his face, fusing as one with the raindrops that had settled upon his chest.

He solemnly remembered that after the funeral cortège had left he had refused to leave Milan in his final place of utter rest.

Molly had come to him in his grief and had read a verse from the book about Hare Krishna he had bought her only two years before when he had become a waged man.

"Hell is a temporary destination after death for people who have sinned greatly while on earth."

She had assured him as their tears had united that Milan was now high up in the heavens, now smiling as he looked down below knowing that he had been loved and was so sadly missed.

As they walked back to the house hand in hand, as they had done so many times before along the path of adventure, she gently retold the story of the magical lake that had been forged as God had taken the stone to create the crescent moon.

Mother and son laughed through their deep grief as Molly recounted how Milan would lead the cattle through the lush summer meadow wildly swinging his underwear above him in the breeze so that his parents would never know he had swum in the forbidden place.

As if to mimic the young Milan she held her own hand to the sky. "He will guide us one day to that place up there amongst the stars, Billy; always remember that, for all time." She wiped the tears gently from his cheeks and held him tightly to her chest.

"One day you too will rest upon its golden banks and stare across at the beauty that Milan missed so very much."

With this, Molly had pushed him gently away, picking up a discarded branch and galloping her own white stallion, cutting down the enemy nettles that dared to stand upright in her path.

The sound of voices approaching dragged him from his thoughts and he turned to see an elderly woman gingerly bending to arrange her own offered flowers upon the grave before her.

As he scanned his surroundings he saw that others were slowly walking towards him along the tree lined path that split the cemetery into two halves. Turning to wipe the tears from his face he cleared his throat, gathered the remnants from the dying flowers that he had removed from the glass vase, and left the place of his sorrow.

Victoria had become his rock whenever he had felt the need to hold onto something tangible and secure.

Billy never forgot the times that he had needed her most and she had rose to the challenge without hesitation or thought for herself. In her eyes, the reckless, sometimes idiotic boy was all that mattered and she would do anything to keep him from harm.

Even Roger, it appeared, had softened as the years took their gradual hold on him and he had warmed to her company in the family home after a hard day's work deep underground.

The ridicules from him were meant and taken with a light heart as he would enter the room to find Molly and Victoria engrossed in the Hare Krishna book that Billy had bought as a gift.

"Mumbo bloody jumbo!" he would announce, exaggerating his dismay at the burning incense sticks. They would rise to his gentle mocking, reciting the sixteen word mantra in defiance whenever he dare utter a word against them.

Billy would attempt to take the side of the man and dismiss what he said was their ramblings but would always resign himself to the silence of the defeated as his gaze was met with the two women that he loved the most.

Since that fateful day which had resulted in Billy being taken to hospital suffering psychosis, after foolishly taking the hallucinogenic mushrooms to impress his friends, he had become ever closer to Victoria. He had sought out her company more than that of the boys with which he had formed the bond of friendship throughout his childhood years.

Blake and Jowett had continued with their experiments with mind altering substances and Billy had laughed at their foolishness as they attempted to seek out never-ending ways to induce the high that they craved.

The day that they had smoked the dried out skin of a banana had been particularly hilarious, as he had watched the hapless pair draw the pungent mist deep into their lungs until their chests had screamed out in agony against the unnatural intrusion.

Ground nutmeg in black coffee had been another claim to their fame and the clowning duo had drank so much that sleep had evaded them for the next two days, the high levels of caffeine sending their inbuilt metabolism into high-speed orbit.

Probably their greatest breakthrough in chemical science had been the notion that cigarette ash, added to apple cider, would reach the parts that other beers could simply never reach.

Billy and Victoria had laughed until the tears had ran down their cheeks and their sides ached as they had found the two jokers totally intoxicated from only the effects of the alcohol, their teeth stained black from the burnt deposits that had settled like coagulated mud, forming a crust on the liquid they had drank.

Their laughter had reached its crescendo as they had looked back from the vantage point of the elevated railway line to witness the local grounds-man chasing the drunken duo, whom had vomited on his carefully laid out grass in readiness for the day's cricket match between two of the local teams.

Victoria had been to Billy his personal saviour. Without her he would have drifted down along the spiralling path that his closest of friends had chosen - of drunken nights, drugs and police involvement.

The subject of ridicule from those that he had known and trusted had been a hard, bitter pill for him to swallow, but swallow it he had done with pride.

He would never forget one of the last conversations he had engaged with Milan before the seeds of cancer had woven their deadly path into his mind and rational thinking.

The old man had gripped him firmly across the shoulders as he had looked deeply into his eyes.

"Billy, my child," his accent thick, despite the forty years he had spoken the language of the country that had offered him respite from the fear he had fled.

"Never be a follower to the idiots that are, and always will be, around you."

The old man had pulled Billy tighter into his embrace.

"Be the leader for all, and always point out the direction that you wish to take because not only will that take you to your own life, but it will also take with you those that you love dearly."

Billy had taken the ramblings of the old man to his heart and had followed them to the best of his ability, the direction in life he had been guided.

His chosen path of leadership had been duly noticed by the powers that ruled everything that the price of coal gripped tightly within its marketable grasp.

Billy had seized the charging bull of opportunity by the horns. From boy to man he had progressed in as little as two years of his working life.

The lowliest tasks he had endured without fuss as these had been expected of all newcomers to the underground kingdom of coal.

Wearing the yellow helmet that announced to all that he was fresh blood for the taking, he had walked the walk of the man as he had stepped for the first time from the cage like lift that had plunged him down into the darkest depths. The sheer speed of the drop had taken him utterly by surprise.

The old colliers had warned him as they had stripped into the dirty, stinking clothes that were to be their attire for the coming day, but nothing could have prepared him for the feeling of free fall as he had been plunged into complete and utter darkness.

He had spent his first forty days of underground life assigned to the supervision of an old collier who would teach him the basics, or pit sense as it was known.

Old Walter had worked at the colliery from the tender age of thirteen and had fifty years of mining experience under his belt. He had started his working life as a boy, still not wise enough to look after his own well being but had learnt the hardest of ways.

Now, fifty years on, he would soon end his working life as the boy that he had once been. Walter was a walking example of the pit man's saying, "You start as a boy and you finish as a boy."

Pit work was rigorous and challenging, drawing on strengths that the human body simply could not endure forever.

The vigour and spark would be all too soon diminished and by the time the average miner had taken his seat into middle age, the flame had gone.

Old Walter's spark of agility and strength had slowly been extinguished and soon even the menial task of learning the young the tricks of his trade would become too much.

Within another year he would sit out his fading career alone, left to operate a power switch that would operate the conveyor belt whilst the agile working men would cut the coals and ensure continued prosperity. He had taught Billy well and had instilled in him a deep respect of the dangers that he would face in his new career.

Walter had given Billy the very best of starts and smiled with pride two years later when he had heard the news that his young prodigy had been selected to undergo his coal face training.

Billy was indeed the man that he had been destined to become.

He had reached the very top of his profession at the tender age of eighteen and would be envied by others held within the lower ranks without hope.

The coal face worker was the elite of the workforce.

Coal was king and it was the face worker that gave out his heart and strength to win over nature and ensure that the black rocks were torn from the anchors of the earth, winning over the nation's wealth and future standing.

Billy had taken the badge of collier as if he had been handed down the Victoria Cross from Her Majesty herself.

Billy the collier was now a force to be reckoned with.

He had grabbed at the challenge with both hands and rose to meet whatever the colliery had to offer.

Roger smiled with pride as he watched his son crawl past him with expertise as he guided the cutting disc into the shining coal that lay exposed before them.

"That's my boy, Mister Cartwright," he said, as he placed a fresh piece of chewing tobacco into his mouth.

"Yes, Roger," the colliery under-manager replied.

"He's a fine boy and has the making of a true pitman," he paused to sneeze as he deeply inhaled the line of aromatic snuff he had spread along the top of his hand like some movie celebrity taking in the pleasured rush of high class cocaine.

"He'll go a long way, that lad." The noise reached a deafening crescendo as the coal cutting machine passed slowly by.

* * * *

Chapter Eighteen – The Blackbird and the Clock

The music was at a deafening pitch as Billy joined the others on the small, tightly-packed dance floor of the local nightclub. He had been watching the dark haired girl for most of the evening as she sat in the corner opposite, laughing and drinking the concoctions that the club proudly offered as the "in thing" in cocktails. Like a stalker with its prey he had seized the moment when he was alerted to her presence on the dance floor before him. Not a natural dancer, he had succumbed to the age old charm of alcohol induced courage. With each drink he had felt the essence of John Travolta slowly being inserted into his soul and now, after consuming vast amounts of Travolta's essence he was ready to shake his stuff like never before.

Like the performer on display he took to the floor as if dance was within his blood. The master was now present and the packed dancers parted to make a pathway just as the biblical Moses parted the waves to allow his people passage across the ocean.

As if by some unseen magnetic pull the girl of Billy's attentions was slowly drawn towards him through the parted waves that Moses had beckoned. As the dark haired beauty danced closer and closer, Billy wrapped his arms around her bare shoulders. With the coming together of the sweetest of kisses he closed his eyes and welcomed the feelings of warmth and passion that were slowly spreading over him.

The music rose to its crescendo and Billy opened his eyes. The flashing lights of the dance floor slowly faded and the blurriness of his vision returned.

BBC Radio One had stirred the awakening and it was Michael Jackson's Thriller that now replaced the hypnotic throes on the dance floor.

Billy rubbed his eyes in the darkness and slowly the reality swept over him; the dance floor had been a dream and it was the radio that now beckoned him to wake as he had commanded it to do so the setting of the alarm, hours before.

Wearily, he reached over and turned off the music. Molly had always been a light sleeper and she would constantly complain that she was woken by the sound of the alarm clock that beckoned the men to their work.

Rubbing the tiredness from his eyes he eased himself up from the bed. In the darkness he fumbled for the cigarette he had left on the windowsill the night before. Gently, he eased open the window, leaning out to strike the match on the coarse brickwork. Inhaling the smoke, he looked out at the scene before him as he had done so ever since they had moved houses seventeen years ago. All was quiet as he scanned the rooftops. Old Red the cockerel had long since gave out his last greeting of the awakening day and sadness settled onto Billy as he peered to his right towards the wasteland that had once been a thriving community of men working their individual plots of land. Milan's own plot lay directly parallel to the house and it was with a tear welling in his eyes that Billy looked closely at the place that he had referred to as his own little paradise.

Movement caught his attention and he smiled happily as Milan turned and waved. Sweat glistened on the old man's body as he leant upon the ancient scythe that he always used to clear the soil of unwanted grass and weeds before digging and sowing the seeds that would, as always, bring about a bumper harvest of fruit and vegetables.

Searing pain spread across Billy's fingers as the cigarette burnt away and the scorched glowing tip had bitten into the delicate skin between work hardened fingers. He cursed under his breath and tossed the glowing ember onto the garden below, watching the plume of smoke as it spiralled its final descent.

Milan had now gone and the place of paradise was again turned into a barren space of wasteland. The collection of huts and sheds now lay rotting on the earth weeds were reaping their revenge for the years they had been cut down and forced into submission by the relentless scythe.

Wiping the tears from his eyes Billy closed the window and quickly dressed, before quietly avoiding the stairs that let out their creak when he descended.

He hated Mondays; the start of yet another working week with little left of his wages that he had collected just days before, on Friday.

Billy had done the best he could to help out financially within the family unit. At the age of eleven he had secured himself a part time job as newspaper delivery boy and had then progressed, at the age of fourteen, to that of milk delivery. The work had been hard and the early morning start at four o'clock would see him constantly being held in detention at school as punishment for falling asleep in class. Although the meagre wages he'd earned did not directly contribute to the household income, it did mean that Molly could concentrate her own budget without having to worry that her son needed an allowance each week for the latest items of fashion that would enable him to stand proud amongst the other teenagers of the town.

At sixteen, he had found full-time employment as a miner and his wage packet each week would be given to Molly unopened. From that he would be handed back an allowance, the rest supplementing the weekly household outgoings. Billy would face ridicule from those around him that the boy would give his precious mother the wages of his toil like a child that had not yet progressed to manhood. The result of the ridicule had always been the same. The laughter would cease with one strike from Billy's fist. Countless bloody noses had earned him the respect that Billy the joker was not an open source for public humiliation and the men folk both at work and in the bars and clubs that the town provided would always remember that.

Billy could not shake away the tiredness that clung to him as he fumbled through the darkness into the kitchen. He had gone to bed early at 9 p.m. as most of the mine's early morning shift would have done, knowing that nine hours later they would be deep underground and travelling on the small scale locomotive that would speedily take them the six miles from the vertical shafts, carrying them underground to their allotted places of work. He had, however, failed to find comfort in sleep and had tossed and turned for most of the night. His mind had relived the life that he knew, from his earliest memories to those of the present day and, desperate as he had been to find solace in sleep, the memories continued to flood over him in relentless waves.

Maybe, he thought, he should simply take the day off. After all, out of the twelve hundred men that worked at the mine, production would not grind to a halt just because he had decided to idle away the morning lying in bed watching television. As tiredness continued to trouble him he needed little persuasion and began to think of excuses that he would use to explain his absence. Billy was the master of the excuse. He smiled to himself as he remembered with amusement the time that he had been called into the manager's office to explain the reasons for his most recent failing to attend for work. The union official had attended, fearing that Billy could be dismissed from employment and had ushered Billy into the office to stand before the seated colliery manager.

Mr. Bottram had never failed to amuse Billy with his strange appearance. Always dressed in English tweeds with a checked waistcoat he looked like he had been plucked from some 1930s film set that chronicled the British aristocracy. He would constantly reach for the gold chain that hung loosely from his side pocket and gaze at the heavily engraved watch, as if addicted to time itself as he peered with lacklustre interest at the lowly subject before him.

It was with this same disinterest that Mr Bottram had peered up at Billy and simply said, "Okay, explain yourself." Fighting back a smile, Billy looked him in the eye and began, "It's like this, Mr. Bottram, sir, knowing I had to wake early I made a point of going to bed." The union official closed his eyes and feared the worst as he had experience of such dealings with Billy.

"To help me sleep I decided to take with me a glass of warm milk and a piece of mam's iced cake upstairs with me. Well, boss, the milk worked its magic and the next thing I knew I was awoken by the sound of a bird's wing fluttering around the bedroom."

The union official looked down at the floor now in dread and bewilderment.

"As my eyes focused I saw to my surprise an ugly looking blackbird proudly sitting on top of the wardrobe preening its feathers. To my horror I glanced at the clock and it said that it was 7.30a.m., three and half hours later than I'd set the alarm to wake me."

The union official now wished that the earth would quickly open up and swallow him away from scene.

"At first, Mr. Bottram, I couldn't understand what had happened, but then it came to me. The bird must have landed on the ledge outside the open window and seen the crumbs from the cake. Hungry, he must have flown into the room and perched on top of the alarm clock to reach down and eat the remnants of the cake. His weight had simply pressed down and turned the clock off."

Mr. Bottram stared up in disbelief, the monocle falling from his eye, clattering onto the desk below as he stood and simply pointed to the door. Smiling widely with satisfaction, that the master of the excuse had won over the day, Billy turned, held his head high with pride, and left the office in victory.

The smile left Billy's face as he stared at the neatly wrapped package Molly had left for him on the kitchen's work surface. Struggling to make ends meet, she would always make sure that her son was sent to work with the best that she could produce. Today the package announced that roast beef adorned the bread from yesterday's roast. Molly had written the word, "enjoy" and had placed the paper on top of the package with care so that it would be read easily in the gloom that the early morning offered its intended. The excuse to simply return to the bed that he craved had been taken away from him in that one kind gesture of love. He picked up the package and imagined his mother carefully carving away at the remains of the Sunday roast they had shared, making the most of a traditional family meal, even if the family did only consist of three. To turn tail now and quietly ascend the creaking staircase to his room would be regarded as selfish by Molly when she woke to find that her efforts had been wasted. That the package of sandwiches remained on the work surface untouched and that Billy had given into the same inner laziness that had been genetically passed down from father to son.

As if sealing the final thoughts of what he was to do, Billy was broken away from his thoughts by the sound of a horn bleating its rising pitch across the silent rooftops of the sleeping town.

Like most collieries in the area, a steam-powered horn would trigger to alert the men folk that they should now prepare themselves in readiness for the short walk from their homes to the mine, and that it was only forty-five minutes before the first men of the day would be lowered at speed into the darkness and heat that they would endure until their day's work was completed and they would once again be lifted into the daylight of normality and safety.

With a heavy sigh, Billy picked up the wrapped parcel of food and opened the kitchen door. The coldness of night hit him as he stepped out onto the concrete path that cut its way across the small lawn of neatly trimmed grass. The coldness wrapped its icy fingers around him like some deep hostile ocean beckoning an offshore fishing boat within its swell.

Closing the door, he quickly fastened his jacket against the advancing chill and walked briskly out onto the main street that snaked through the town. Rounding the corner that led to the row of terraced houses forming the next uniformed street of dwellings he looked in dismay to see that the third house on the row was in darkness.

Jowett had complained throughout the previous week about having to work in the hell hole that he had been allocated by the colliery over-man, whose first job of the day was to deploy the miners to their places of work underground.

Like Billy, Jowett was the elite amongst miners; his job was to work on the coal faces that fed the conveyor belts of their precious cargo which would be sent to the surface, washed and sold to the local power stations to feed the nation's need for electricity, energy and warmth.

The coal face to which Jowett had been deployed had been suffering geological problems during the previous two weeks and had made the already arduous task of working in cramped conditions even more unbearable. The mine's surveyors had speculated that the reasons for the constant water spraying down from the unstable and fragile roof of stone above the miner's heads; the coal face had entered a shattered area of the earth's geology, and this broken area had become porous and was now simply, with mankind's breach of the seal containing the stinking remnants of the rain from prehistoric times, releasing the precipitation to fall as intended thousands of years ago.

Billy looked up at the darkened window that he knew was in Jowett's bedroom. The bastard, he thought ,would have given into the pressures of last night's entourage of drinkers and would have succumbed to the rising feeling of merriment, drinking himself into oblivion in one of the town's bars and clubs. His mind distorted and clouded with the effects of alcohol, Billy readily guessed that Jowett would have remembered the week's previous hell of being drenched in the stinking ice cold broth. That there had been no escaping this new horror as he crawled amongst the darkness, heat and dust in the collective attempt to overcome yet another obstacle set down by Mother Nature, to win for mankind the coals that the once mighty kingdom needed to survive in the unsteady financial climate of a rapidly changing world.

Not wanting to awaken his friend's parents, Billy decided against knocking on the door, turning round instead, walking back the few steps to where the street joined with the town's main street.

To his left he could see the darkness illuminated by the powerful lamps that surrounded the mine's perimeter. To his right beckoned the warmth and security of the bed he had left behind as the alarm clock had alerted and welcomed him to yet another working day.

Again the magnetic pull of home beckoned and chipped away at his thoughts as he struck a match against his jeans to light the cigarette hung loosely from his mouth like those he had seen in some bygone Hollywood movie. Again, the rebel without a cause won the day in Billy's mind and he gave in, once more like the racing pigeon, to the pull of home and security.

Billy turned to his right and headed for home, thinking what the master of excuses could present tomorrow to explain yet another absence to the colliery officials.

Returning the cigarette packet to his pocket he felt the paper wrapped package that he had placed there as he left home. Realisation again washed over him. Molly would be so disappointed when she woke to find Billy sleeping the morning away after she had gone to so much trouble preparing his underground meal that he would be proud to show off to his colleagues as they sat huddled together in the darkness, taking a brief respite from their labour as they refuelled the energy within themselves in readiness to once again push themselves to the limit in their work.

With a deep sigh he stopped and turned around yet again, kicking out at nothing in frustration. He began walking towards the brightly lit mine that had breathed life into the town for a hundred and fifty years.

* * *

Chapter Nineteen- The Human Apple

The locker room was bustling with men changing from their clothes of everyday living into those of underground fashion. The heat from the huge communal shower hit Billy as soon as he opened the door, making his skin tingle with prickly heat.

Laughter here ruled as the changing men exchanged their adventures from the two days rest that the weekend had offered.

Stories of fights won in the local ale houses and sexual conquests ruled the roost here and the audience of listeners revelled in the never-ending and often exaggerated tales of fun and mirth.

Billy stripped naked and threw his towel across his shoulders as he passed through the double doors that separated the clean locker room to the one that was used to store the working clothes of the miner. This time, however, it was not the heat that clawed at his nostrils but the smell.

Not everyone took their clothes home to be washed on a weekly basis and the stench of stale sweat and stinking feet rushed forward to engulf the unwary as soon as the doors were opened and the seal was broken.

Billy too had been guilty of adding to the stench today. In tiredness he had forgotten to take home his own clothes of the previous week and now grimaced as he hit his stinking stockings against the steel rail of the metal lockers to soften the woollen fabric that had hardened like leather since they had last contoured themselves to the shape of his feet.

Silently, he dressed, oblivious to the mayhem and laughter around him. Once favourite items of clothing that had outworn themselves in the local bars were now destined to a life of underground drudgery. The Levi jeans that he had been so proud to wear were now a puzzle of holes and hanging threads as Billy sat on the narrow steel plinth that ran at thigh height. He buckled the rubber knee pads that would cushion the effects of having to crawl like some lowly hound until the working day was done.

Finally dressed in his shabby and filthy attire Billy reached into the locker and retrieved the helmet that he had been given eight years previous when he had begun his first working day. The helmet was heavily scarred from countless battles of falling rock and, to the miner was a trophy of his toil. The more scarred and damaged the helmet, the more the miner could walk with pride amongst his colleagues.

With this pride he carefully placed the helmet upon his head. With one final gesture he pulled it sharply so that it slanted down towards his ear as he had done so from the very first time that he had worn it eight years before. Turning the key to secure the locker, Billy turned and walked briskly to the doors that led outside.

As he neared the building that held the lamps fastened to the miners' helmets to illuminate the darkness that engulfed them, the door swung open and remnants of the men from the previous night shift came into view as they headed for the locker rooms that Billy had exited. The men were black and filthy from the grime that they had been working in whilst the rest of the town had slept comfortably and safe within their beds. Billy noticed that some of the men were smeared from the stains of having been exposed to water underground and he hoped that he would not be deployed to work in that area of the mine to replace the sleeping Jowett, who would spend most of the day nursing a hangover from the previous night's festivities and fun.

Joined now by others that he had mostly known all his life, he walked slowly towards the huge steel lattice tower that held aloft the impressive spoked wheel that fed the steel rope from the winding engine room onto the roof of the lift that would lower and raise the men almost eight hundred metres underground.

As they neared the imposing structure of Victorian craftsmanship the air around them dropped in temperature considerably as the huge underground fans could be felt to pull air from the surface and ventilate the many miles of tunnels that had resulted from a century and half of coal extraction.

The men whose job it was to oversee the safe operation of loading their colleagues and the much needed materials to be used underground were in a constant battle against the icy wind that that bore at the flesh in an attempt to drag anything in its icy way with it into the man-made abyss. Strategically, they would place redundant containers that had once been used to store oil around the shaft's perimeter and constantly fuel the fires within the timber.

Although offering the merest of warmth from the numbing wind, the fires added to the unpleasantness that Billy and the rest of the men felt as they boarded the cage-like lift that would soon plummet them at speed into the darkness that would be their companion for the next eight hours.

Billy hated the descent and despite having gone through this ritual each day of his working life it was still the one aspect of his job that he feared the most.

The eight hundred metre deep shaft was circular and housed two lifts or cages as they were called. These were counter balanced and travelled in unison. Whilst one was at the surface, the other would be at its place of rest at the bottom of the shaft. As the cages passed each other in mid shaft it was obvious that it was only centimetres that separated the high speed collision and as the air was displaced the men inside would be jolted inside as if on some fancy fairground ride for the foolish that would pay the price for inflicted fear.

As the surface banks man lifted the flimsy wire meshed safety restraint Billy jostled himself for his favoured position in readiness to board the cage. Having three levels, each one safely having the capacity to tightly squeeze in fourteen men standing two abreast, Billy always tried to board the upper deck.

Twenty years previous there had been a disaster at another local mine when the braking system on the winding engine had failed. As a result of the freefall into hell the men that had boarded the lower deck had become pulverised into one gluttonous mixture, like some huge macabre smoothie ready to be poured into iced glasses from a kitchen blender. The bodies on the middle deck had become a puzzle of dismembered limbs and many were simply pieced together for burial from the clothing that was still attached to skin and bloodied bone in tatters.

Half of the men on the upper deck had been lucky enough to escape the descent. They would spend, however, the rest of their lives sat in the wheelchairs that gave them mobility without the use of their legs and relive the day they had simply fallen to the centre of the earth.

Today, Billy was in luck, as the wire mesh gate opened for admission to the upper deck and he was in pole position. Immediately, he stepped aboard and gingerly stepped across the raised metal work guiding the steel wheeled locomotive cars that were also transported underground carrying vital steel and timber roof supports to the newly opened areas of the mine. He positioned himself at the rear on the outside of the steel tomb-like structure which was closest to the circular brick wall of the shaft. This was another trait of fear that he carried with him. His rational thinking, if just a little misguided, reassured him that if there were to be some collision between the ascending and descending cages then it would be the unfortunates at his side that would bear the brunt of the collision and that, selfishly, their shattered remains would cushion and protect him from the full force that had carried them to oblivion.

As the last of the men jostled for position the unmistakable sound of three low rings of the bell that instructed the engine winding man could be heard above cramped bodies pushing and shoving at each other for comfort in the tight confines they had entered.

Three sounds of the bell indicated to the engineman that all was ready for him to start the descent and Billy felt a sudden clatter as the cage was lifted slightly, in order that the hydraulic supports that had taken the burden of the cage's weight from the steel rope could be retracted in readiness for descent.

Maybe it was the combined fear of the masses confined so closely that sparked the behaviour which immediately followed, as the cage was plunged into the darkness. Whatever it was that ignited the foolery was always sparked as the descent began.

The usual screeches and pushing began today as they always did.

Billy's own fear was replaced as he grabbed the man in front of him and, with his left hand, held him close to his chest in an unbreakable headlock. Poor "Alfie Apple" was defenceless from the sudden grip and could only manage to push his body weight backwards against his attacker in the cramped confines.

Alfie was coming to the end of his working life after having spent fifty-two years winning over the nation's fuel was due to retire in six months time.

Like those of his time he had descended into the depths at the tender age of thirteen years and had earned his pittance of wages taking on the menial work of a boy. As maturity blossomed so too had his capabilities and he had rose through the ranks from useless boy to respected pitman. The natural "pit sense" of only those born from mining stock shone like a beacon and Alfie had adapted to every aspect of underground work, earning good wages from being one of mining's elite.

Unfortunately, Alfie had followed the natural progression of the generations before him. With the peak of manhood so too followed the sad demise that old age brought. As the years beckoned then so did his capabilities, as his body and mind dwindled after relentless torture and once again the boy was returned to carry out the menial tasks that only the boy could complete.

The more Alfie struggled the more Billy tightened his grip, and quickly the old man accepted that the fight was long lost and that he should succumb now to the domineering strength of his unseen attacker.

Now limp in his grip Billy reached down and unhooked the water bottle that was fastened to the belt around his waist. In the tight confines and darkness he carefully placed the bottle neck in front of him and pushed it firmly above Alfie's buttocks and simply whispered in the old man's ear, "Ey, who's the daddy now?"

Fearing the worst, the old man again struggled in vain against the overwhelming odds but was subdued by brute force and exhaustion that old age brought even to the strongest.

Billy, realising now that the game had reached its crescendo, removed the pressure from his victim and pulled the bottle away. With the pressure and threat removed, the old man found renewed vigour and began again the limited fight back against his would-be assailant.

"Ey, Alfie, it's me," Billy reassured him in the darkness, against the feeble and exhausted struggles that were offered in retaliation.

As the sudden lurch of the winding engine's brakes took hold and slowed the descent into the gentle lights of the shaft's bottom, Alfie looked over his shoulder and a wide, toothless grin contoured his darkened features.

"Bloody hell, son, I was ready to tear your guts away had you not released me. Imagine me having to tell old Milan at his grave that I had just laid out his golden boy in a fight of fair knuckle underground...."

Billy placed an arm around the old man's shoulders as they slowly made their way from the uneven flooring of the cage and stepped onto the solid rock floor of the brightly lit tunnel born from the sweat and toil of bygone miners - and which now acted as the main artery of the sprawling underground mine workings that would feed its vital organs the much needed men and equipment vital for its continued existence.

Despite the earlier foolery to mask out his own fear from the descent into the man made hell, Billy held the greatest of respect for the old man. Standing at less than five feet in height, he was remembered as having the heart and strength of a lion by those of his own generation. The stories were never-ending of his once proud courage whenever he had been faced with danger and it was said that he would put his own life before that of his fellow miners'.

Only behind his back would the younger generations refer to Alfie as being connected with the word apple. "Alfie

Apple" they would whisper to each other as the old man approached from the darkness.

Despite being somewhat short in stature and with a lower center of gravity than the taller person, the law of nature had continued to take the course that old age unfortunately accelerated. The once muscle-bound upper torso of the old man had gradually loosened its grip to the age old pull of the spinning earth and over the years his once proud bulk had come to settle around his midriff and thighs.

In the silhouetted darkness Alfie now gave the impression of a plump, ripe apple, with short, swinging arms stuck artificially on his body, as his thick legs carried him along, fatigued forever with the burden they now had to bear.

The hero long since gone, Billy respected the shadow of what once had been, giving Alfie the friendly hug of comradeship and respect that only one man can give to another.

Rumour was that poor Alfie had gradually become blind with old age but had tried to keep this a secret as he feared that his disability would lose him his job and effect the pension that he would receive when he finally retired after fifty-two years of suffering hard labour underground.

It was said that he had become accustomed to the different noises that individuals made as they walked about their daily business. The rattle of tools that the miners hung from their belts he had memorised and he would shout out his greeting, not to the man but to the noise that they made in their approach. Alfie had also familiarised himself, like the blind do, to the layout of his surroundings and had learnt by counting his steps, noise and smell, exactly where he was in the mine.

Like many of the miners building up to retirement he had been given the simple task of sitting alone, miles from the areas of coal production, overseeing the transfer of coal from one conveyor belt onto another. In seven hours of work all he would have to do is listen for the noise of the leading conveyor to stop and, if this happened he would press down on the large brass button that would then stop the running conveyor belt from shedding its load onto the stationary one in front.

Even the young boys whose first task on starting their employment adapted themselves quickly to determine the noise; even in sleep when their conveyor belt was slowing coming to a halt. The "button boy" would instantly rise from his slumber and press down on the power switch to avoid any spillage of mineral onto the tunnel's floor; after all, it would their responsibility to then, in the heat and the dust, shovel the heavy spillage onto the conveyor belt when power was resumed.

Billy had put the rumours of Alfie's blindness to the test.

He had raced on ahead of the old man and had placed an empty oil barrel in the uneven walkway that he knew Alfie would soon take. With cap light dimmed he had sat waiting for the unmistakable sight of the round, old man as he turned the corner, heading on a collision course that he had not expected.

The rumours had proved themselves correct and poor Alfie had ended up flat on his face in the dust that bellowed upwards as heavy body made contact with the ground.

Billy had felt sad as he watched the helpless old man struggle in the darkness and leapt from his hideout and offered aid to his stricken comrade. The wave of shame rode over him in that instant as he pulled the old man from the floor.

That day had formed a union between the two men. The coming together of old and young was formed and Billy would become the protector and sight of the man that had now succumbed to the weakness that the passing of years handed down, even to the strongest.

As the unmistakable silhouette of the human apple disappeared round the corner, Billy once again focused his thoughts and attention on the scene before him.

Coal mining ran thickly through his blood and it was this heritage that he proudly wore with the badge of pride. It never ceased to amaze him each day as he walked the mine's path, just how perfect his Victorian ancestors had been.

Meticulously they had laid out the tunnel leading from the shaft with a pride that had long since been forgotten. The square, brick-lined walls had been erected like those of some neatly fashioned house and had been painted the whitest of whites in an effort to ward away the true blackness of a place that would remain so far from even the slightest glimpse of sunlight.

History had recorded that English hierarchy had been ruthless in their pursuit of wealth against all odds. That the humble, lowly worker could be sacrificed against the need for profit, and that it was profit and wealth that rose above the human suffering it needed to feed upon if it were to prosper at all in the expanding industrial world.

The sight that met Billy each day told that of a different history to which had been written in the history books of the working classes.

All around him now Billy saw perfection; the neatly appointed brickwork, the smoothness of the carefully laid out timber work above that had fought against nature's need to fall for over one hundred and fifty years. Each day Billy had felt himself being slowly drawn into the very fabric of the mine and its rich history of man's struggle against the forces of nature.

Even the aromas reached out and pulled the underground traveller into the mine's fabric and cast their spell of magic, to those of only mining stock and breeding, deep into its spellbinding pull of belonging.

The air took on a very different smell deep underground - a smell that only the miner could identify with and recognise in an instant. As the wind was drawn sharply down the intake shaft it took on the stench of bleach, clawing at the nostrils and taken gently at first like a newborn taking in the first breaths of life. The miner would never forget this smell and it would become entwined forever into his subconscious, stirring age old memories whenever the aroma was detected.

Billy's thoughts were interrupted as he approached the gathered men that had stopped to congregate around the rough wooden door concealing the entrance to the shaft side, that gave respite and shelter for the men whose task it was to load and unload the men and materials that were constantly being transported up and down the shaft that he had descended.

Although conditions for these men during the summer months were pleasant compared to those endured by their colleagues who toiled further into the mine's interior, in winter, the men faced the hardship of a biting cold that could not be escaped. As temperatures plummeted on the earth's surface to ring out its picture postcard blanket of snow and ice, temperatures here were amplified greatly with the wind chill factor of the frozen air being pulled sharply downwards, exposing the men to arctic-like conditions. No amount of extra clothing could ever ward away the deathly cold grip of numbing ice, and the men of "Siberia" had graciously accepted the touch of human kindness that the coal owners had offered when they had ordered a hole to be cut into the stone for at least an allotted twenty minutes of each working day could be spent to eat their sparse sandwiches in relative comfort.

At the beginning of each of the three different working shifts for the day the simple shelter against the elements served another purpose.

Equipped with a telephone, the brick-lined cavity acted as the place for deploying the men that had not secured a permanent role within a specific area, or district as it was known within the mine.

Here the colliery deputies ruled supreme and it was their job to select the men that they needed to carry out a particular task for which they were ultimately responsible. They were the overseer, the safety delegates and the payer of wages to the men that they had control over; they would haggle and jostle with each other to secure whom they saw as the best man for the job within the team they were to supervise.

This humble place of gathering was another where Billy would feel himself drawn to the aromas that reached out into his inner self, and with the trickery of an illusionist, the sweet smell would hold its captive audience in trance until the spell was interrupted with that of reality.

The mine's deputies carried with them a heavy brass lamp whose tiny flame was fuelled by oil. It was the combined burning of this oil in the tight confines that let out the sweet smell Billy associated with his favourite boiled sweets of childhood, and he would take in this essence as he had taken in the warmth of the sunshine on a summer's day, laying amongst the flowers watching the tireless Milan go about his day's labour on his treasured allotment.

Billy waited outside the makeshift office with the others until their names were called out, sending them to their allotted place of work. The group resembled lost souls emerging from a holocaust of destruction and depravity. Shabby in their appearance, their clothing was soiled from the sweat and filth that coal mining offered to the luckless that had chosen its path in return for job security and a weekly wage.

Laughing and cajoling each other Billy knew deep in his heart that he was amongst the band of brothers that he would not have exchanged for anything that could be offered as a replacement.

Young and old together they had formed a closeness that ran thicker than the tie of family blood and the connection could never be broken.

It was here that Billy felt his place of true belonging and thrived on the closeness that engulfed him in his working class pride.

Here were the true characters of life, Billy thought to himself, as he scanned their smiling faces. Books could be written about each and every one of them and would have the readers in hysterics when the pages would reveal their daily antics of fun and strife.

'Colin the cobbler', to Billy's right, who had once stopped the entire coal production of the nightshift when he had raised the alarm that he had seen a young boy walk past him and disappear into the darkness.

The entire district of the mine had been searched but no boy was ever found - only the intermittent tracks of tiny bare footprints in the flour-like dust that settled everywhere were evidence that the boy had not simply been a figment of his tired imagination.

It was only when a written statement was taken from him that Colin had realised the true realisation of what he had seen. The boy had been a black and white image, like some sepia photograph taken from a time long since past. On closer inspection, the boy had not simply vanished into the darkness as he had first reported but had in fact appeared to have stepped out of sight as he had passed through a brick wall that sealed away old mine workings of the Victorian era.

Mining historians had researched the area of the mine and had found that children had been employed in that area to do menial tasks at a fraction of the cost of employing a man.

Colin had simply seen a snapshot of a time long gone and the boy, even in death, was simply continuing the daily ritual of work which he had known best.

'Lend a Hand Dave', to his left, let out his guttural laugh upon the announcement of the punchline to the joke that was now being told.

Last year, Dave had the misfortune of having his hand cleanly amputated in a tragic accident that could have cost him his life.

Billy had witnessed the accident and, like the others present, fell into blind panic when Dave had lifted the bloodied stump in his own shock and disbelief.

Yearly first aid training vanished amongst the men as each one in turn tried to administer the pain relieving injection that was vitally needed. Like the others before him, Billy's hand trembled and the syringe resembled that of a vibrating needle of some insane tattooist trying out his latest piece of artwork on some unwitting and unfortunate customer.

In fear that he was to be subjected to even more pain from the injection that was supposed to bring about relief, Dave had snatched the hypodermic syringe from his supposed saviour's hand and had sank it deep into the muscle of his right thigh before drifting into the welcomed unconsciousness that shock offered to the victims of acute pain and trauma.

These were merely two of the never-ending faces that surrounded Billy in the confines of his world deep beneath the earth's surface.

The stories were countless of man's laughter against the constant fear that was all around. Each day would bring about its own episode that would be replayed over and over to amuse the audiences of the local Working Men's Clubs until something even more amusing would be brought to their attention and create even more amusement than the previous story had done.

From the sweetly scented confines of the makeshift office Billy heard his own name being called. Pushing his way through the crowded laughter he peered through the makeshift entrance of roughly sawn timber to see his father, Roger, hurriedly writing down notes in the tattered notebook that the colliery deputies would carry with them in their breast pocket. As if drawn to his son's gaze amidst the commotion, Roger glanced up and with the simple gesture of nodding his head towards Billy and pointing his finger at his own chest Billy understood that he had been deployed by the colliery over-man to work on the coal face that was under his father's jurisdiction.

Jowett had failed to report for work and it was Billy that would act as his replacement. He recalled how his friend had complained bitterly throughout the previous week about the conditions on WH 14's coal face, as he had been drenched constantly with the seeping foul water that was being released from the rock that had held it for so long. He remembered too the tired and weary faces of the previous men of the night shift as they had passed him, their clothes almost turned to stone from the minerals the water had collected from time spent confined in the rocky tomb of Mother Nature.

Colin the cobbler broke Billy's thoughts with the unmistakable laugh resembling a mule's than man-like, and Billy bent to pick up the plastic disposable shopping bag that Colin had thrown at his feet. The bag was empty and on closer inspection Billy noticed that both bottom corners and been torn away to reveal leg size openings.

"Okay, ghost man, what's the joke?" Billy shouted over the heightening roar of laughter.

"Waterproof underwear, son," came the witty reply, "At least now poor old Roger can make sure you're nice and dry again for when he returns you to dear Molly!"

The laughter rose as Billy threw the weightless bag in the direction of the laughter, only for it to be dragged to the dusty floor and sent rolling into the darkness of what awaited the men, like some stage set tumbleweed used to add character in a wild west ghost town that John Wayne would ride with his posse of armed men.

The laughter was quelled with further names being called from the underground office. Billy smiled as Colin's grin turned instantly to that of a grimace as he too was deployed to work on the dreaded watery hell and Billy shouted that maybe he had wasted the waterproof underwear in haste.

One armed Dave's smile also fell as did others when the final deployment of the stragglers was concluded.

The unfortunates of the day came together again in laughter and joke and formed the band of brothers that had held them close in comradeship as if they were siblings from birth.

Rounding the corner that would lead them to the waiting locomotive, Billy smiled as he saw that the waterproof underwear that Colin had fashioned now flapped violently in the man made breeze, caught against the steel mesh that lined the arched tunnel to prevent loosened rock from falling out onto the walkway. He snatched the tattered plastic bag and threw it into the air, sending it again on its tumbling journey of never knowing before them into the darkness.

* * * *

Chapter Twenty- Lonely This Christmas

The whiteness of the Victorian brickwork gave way to the stark reality and reminded the traveller that this was no illuminated coal cellar but that he was in the depths of the earth itself.

Arched steel girder work replaced the comfort of enclosed whitened brick and between the metre-lined symmetry of the steel, nature pressed down her force with a vengeance to take back what had once been hers.

Steel held firm against nature, preventing collapse, but her never-ending pressure distorted the steel work as if it were simply made from darkened toffee; soft and pliable to the pressure of touch. The touch this time, however, was not that of the childish finger impatient to taste the sweet offering. This time it was the weight of the world itself which presented the constant danger of sudden collapse and the snuffing out of human life in an instant.

Over time the steel had succumbed to the relentless pressures that it faced and once symmetrical curves were now twisted and contorted out of shape, now requiring the added assistance of strategically placed wooden supports to ward away the natural force of gravity fighting to seal the openings that man had created.

Wood had always been the miners' friend. Steel was robust and strong but it was the timber supports that let out the creaks and groans of discomfort that alerted the vigilant miner that old Mother Nature was again pushing down in a contraction that would not give birth to life, but instead would be capable of taking life it had once bore away in the cruellest of crushing blows.

    The locomotive waited patiently beneath the distorted steel work that continued in its everyday struggle to ward off the natural force of gravity and to make the passing of the men below as safe as possible, in a world that intruded against the natural laws of science.

One hundred and twenty years of scraping out the black diamonds of energy had forced the coal owners to chase the rich seams far out into the subterranean horizons that were now out of sight from the comfort and safety of the vertical shafts sunk down into the earth in the quest for wealth.

The drive for continued financial prosperity now took the weary miner seven miles of underground travel to reach his allotted place of exhaustion.

The advent of the locomotive was not to ensure their comfort along the way but was merely a means to take away the time that they would spend marching rather than time spent actually fighting to win out the profits deserved only by the already wealthy in English society.

The locomotive itself seemed as old as the mine's fabric and added to the atmosphere that Billy drew with every breath he took. With each breath that he inhaled was the spirit of miners past that would fill his own self with the pride of what had been.

    The Hunslet factory in Leeds had been renowned for its expertise in providing the nation with its pulling power of man-made strength, to overcome the limitations that the mere human could offer. The horse had been the first to show its strength against the common man and had proved its worth for generations, wearily hauling the burdens that man had found too tiring in his normal working day to undertake.

Now it was the diesel driven horse that ensured the swift passage of both men and supplies of raw materials to feed the coal faces. This morning it was the men that it patiently waited for, sat in readiness to once again enter the darkness and gloom that man had created in his quest to win over the coals that nature had provided.

The acrid smell of burnt diesel fuel filled the narrow passageway as Billy made his way along the battered steel structures of the miniature carriages that had transported generations of miners to their allotted places of work. Comfort was not an issue and Billy hauled himself through the narrow opening and sat on the rough wood planking that crudely acted as a seat.

Colin the Cobbler followed him and clambered over Billy's knees in the cramped confines to ease himself aboard. As he did so he broke wind and smiled smugly as he saw with obvious pride the look of distaste on Billy's face.

In childish retaliation Billy turned and faced him. When he felt that the target was within his sights he reached towards the battery powered spotlight that hung from the battered bracket on the front of his helmet. Without warning, he turned the switch dazing Colin's sight that had accustomed itself to the blackness all around. This time it was Billy that gave forth the smug smile of satisfaction as once again the light was dimmed allowing natural darkness to descend around them.

Both men, now content that they had each scored points against the other, settled themselves for the forty-five minute journey that would take them to the coal face where they had been deployed.

In the darkness other men clambered aboard the steel hulls of the man-riding carriages until finally the diesel engine revved to indicate it was time for the journey to begin. The ride was a far cry from the luxury offered by the Orient Express and Billy held himself rigid against the sudden jerk forward that would catch the unwary traveller by complete surprise.

Slowly the locomotive snaked its way round the tight right-hand corner, before building up speed as the track straightened, heading into the complete darkness that lay ahead.

Although the journey was a far cry from one of comfort, Billy felt his inner spirits being lifted. Deep within him the age old pride manifested itself that what he now saw before him was the work of countless generations that he had been linked to by blood.

Each turn of the track revealed a now dormant tunnel of blackness and decay and it never ceased to intrigue him of times past of long gone miners that would have wearily made their own way into the darkness once bristling with human activity.

Although the laboured spirits had long since succumbed to the darkness and abandonment, with each clattering turn of the diesel Billy could feel the energy of their presence and the hope that had filled their earthbound lives willing them onwards against the many hardships that they had suffered.

Many of the miners made good use of the travelling time aboard the locomotive and would drift into sleep, aided by the rocking movement created by the uneven surface over which they were travelling.

Others would use the time for endless humour. Billy fell into this category and would have his audience laughing until their sides hurt with his endless bombardment of jokes.

These were before the days that political correctness had gone totally crazy and the jokes would cover almost any topic known to man.

"Lend a hand Dave", sat in front of Billy, suggested that maybe he had picked the wrong profession and that stand up comedy should have been his thing. Billy agreed but then went onto say that the biggest difference was that here he only had idiots to listen to his wit and humour.

Aided either by sleep or by laughter the journey passed all too quickly as the locomotive slowly came to rest indicating that it was time to leave the relative comfort that the man-riding carriages had offered before the strenuous task of winning the coals that lay ahead of them.

Billy hauled himself through the narrow opening and joined the gathered group of men that had congregated around a crude bench erected from lengths of sawn wood and which rested on blocks fashioned from concrete.

The stench that was being carried in the breeze from the darkened tunnel immediately passed the bedraggled crowd and clawed at Billy's nostrils. The stench of decay and rotting eggs he knew from experience was being caused by the stagnant water that was seeping through the strata onto the coal face ahead.

Again, the never-ending master of the centre stage, Roger was holding court as Billy approached the gathered men. Although he had risen through the ranks he had retained the down-to-earth spirit that had gained him the utmost respect from the men now under his control.

The joker had too retained itself within him as he coaxed his now-gathered audience around the master of both fun and respect.

The underground telephone that Roger held constantly rang out as he received orders from the mine's control room high above their heads. He relayed the messages from above that the night shift had encountered problems throughout the early hours, and production of the precious coals had been hindered constantly from rising methane gas levels that the water-drenched strata had allowed to escape into the atmosphere where the men now toiled.

Methane gas had been the miners' enemy ever since the first coals had been cut hundreds of years before. Being the waste product of vegetable decay it was highly combustible and countless lives had been lost in explosions on man's quest to seek out the energy sources he needed to fuel his progression in an age of industry and wealth.

Billy joined the gathered group of jokers and circus clowns as they waited for their orders of deployment.

As he scanned the faces he realised that here was his true sense of being. These were the very people that were deeply embedded into his very fabric of existence.

Pride pulsed through his veins as he sank into the sanctuary and security that he felt within the presence of those that were just like him.

Richard, to his left, whom he had known all of his life; Mark, the short-sighted kid others had cajoled and mercilessly bullied at school for no other reason other than he had been forced to wear spectacles to aid his failing eyesight; Blake, the envious beholder of the precision rifle that had been carefully crafted by his father to give him the ultimate edge in the never-ending make-believe battles acted out on the cobbled streets. These were his people, the friends that could only be conjured within the dreams of wishes.

Despite the stench from the darkened tunnel beyond, the bond of friendship rained out its embrace that brought the bedraggled gathering closer together in unity. Laughter and light hearted banter ruled supreme amongst the gathering of men in their underground surroundings. A world so alien to man had become so ordinary and day-to-day to those that now stood encircled around the showman with the telephone in his hand.

Orders were relayed to the waiting men and their numbers gradually diminished as the ordered took on their directions for the day.

"A pint after – okay?" Dave called back as he followed Colin round the darkened corner.

"Two pints at least," Colin added as the pair disappeared into the darkness.

"What's the point of one pint?" Dave's voice echoed away as complete blackness swallowed them from sight.

"Take no notice, son," Roger's voice broke the silence. "Prove yourself for me today and the first four beers are paid for."

With the promise came the smile that could only connect a father to his son.

Biting down hard to release the juice from the dried out tobacco, that most of the miners chewed to produce saliva against the dust filled environment to which they were exposed, Billy turned and took the final steps to his own destiny.

The coal face lay five hundred metres along the dark, semi-circular tunnel that he now walked. The rest of the men had chosen to walk along the tunnel that ran parallel to his right as the steel girders were less buckled along its length and the walkway provided easier passage for the traveller.

Roger had used his position of command to ensure Billy had a relatively easy job ahead of him today and at least would remain dry away from the worst of the stinking waters that were seeping from the roof and walls, adding misery and discomfort to those that were exposed to its ice cold touch that would irritate the skin for days to come.

Roger had assigned his son to operate the stage loader. This simple job would normally be undertaken by the less skilled man on a lower wage but the management had agreed that given the current bad conditions, it would have been unfair to submit the lower paid members of the workforce to endure the added discomfort that they may be exposed to.

It would mean Billy was to sit out the working day alone. He was to ensure that he stopped the feed of coal that was being pushed along the coal face if the receiving conveyor belt - for whatever reason - came to a standstill, avoiding a pile of coal that would then have to be shovelled away manually.

His only regret was that had he known that he was to spend six hours practically alone with very little to do, he would have brought something to read to pass the time. Sleep was out of the question as had to remain vigilant, in case the outgoing conveyor belt stopped - causing a huge spillage of coal if he did not stop the flow that the cutting machine spewed out from its advance.

As he walked along the darkened tunnel it never seemed to amaze him just how black darkness could be. He had been exposed to nightmares that the shadows of the night had offered to him as a small child. These same shadows had crept from the darkest recesses and again entered his world without welcome during his teenage years.

As he walked the darkness before him held no shadows. Darkness was complete as one without the need to slowly look from side to side. Even the darkest of shadows could never penetrate the blackness now as he steadily walked to his destination.

Darkness was indeed his friend and he had come to talk with it once again.

Slowly, the dimly illuminated lamp that heralded the newcomer to the forefront of coal production gave out its dull glow. Here was the beacon that softly called the men from the darkness to their allotted place of work for the day.

As Billy approached the illuminated area before him he caught sight of movement. Instinctively, he pointed the narrow beam of light, from the lamp that slotted into the front of the safety helmet he wore, into the direction where the unexpected movement had come from. The beam of light revealed a figure seated on a pile of timber that had earlier been transported, ready to be used to support the fragile roof of the coal face beyond.

"Don't shoot lad, am unarmed," came the unmistaken dulcet tone of old "leatherneck" - the deputy that had started his working day earlier than the other men in order that he could check for any build up of gasses prior to work commencing.

Leatherneck had earned his nickname from the leather dog collar that he always wore around his neck. He had worked on the colliery's coal faces for most of his life and had been a deputy for over twenty years. Crawling along the metre high coal faces had presented itself with the problem that he had constantly damaged the brass oil lamp that all deputies had to carry for the purpose of gas testing. As a gesture of fun one of the miners had told him that if it were him then he would simply hang the lamp around his neck.

Leatherneck had heeded this advice and had turned up for work the very next day sporting a leather-studded dog collar, much to the amusement of the men under his command.

"Sit down, lad, seat's nice and warm," the old man gestured as Billy neared. Billy took the advice of wisdom and lowered himself down onto the old wooden boards forming the makeshift bench.

No sooner had he made himself comfortable the sound of two electronic bell ring tones rang out, alerting him that the men had arrived on the coal face and wanted Billy to turn on the power supply that would start the conveyor belt in readiness for coal production to begin.

"No rest for the wicked, son," Leatherneck sighed, as he heaved himself up and slowly hooked the brass oil lamp onto the leather collar around his neck.

"Keep that seat warm, lad, I'll be back," he voiced as he walked into the darkness.

"I'll be back!" Billy mimicked under his breath as he reached out and pulled the brass switch that operated the conveyor belt.

Placing his hands over his ears to cushion the thundering sound of the five hundred horsepower gearbox breathing life he sat himself back down on the wooden bench.

Two lights appeared up ahead, signalling the arrival of Tony and Albert, the two men that had the job of ensuring the coal cutting machine could be turned round, ready to travel the one hundred and eighty metre length of the coal face without delay.

It was not long before the thick black dust crept over Billy and gave the whole tunnel the appearance that it had filled with smoke.

"Shit," Billy said out loud, as he quickly placed over his mouth the paper dust mask that would offer him some protection against the deadly particles of airborne coal. All too well he knew just how deadly this dust was. The older miners all showed symptoms of "Black Lung" as they struggled for their breath as they walked.

Waves of tiredness washed over him as time slowly passed and eventually he gave into the sleep that reached out to take him in its warm embrace.

Colin the Cobbler looked at the watch that he kept wrapped in an old handkerchief in his breast pocket. 9.30 a.m. the hands announced. Wearily, he placed the timepiece back into its protective covering and returned it to his pocket.

His knees had become sore as the water that seeped from the strata all around him had soaked the rubber pads to protect them as he crawled behind the coal cutting machine.

Roger crawled ahead of the cutting machine, pausing occasionally to take gas readings. The water that had been raining down on him had begun to irritate the bare skin of his shoulders and arms, and he knew that even after showering the prickly sensation would continue long into the day. As his mood slowly dipped he reminded himself that the shift would soon be over and he would reward his endeavours with a well earned drink before returning home.

Lend a Hand Dave had taken shelter from the droplets of water whilst he ate the sandwiches his wife had made for him the previous night. Cheese and pickle had always been a favourite of his and his mood lifted as he savoured the sweet taste.

His thoughts drifted away from the discomfort that he felt as he focused on the meal that he had planned later in the evening.

Fifteen years of marriage had presented the inevitable problems that often faced man and wife but the good times had outweighed the bad. To show his appreciation to the woman that he loved he had secretly booked a table at her favourite restaurant that evening.

Leatherneck sat shielded against the cool breeze in the tunnel that ran parallel to the one where Billy now slept.

Blake, Richard and Mark were labouring twenty metres away, unloading a fresh supply of steel girders that the locomotive had delivered.

Old Leatherneck was studying financial figures from a tattered notebook he had taken from his jacket pocket. He was due to retire in three weeks time and he was scrutinising the financial standing of the retired man.

He had dreamed of this day for the past five years and saw before him a man of leisure and rest.

Molly switched on the kettle as she took a well earned break from the mountain of ironing that now lay on the kitchen floor. The washing machine repeated its cycle as she had just refilled it with more soiled items she had collected from the laundry basket.

She cursed to herself each and every time she did the family's washing and could never understand how two grown men could change into so many outfits each day, leaving the discarded items of clothing for her to wash unnecessarily.

The whistle of the kettle brought her from her thoughts and she leant forward to pour the boiling liquid into the cup she had placed on the work surface.

Without warning the water crashed against her heels causing her to drop the kettle onto the carpet at her feet. Shocked, she spun around and was horrified to see that the circular door on the washing machine had somehow become unlocked, unleashing its load of water and drenched linen across the kitchen floor, soaking everything in its path.

Victoria woke from her delicate sleep and stared at the darkened ceiling above her. The unease that had settled over her had continued throughout the night and offered no respite as her eyes opened to wakefulness. The pain within her stomach had intensified each time she had awoken and an inner thirst for water had prevailed until she gave in to tired resistance. Quickly dressing against the cold, she descended the staircase to face another new day and realised that finally the secret would have to be shared.

Deep beneath the earth's surface Colin the Cobbler sensed an unusual rumbling that at first he thought was coming from the coal cutting machine that he operated. Fearing that there was some possible mechanical failure he instantly reached and pulled the emergency stop button in the hope that further damage could be avoided. As the cutting disc slowly ground to a halt the deep rumbling continued and seemed to be coming from the wall of coal immediately in front of him. Water now sprayed from the fissures that appeared in the black rock. As each fissure opened more and more stinking water gushed out with increased pressure.

"Shit!" Colin called out into the darkness as he desperately battled against the rising pressure of water that was pushing him backwards against the hydraulic roof supports behind him. In desperation, he tried to turn and reach for the tannoy system to warn the men that there was an inrush of water.

Before Colin could move any further, three and a half million gallons of water were unleashed. The wall of coal buckled and exploded forward as if ignited by some huge catastrophic bomb.

Death came to him instantaneously, the sheer force of the water, as it crashed into his soft flesh tore his body apart and reduced bone and solid matter to liquid. The treasured watch that he had moments before held in his hands was instantly transformed into a flattened piece of worthless metal that would never herald out its call of time again.

Leatherneck was snatched from his financial thoughts as the ventilation suddenly seemed to stop and shudder before a strong, almost gale-like gust of freezing air rushed from the direction of the coal face ahead. Dust that had settled on the floor was violently whipped into the air forming a thick blanket of impenetrable blackness.

The notebook, which contained his financial calculations for the life of leisure he had worked all of his life in preparation for, was snatched from his grasp and was lost forever in the complete blackness that had swept over everything.

Instinct told him that an explosion had occurred within the confines of the coal face and he hurriedly sprang from his sitting position. With no thought for his own safety he desperately fought against his natural instinct of self preservation as he desperately felt his way towards the coal face ahead of him.

Ironically, as he struggled to feel his way forward he recalled his life long friend Alfie. Poor Alfie, he thought, as he too felt the blindness that had overcome the human apple gradually as the years had passed.

The wall of water and debris struck him without warning, sending him backwards with a speed that made him feel nauseous. The blackness now pressed into him and he felt himself slowly being overtaken by a deep sensation of total paralysis that bore into him with a ferocity that he could not control. Thick mud forced its way into his open mouth which contained the silent scream that was to hang unheard for all eternity.

Blake, Richard and Mark were taken by complete surprise as the ventilation turned round and they were suddenly faced with the ice cold gust of wind coming from the direction of the coal face ahead of them.

"What the fuck?" all three shouted out in unison as the wall of slurry raced towards them with speed and destruction for everything that lay in its path. The steel girders of support were wrenched away and distorted beyond recognition as if made from pliable rubber.

Richard was knocked over even before he even had the chance to take on the stance of the sprinter before the race.

Death came instantaneously to him as the steel girder dislodged and struck his head, taking him away from mortal existence instantly.

Mark was a little more fortunate. Quicker off the mark, he had time to turn and hurl himself away from the wall of death that had attacked without warning.

Always the sprinter, he had the legs of a gazelle which had propelled him and coasted him through the rugby career of his youth.

The gazelle, however, could not match the speed the wall of blackened death had to offer in its haste to carry the ball of final destiny across the finishing line.

His Final destination he could not stop as he raced towards the finishing line of life. Black, cold hands wrapped around him as he took in the final breath of the life that he had ever known and had ever loved.

Blake had been chosen as the lucky one. He stood aloft the pile of timbers, horrified at the scene that was playing out before his eyes. Miraculously, he had been spared from the onslaught of total destruction that had brought with it havoc and death for all that had stood in its way.

Numbed by deep shock he slowly realised that the recess in the tunnels wall where he stood had saved his life. With total disbelief he looked out at the carnage that now lay before him. Thick mud spewed through the tunnel like the solidified lava flow from a newly-erupted volcano. Steel girders that had once carried the weight of the world were now buckled and twisted as if they had stood before a great tornado.

His attention was drawn to a tattered notebook that lay on the surface of the flowing river of mud and smashed machinery. "Leatherneck" was clearly scrawled on the tattered and sodden page as it drifted past out of sight.

A loud bang jolted Blake back to his senses and he felt the strata around him shake and vibrate violently.

He felt no pain as the roof gave way, crushing his body to the same consistency as the river of death which had attacked without warning minutes before. Mud and human matter became one as Blake was slowly carried into the darkness of the tunnel that he had walked only hours before.

Roger immediately knew that something catastrophic was happening as soon as he heard the deafening crashing sound coming from behind him. The narrow confines of the coal face shuddered angrily as if gripped in the throes of some underground earthquake. He turned and shone the narrow beam of light from his helmet lamp back towards the coal cutting machine that he had only moments before crawled past, pausing momentarily to exchange pleasantries with Colin the Cobbler.

At first Roger could not comprehend nor decipher the information that his eyes were sending to his brain. Hydraulic supports that he had moments before crawled under, as he slowly made his way through the coal face, were being ripped from their moorings as if they were made from paper that was being scattered before a winter's storm.

The stench that came with the sudden blast of ice cold air hit him with a ferocity he had never known. It was as if a million raw eggs had been thrown at him simultaneously and he immediately retched as the putrid odour entered his mouth and nostrils.

Instinctively Roger realised with horror what was happening around him. The coal face had suffered an inrush of water and in that second he prayed that the damage would be minimal and that no one had been injured. Little did he know that death had already paid a visit and that his own prayer now would be wasted on ears that would never again hear any sound. Desperate to alert the other men of the danger he clawed at the tannoy system immediately in front of him. Hands trembling in panic and fear he pressed the small concave steel button that would allow him to broadcast his message to the men under his command. The deafening noise drowned out his words of warning as the coal cutting disc was torn away from its base by the sheer velocity of water that gushed from the fractured strata.

Death came to Roger instantly as the diamond cutting discs of the machine tore through flesh and bone without resistance. Flesh and bone that was not cut was crushed from existence with the sheer weight of both water and distorted machinery.

Like that of Blake's destiny only moments before, Roger's was that he also would became as one with the black tide of death.

Billy lay beside a bubbling stream with fishing rod in hand. The gentle breeze warmed his cheek as it made the grass around him swirl in dance with its magical touch. The golden sun dipped behind the tree line ahead as the darkened shadows stretched out their fingers to touch him. The gentle breeze cooled and Billy felt the cold claw its way slowly across his skin, making the hairs on his exposed arms rise to trap some of the warmth that the golden sun had offered.

The dancing grasses of the lush meadow shook violently as the blast bore down on the valley, shaking the trees with such a force that it seemed they would be ripped from their roots at any moment. Instinctively, Billy opened his eyes. The crisp, clear waters and the meadow vanished as the shadows advanced at speed, bringing darkness with them.

Momentarily confused, the realisation that he had been dreaming bore into him as he was shaken into reality by the sound of desperate shouting coming from the blackness beyond where he was sat.

Tony and Albert ran towards him as if they were on some crazy one hundred metre race. The speed at which they bore down on Billy was exaggerated with the strobe light effect that the lamps on their helmets made as they were bounced from side to side with the men's haste.

Pulling himself to his feet Billy pointed his own helmet light in the direction of the two crazed racers. As if by the trick of a conjurer's magic the two lights vanished and the desperate screams were replaced by utter silence. Tony and Albert were encased for eternity in a tomb that nature had created in an attempt to win back from man what he had been taking for hundreds of years.

As sudden as it had descended the silence was broken by the deafening roar that the tidal wave of death created as it crashed headlong towards its next stunned victim.

The flight or fight instinct within Billy immediately chose the former as he turned and ran like he had never run before. The curved girders of steel that lined the tunnel became one solid mass as the momentum of total fear carried him forward at breakneck speed.

He desperately fought against the growing desire to turn and check on his attacker's distance but he knew that if he were to do so then his speed would lessen momentarily and that ground would be lost. The noise behind him grew and it felt as if the whole tunnel was being shaken by the force of some huge unseen hands, hell bent on destroying everything that was within its grasp.

The wall of thick mud and accumulated debris hit Billy with such a force that sent him somersaulting forwards. His face smashed into the steel locomotive track with a sickening thud that instantly stunned him into submission and he lay helpless and unable to move.

The deafening noise subsided as if it had never been there and complete silence settled all around him.

The pitch of the skylark broke the absolute quietness and once again Billy felt the warmth and comfort of the rising sun as its dappled rays beat back the encroaching shadows through the leafy tree line before him.

The gushing stream was again within reach of his fingertips that had clasped the fishing rod before the nightmare had begun.

Once again, Billy pulled himself up into a sitting position and looked out across the dancing meadow of grass and summer flowers. The tree line was now gone and was replaced by the familiar sight of the uniformed houses of Castlefields.

The sound of laughter caught his attention and he watched with a smile as the children on the cobbled street played their games of hopscotch and hide and seek.

The houses gave way to greenery and tranquillity that paradise offered amidst the dreariness of its surroundings.

His attention was drawn to a boy sat watching an old man work the soil with a hoe. Sensing his presence, the boy slowly turned his head and waved in recognition, the warmest of smiles spreading across his young face.

The sound of laughter made him turn to his left. The young couple that walked across his vision against the backdrop of the colliery waste heap appeared so very much in love.

Hand in hand they appeared not to have a care in the world as they walked along the footpath towards the houses that spread out before them. In her free hand the woman carried a basket of the finest summer blackberries that would fill a thousand pies.

As he watched, another figure appeared before him on the footpath that stretched out into the distance.

Victoria stood amongst the fragrant flowers as beautiful as always, as she looked lovingly at him in her floral dress. Her hair was gently blowing in the gentle breeze and she slowly raised her arms towards Billy to form a loving embrace. Overcome with loving emotion Billy instinctively raised his arms to meet hers and as their fingertips met Billy once again felt the rays of the sun diminish, allowing the darkened shadows to creep forward.

Darkness overwhelmed him and he panicked as the temperature around him plummeted. In desperation he tried to fight away the oppressive feelings that were now sweeping over him in relentless waves but was helpless as total paralysis slowly took over his entire body.

Darkness turned into complete blackness as he desperately tried to take in breath and he realised in his last second of life that he was dying, that he would be no more.

Panic gave way to a deep feeling of happiness and comfort that he welcomed without further resistance and he took pleasure that this new sensation offered.

The sudden grasp that he felt around his wrists dragged him suddenly from the feeling of ultimate pleasure and brought him again to his senses. Strong hands had found his own and were now pulling him from the clutches of death.

He felt immediate release from the constraints that paralysis had forced upon him as he was dragged to safety by his unseen rescuer. Slowly, as he was lifted from the tomb that was to be, he opened his eyes to the rescuer that had snatched him from the jaws of dearth.

Peter looked down at him with a loving smile of reassurance.

Peter, whom Billy had last seen as he smiled his final farewell almost twenty years previous, before being crushed from existence whilst winning out the coals from deep underground.

Peter's smile brought the light of a thousand sunrises as Billy looked out at the scene before him.

Milan turned slowly and set the scythe gently down onto the dancing grass underfoot as he placed his arms around his loved one.

Alison paused from kneading the dough that was before her in the earthenware bowl that rested between her knees and smiled the loving smile that had never failed to comfort him as a child.

The small boy appeared from behind the blackberry bush and stepped towards him. The grin on his face was familiar as he held out his hand to reveal the toy car. Billy paused and finally held out his own hand to accept the gift that was being offered. With lightening speed the boy withdrew. "Boo," he said with childish laughter, then turned and ran with a skip in his stride into the lush meadow grass which swallowed him in its gentle breeze-swept dance.

Doctor Forster who had last seen Billy in birth wiped the tear from his cheek before turning to embrace his ever loving wife.

The sound of the skylark again filled the air with the richest of songs as the sun finally broke through the shadows of the tree line that lay before them across the never-ending meadow of tranquillity.

Victoria leant against the bowl she had set before her, waiting for the retch that would bring final relief from the sickness that she felt. The same nauseous feeling that she felt each morning as she woke had strengthened with each passing day and she knew that today would be the day that she would have to tell Billy the truth.

He had cajoled her for weeks that she should maybe ease a little on the food that she ate as he could see that her girth was widening.

She had known that she was carrying his child since the doctor's examination four weeks prior but had waited in earnest until the signs were visible for all to read.

Today, she thought, as she retched glutinous bile into the bowl before her, she would make Billy the happiest man alive.

Molly wiped the sweat from her brow as she looked at the brass clock Billy had bought for her from his first week's wages when he began work at the mine.

9.37 a.m. the ornate hands called out to her as she continued mopping the water that had soaked every corner of the kitchen.

With a smile she knew that the two men in her life would soon be home and that the damage would be cleared with their help.

Leaning forward she turned on the radio that Roger had bought to replace the recording equipment he had broken years before.

The fragrance of the sweet red rose Billy had kindly cut from the garden and left for her in a glass tumbler before he'd left for work filled her nostrils as she leaned over the radio to tune into her favourite station.

Nostalgia filled her heart as a 1970s pop group sang out one of their classics.

As she cleaned away the dirt and grime that the deluge of water had created, her own voice joined that of the singers as they sang out the opening chorus in unison.

"It'll be lonely this Christmas,"

"Without you to hold,"

"It'll be lonely this Christmas,"

"Lonely and cold…"

* * * *

Chapter Twenty One – Life For Life

Victoria closed her eyes and listened to bird song that seemed to fill the air with its beautiful chorus. A skylark, high overhead, announced its existence to the world below, as did a watchful blackbird with a shriek from the juvenile hedgerow of elderberry and blackthorn.

The warm air, stirred by the soft summer breeze, stroked gently at her cheeks and cooled the tears that had broken the barriers she carefully erected each and every time she visited this place of beauty and tranquillity.

Her eyes slowly opened to see the scene that had been set out before her. Long gone was the industrial blight of the town's colliery that had polluted the skyline with its foreboding presence. Closed, due to economic reasons, two years after the tragedy that had stolen away the loved ones of so many. The landscape had once again been given back to nature's mother. The grey, rolling contours of the waste heap had been levelled and landscaped to a place of colour and greenery, offering the visitor respite from the rigours of modern life.

Boyish whoops of laughter and fun drew Victoria from her thoughts. She glanced across the meadow of grass and multi-coloured wild flower, to see her son galloping on a make-believe charger. He drew a sword of willow against the flowing enemy, who dared to stand in opposition before him. With precision and care she placed twelve red roses against the brass plaque that had been set into granite stone to mark the location of 'number one shaft'; the place where generations of men had travelled into the depths of the earth. Tears welled from her eyes and ran unopposed down her cheeks in constant and never-ending grief.

Here was the spiritual final place that kept the connection alive to those that she had once loved and lost. Billy, Roger, Milan, Alison and the friends she had known and loved from childhood, were all now together, united as one in this place - to share in the beauty they had never known. The wooden bench offered the mourning rest from their endeavours of walking the slope to the gentle crown of greenery that now overshadowed the small town. The ageing timbers held their poignant memories close to her heart as she remembered the times she had sat with Billy at the mine's entrance, simply watching the world go by.

The steady ticking against her chest brought her thoughts back from recollecting summer days and she reached out the highly decorative hunter pocket-watch that she had always kept close to her heart ever since that fateful day when Mother Nature's waters of death had given way. The watch had been Billy's most prized possession and now it was hers to preserve and keep until her own time of passing fell over her. 6 p.m. the ornate hands announced to the holder, as the closing sunlight shimmered its dance upon the white face of time itself.

"Milan," she gently announced, her voice carried by the warm breeze across the swaying seed-filled stalks of meadow grass.

"Nana Molly and the fireside people will be waiting; it's time to go." With a smile, the boy released his horse of imagination and cast the sword of bravery into the hedgerow at his side.

"I love this place, mammy," he said, as their arms enveloped each other in the mark of true love and togetherness.

The breeze lifted slightly as they turned, hand in hand, making their way slowly towards the town below. As she turned, she felt the slightest fluttering feeling within her as the forming foetus turned, and once again settled. Jowett stood, rested with his weight against the moss-covered boundary fence that enclosed the final resting place of his friends and loved ones. He too had suffered the burden that the disaster had unfolded, but his had been the weight of not only loss but that of guilt. Billy had taken his place, and that place had indeed been final. A place now he could never repay. He now watched through tear-stained eyes as his wife and stepson slowly made their way through the meadow grass towards him. He wondered, within his heart, if he might ask that their unborn son be named after the hero and friend to all….. Billy.

* * * *

About The Authors

Andy Evans was born in the gritty coal mining communities of West Yorkshire England.
After leaving school at the age of sixteen he followed the generations of school leavers before him to work in the local coal mines.
Following the demise of the coal mining industry he now works within the Criminal Justice System.
Andy is married with two children and has a granddaughter, Ava. He continues to live in his native West Yorkshire.

Vesna Kovac was born and raised in her native homeland of Bosnia.
Her home town is Novi Travnik. After leaving school she went onto graduate as an engineer at the Military Academy in Zagreb, Croatia and went onto work at the Bratstvo Armaments factory in Novi Travnik.
She remained in Bosnia until the end of the war and now lives in the USA with her husband and two sons.

Other works by the authors

In Search of the Displaced Persons
Our lives So Differently Told
Andy Evans and Vesna Kovac

For most of us genealogy is a subject we are drawn to. Whether it is our curiosity to uncover distant ancestral roots or to expose the blue blood of a long lost royal connection, many of us have become fascinated with researching our past.

With this rising trend genealogy has become big business with websites allowing access to vital records, at a cost to the researcher. Find My Past and Ancestry, to name just two have helped transform us into private investigators. The magnifying glass and smoking pipe have long since gone, but the desire to seek out what was once lost, remains within us.

Genealogy in the United Kingdom has been made easy with online records of the ten yearly census records being made available one hundred years after they were originally carried out.

With 2011 rapidly approaching we will soon have access to the national census that was carried out in 1911. These records are extremely accurate and give us a detailed account of our ancestors, information that would have been otherwise lost from memory.

As a nation we are lucky. Despite being embroiled in countless battles and wars overseas. Not a shot has been fired in anger on English soil however since Oliver Cromwell took a disliking to the king over three hundred years ago. Marriage, birth and legal documents have been painstakingly preserved for centuries, most being open to public viewing.

Imagine researching family history within a country that simply forgot to add the word peace into its vocabulary. A country cursed with centuries old bitterness and hatred held deep within its people. Civil war and killing was never enough to settle the appetites of the warring factions. Elimination of life was always just the beginning. The total elimination of history ultimately was the goal.

It is all too easy to dismiss such an account from some distant, impoverished third world country. A place so far away distance gives us comfort. Comfort because such a thing never actually happens within our own back yard of security and safety.

How so very wrong we are. In Search of the Displaced Persons tells the story of a twenty year attempt at uncovering family history from the former Yugoslavia. A country submerged in ethnic and religious indifference culminating in the latest civil war in the 1990's.

There are no Ancestry or Find My Past websites offering information to the novice investigator. Church records have long since been destroyed, graves destroyed by explosives and whole families exterminated without heirs to carry forward the genetics into the future.

* * * * *

Printed in Great Britain
by Amazon